The Pandora Box

*A tale of
adventure and
betrayal on the
high seas.*

Lilly Maytree

LIGHTSMITH PUBLISHERS
Thorne Bay, Alaska

Lightsmith Publishers
P.O. Box 19293
Thorne Bay, AK 99919

www.LightsmithPublishers.com

Ordering Information:

Quantity sales. Special discounts are available on quantity purchases by corporations, associations, and others. For details, contact: info@LightsmithPublishers.com

Lightsmith Publishers is an imprint of the Wilderness School Institute, a nonprofit educational organization that offers outdoor youth activities in wilderness settings, including training in wilderness skills and nature studies, as well as the publication of curriculum on related subjects, through the Wilderness School Press, and their children's imprint Summers Island Press.

The Pandora Box/ Lightsmith Publishers Edition/ Paperback

*To my wonderful Captain Husband,
who took me on my first adventure.
After which I never looked back.*

1
The Assignment

"How will you get me out," I asked my editor,
"after I once get in?" ~ Nellie Bly

It was visiting day in the psychiatric hospital. Dee Parker sat at her usual table in the lounge, next to a foot-wide floor to ceiling window that allowed only a narrow view to the outside lawn. No need to attract any undue attention. It was not an opening window and there was no way of escape. There was that word again. Kept popping up every time she turned around. Honestly, if people could read each other's minds, they'd all be staring at her right now.

Better get a grip. This was the day. The real deal.

Today, she was going to help Nelson Peterson escape from Wyngate State Hospital. Of course, that was not part of her original assignment, and her editor would probably hit the roof when he found out. But she would deal with that after she got Peterson safely out of here. For weeks now, she only had to come as far as this visitor's lounge to talk with the old gentleman. Just the thought of having to live here was enough to give her nightmares. But it would soon be over.

Dee felt again for the sprig of miniature roses she had tucked into the band of her straw hat (the smell of roses was supposed to have a calming effect on people) and forced herself not to look around so much. There were too many people here who were getting used to her weekly visits and might engage in conversation if they caught her eye. Today, of all days, she did not want to stand out or be remembered. Except this afternoon, there was something troubling in the atmosphere. She could sense it. Then again, maybe it was just her own nerves.

She watched one of the orderlies escort a disheveled woman across the room in much the same way a person might take a dog out for a walk, then rather abruptly seat her at a crowded table of waiting visitors. It was Iris Kitner, with an inside-out pajama top on instead of something more suitable that went with her skirt. Hadn't anyone helped her dress today?

The hum of their voices was too far away to make out what anyone was saying, but Dee had heard enough past conversations to know things were progressing the same way they did every week. They would all have a lively visit among themselves, with little or no interaction with Iris. Then they would say their goodbyes. After which, Iris would have a few moments of free rein with the complimentary coffee and cookies set up on the long table against the farthest wall, before another white-coated somebody took her back upstairs.

Only, less than five minutes later, she popped up from her chair with an outburst of bizarre babbling and refused to sit down again. Now, that wasn't like her, at all. The plump, forty-something woman (whose auburn bun was always crooked) was fairly complacent most Fridays. As if the thought of coffee and cookies was enough to keep her on best behavior. Which made Dee wonder if these troubled souls might have more sensitivity to otherworldly things than most normal people. Something to look into as a possible follow-up story for the series she was writing for the Columbia Herald. The headline might read: Mental Patients: Is What They See Real? A thought that was interrupted when a self-conscious glance from a teenager in the group collided with hers. Grandson or nephew, maybe, who was embarrassed at the way Iris was acting. Dee realized she was watching people again and forced herself to look away.

Instead, she deliberately turned in her seat toward the green double doors on the other side of the room and waited. What was taking so long? Did Nelson forget what day this was?

"Come on, Nels," she murmured half-aloud. "You're not giving someone a hard time up there, are you? I don't have nerves of steel, like you do. Oh, dear Lord...what if..."

For heaven's sake, Iris had moved into her peripheral vision again, messing around with the refreshments, already. Dee tried not to watch that, either. Except when the unmistakable crash of a coffee cup onto the floor (probably full) caused a momentary lull in the hum of visitors.

She had to do something. Simply because that sour-faced kitchen worker who should never have been hired for this kind of job, was on duty today. In her late sixties, at least, she did not like to clean up messes. Instead, she would complain to housekeeping, which would cause an even bigger disturbance, and Iris would be returned to her room, early. Meanwhile, the family picnic was going on without her, and none of them seemed inclined to come get her.

So Dee slung the strap of her purse over a shoulder, picked up her package, and headed over there. But before she even got across the room, Iris stepped on an errant cookie that had also hit the floor, and the inevitable happened. Ms. Sour-face made an immediate exit through the green doors to tell somebody.

"Hey there, Iris, need some help?" Dee filled a fresh cup, piled an assortment of cookies around the saucer and steered her toward the nearest table. The corners of the woman's mouth turned up in a barely detectable smile, and she settled down with a contended sigh.

"Cream and sugar?" Dee set a few packets in front of her without waiting for an answer and then left her package on the table for a moment while she turned back to clean up the mess before housekeeping arrived.

"Miss Parker?" The tap on her shoulder a few moments later gave her a start.

"Was this ever clumsy of me!" She scooped up the soppy napkins and deftly tossed them into the nearby trash bin before turning around. "Slipped right out of my..." At which point she found herself looking into the magnified eyes of a large-boned, ruffle-haired orderly whom she didn't recognize, at all. Now, which department had he come from? He had thick glasses and was wearing a blue uniform instead of the typical white one.

"Mr. Peterson can't come down today," he

informed her.

"Oh?" She'd been told her dark blue eyes were fringed with unusually long lashes, and he seemed mesmerized by them. So she said the first thing that popped into her mind to break the spell. "Shall I go up, then?"

He glanced furtively toward the green doors as if someone beyond might have heard her say that. "No, I don't think you better."

"Well, I would at least like to leave my package." Dee glanced back toward the brown-wrapped bundle she'd left on the table and inwardly cringed when she saw Iris begin to open it. The visitor's lounge was getting more crowded now, and the place was turning into a hub of confusion. "What room is he in?"

"6B. But Miss Parker, He really isn't up to—"

"Did you say six?" Dee felt a sudden hollow in the pit of her stomach. "Why—that's the violent ward. What on earth is he doing there?" She walked over to collect her package before the contents tumbled out in plain sight, with the orderly following close behind.

"It is often necessary for the safety of our staff, as well as other patients, to confine..."

A textbook answer accompanied a complete shutdown of any previous communication between them.

"Oh, honestly." Dee added more cookies to Iris's plate and retrieved the package when her interest shifted then turned around again, expecting to catch him reading verbatim off some card he had snatched from his pocket. "There must be some mistake. He has his quirks, but he isn't violent. Putting him in with dangerous people could give him a heart attack! Now, who do I talk to about this?"

When she was met with nothing but a blank stare in reply, she closed her eyes for a moment, sighed heavily, and willed herself to calm down. But it didn't have much effect. The minute she opened them, her impatience popped right out her mouth. "Oh, I'll just take care of it, myself!" Then, she whisked past him, her flowery print dress set in motion with a determined stride. At that pace, her yellow heels clicked along the gray linoleum, drawing attention like some bright tropical bird moving through dark forest.

Nearly everyone in the room seemed to watch as she walked through those green doors.

2

Into the Madhouse

*"I went inside with fear and trembling,
for good reason" ~ Nellie Bly*

Leaving the restrictions of the visitor's lounge would, no doubt, bring more than one member of the housekeeping staff out to handle things. Since no visitors were allowed past the green doors, it would definitely be a matter for the security people. Who Dee was convinced, without even having to look back, the blue coat had taken off to report to, because he didn't even try to stop her. Today, of all days! But none of that mattered now. She would probably be intercepted before she even got to the elevators, but she didn't care about that, either. Not any more, she didn't.

She was going to drag old Nelson Peterson out of this horrible place, today, one way or the other, even if she had to call the police. Things had gone way past just getting a good story. Now, here she was, personally tangled up in the mess. Something good reporters should beware of. But that poor old man in the violent ward!

Well, she was deep into it, now, and there was nothing left but to see it through. After all he had done for her, it was the least she could do for him. Besides that, she didn't for a minute believe he was crazy, or she wouldn't even be here. He wasn't violent, either. Troubled, was all it really was, over things that would send most normal people a lot farther over the edge than he was. Which was the very reason she had decided to help him in the first place.

They had worked the escape plan out together. But it was Peterson, himself, who had come up with the ingenious parts. The rest of it was the most farfetched idea she ever heard of. One that would take a miracle to pull off.

Thing was, she had twenty-three good reasons to believe in those kinds of miracles. Besides, just because somebody was old didn't mean they were incompetent. But if he was as sound in his mind as she thought he was...

Why had they put him in the violent ward?

The corridor beyond the green doors was eerily deserted when she stepped inside.

No nurse's station visible or even an open office door to evade. Still, there were probably cameras somewhere, so she hurried to the last door in a row of elevators and pushed the number six button when she got in. The door rumbled closed with the sound of a freight elevator, and it seemed like forever before it opened again. It was that slow. When it finally did, she found the sixth floor was—like everywhere else— buzzing with activity.

An emergency cart passed by just as she stepped out. But it was in no hurry, as if whatever had gone on was finished now. Ahead and a few yards to the left she saw a busy station with charts and people and equipment, and farther down that same corridor she could see a dozen or more doors with windows for looking in. All were closed except one. Outside it, a small group of doctors and nurses were talking quietly as other workers moved in and out. She was halfway past the station before a nurse looked up with a start.

"How did you get in here?" she said.

"Service elevator," Dee replied. "Other ones don't come up this high."

"There's a reason for that, young lady. Come back here, right now!"

The medical people, down the hall, looked toward the commotion.

Then a middle-aged woman in an old-style white uniform broke away from them to intercept her. The nurse's blonde hair was pulled back from beautiful features and there was something oddly familiar about her. Even though Dee had always tried her best to avoid any of the actual medical staff.

They met head on, and Dee mustered her most authoritative tone. "I want to see Nelson Peterson."

The thought of the old man in some sort of trouble for feeding her so much information, all these weeks, was suddenly extremely unnerving. But from the looks of things, she was going to need some serious help.

"I'm sorry," said the nurse. "Mr. Peterson died twenty minutes ago."

The quiet, non-emotional statement hit Dee like a splash of cold water. "What? But..." Her insides suddenly began to churn. "How could that happen? Last week he was fine. He was perfectly fine! And—and—why is he up here in the violent ward?"

The gazes of the two women locked.

"Can I at least see him?" Dee peered over the starched white shoulder toward the open doorway down the hall. Contrary to typical hospital behavior, the remaining staff members around 6B seemed to have their attention centered more on her now, instead of the matter at hand.

"Are you next of kin?" The nurse's tone was cool.

Dee thought about lying but evidence gotten by such means never held up in court. Not to mention any personal morals she believed in. "No...just a friend."

"It's against policy to let anyone but the next of kin inside." The woman looked toward the busy station and raised her voice. "Jennifer? Could you escort Miss Parker back to the lounge, please?"

"How do you know my—"

"You're the only person on his visitor's list, so I just assumed. If you'd like, I can request that you be notified after arrangements have been made."

Dee didn't object. What could she object to? She allowed herself to be led back into the elevator. The dark-haired aide named Jennifer stepped quietly in beside her and pushed the button to the main floor. Probably to make sure she actually left the building. But—like everything else, today—there was something odd about her, too. The proverbial stethoscope was not draped over her shoulders or protruding out of a pocket. What's more, she had jewelry on and smelled faintly of some expensive perfume. It smelled like... like night blooming jasmine. After the doors closed, the girl reached into the pocket of her blue smock and handed Dee an envelope.

"This is from Mr. Peterson."

"Thanks." She shuffled the package that held the clothes Nels was to have changed into, over to her other arm, slipped the envelope into her purse with hardly a glance, and sighed.

Dead—poor Nels! She just couldn't believe it! Maybe this was all too much for him. The stress of what they had been planning. In which case she would feel utterly and totally responsible for bringing it all on. Then again, maybe he had simply suffered a reaction to some medication and gone temporarily berserk. Had to be restrained, so they brought him up here. Worse yet, what if they somehow found out what he had been telling her and—

"Aren't you going to open it?"

"What? Oh. Probably just another list. He likes to—did like, I mean—to make up lists of things he wanted me to bring for him next time. Last week it was a magnifying glass and a world atlas. But I guess he won't need whatever it is, now. When did he give you this one?"

"This morning, after I brought him the newspaper. Sort of cryptic, if you ask me. He told me ,Give it to Dee Parker when she comes by to see me this afternoon. And just when I'm wondering why he doesn't do it himself, he slipped me twenty bucks."

"He paid money for you to give it to me?"

"He paid me to keep quiet about all his lists. Twenty dollars each so I wouldn't hand them over to the psychiatric department for screening. Not much in this economy but I did it mostly as a favor because of his phobia."

"What phobia?"

"Always worrying they won't let him have what's on them. Which they wouldn't. Cigars and good whiskey are definitely not OK around here. But in my opinion? A man that old ought to be able to smoke or drink anything he wants if it makes him feel better. He isn't going to live long enough for it to kill him, anyway.'

"So it was a favor, but you still took the money."

"Hey, this job only pays minimum wage. But where he got all that money we'll never know. Because they don't let the patients keep any. Especially on this floor. He was a crafty one, though. This was the first time he ever asked me to deliver one of those lists to somebody. That's probably why he gave me the extra. Then—not two hours later—his heart stopped. Spooky. It was almost like he knew it was going to happen."

Slow apprehension crept over Dee at the words, accentuated by the vibration beneath their feet as the elevator lumbered its way back down. As long as the aide was giving up information, she'd better continue to press. ,"What exactly went on back there—do you know?"

The girl shook her head and a fresh waft of jasmine released itself from the straight dark hair. "Beats me. I'm never allowed in the rooms during an emergency. Half of them on that floor I can't go into at all."

They finally stopped, and as Dee stepped out, she noticed open-toed sandals instead of the more common, comfort support shoes people who spent most of the day on their feet normally wore. And lavender-painted toenails.

"Jennifer, wasn't it?" She turned back for another look before the doors closed.

The expression she caught on the girl's face was

one of irritation. But it dissolved quickly into a well-practiced smile.

"Well, thanks for everything, Jennifer."

Once inside her own little red car, Dee snatched off her hat and tossed it onto the back seat, letting loose a cascade of honey-colored curls. She retrieved the envelope from her purse, glanced once around the nearby cars in the crowded parking lot to ensure no one had followed her, and tore it open.

It was Peterson's handwriting, all right, but what she saw made her gasp in disbelief and cast another cautious glance around...

Box 127

It's all yours.

Nels.

"The wealth of the wicked is laid up for the just..." Her heart began to pound. Something had definitely gone wrong, and he'd seen it coming. But why hadn't he called her? That's what the emergency cell phone she gave him was for. She would have been here within an hour—with police. This was so shocking and final. Had he sacrificed himself? All hers? She had only known the man a few weeks. He couldn't possibly mean that.

But what if he did?

The thought gave her an eerie, tingly sensation all over. All of everything? Why, if that was true...she could be wealthy beyond...of course, she shouldn't take it. Couldn't even think about it, because... because...well, because why? ,The wealth of the wicked is laid up for the just...' was a verse of Scripture. She wasn't exactly sure where in the Bible it was, but she recognized it just the same. Maybe the Lord was trying to tell her something. Only it didn't feel quite right, somehow.

Then again, everything had felt strange today. So incredibly sad. Lonely, old Peterson...dead. Well. What now? She would have to look into his cause of death. Personal involvement aside, it was her job to look into it. Any good reporter would. She'd bet money Nellie Bly would have done so. That woman was fearless.

Especially where any foul play was going on. Well, there was definitely more than a little of it going on here.

Didn't necessarily mean she was going to accept anything.

3
Tempted

"If there is anyone who can ferret out a mystery it is a reporter." ~ Nellie Bly

As Dee groped for logical reasons why she should let Peterson's whole sordid secret die right along with him she began thinking about what kind of good his money, if it existed at all, could accomplish.

Hadn't she been praying for answers? More importantly, hadn't she been praying all her life to be able to do big things? And now that the opportunity was here, was she going to say, "Excuse me, God, but I didn't mean this big?'

This was big.

Her missionary father always said it took integrity to handle large amounts of money. Well, she was the daughter of integrity. Not once had she ever known him to be tempted by the tremendous sums of money that passed through his hands. Though their own lifestyle was extremely modest, her father had made them feel rich in other things. The kind of things she still valued more than money.

Surely, then, if the Lord moved someone into a position like this, it could only mean one thing. This could very well be her "Divine assignment." The one she had been waiting all her life for.

Divine assignment or a deadly detour.

The only way to find out which one, was to proceed with caution. Wait for a confirmation. Because (to be honest) at the moment the situation seemed more like a temptation in the wilderness than promotion to a higher calling. Not to mention she couldn't exactly picture herself standing up in the middle of the church congregation to announce she felt led to quit work and spend the rest of her life wealthy beyond belief. Funded by an ex-criminal.

Her poor mother would faint. She had a hard enough time thinking anything good could come out of a decent Christian woman taking a reporter job like this in the first place. And why couldn't she be like her brothers and do missionary work—that was exciting wasn't it? Not enough, obviously, since she had been doing that since she was fifteen. Which would always lead to the where-had-she-gone-wrong discussion, and the why-can't-you-settle-down-and-get-married sequel.

No, she couldn't discuss this with her parents yet. They simply wouldn't understand.

Instead, she would wait until the right thing to do became clear to her. And she would do nothing in a hurry, either. This was a time to proceed with caution and find out what these warning signals going off in her spirit really were.

There was every possibility that Nelson Peterson was as loony as everyone said he was. What then? Maybe he hadn't meant a word about repenting of his sins and turning over a new leaf that day they had prayed together. After all, a person had to do something very serious to get themselves committed to a mental institution in the first place. So something was definitely off here.

Maybe even way off. Which meant the secret had to be kept long enough to prove its validity. One way or the other.

She wasn't an investigative journalist for nothing. She would keep doing her job the best way she knew how, until she eventually got to the truth of it all. For poor old Peterson, if nothing else. And for her own peace of mind, too. Yes, she felt a little better now. Bottom line? Nothing hasty.

Dee took a deep breath to calm down, slipped the key into the ignition, and started the engine. She backed out of the parking space with a firm new resolve, drove past tiny islands of manicured lawn with dwarfed trees, and headed toward the gated exit. Thank heavens it was Friday. She could pray and mull this thing over all weekend, if she had to. All weekend...

But couldn't a person get to that little town on the Oregon coast and back in a weekend? That's what Nels had told her. And that's all it would take for her to figure this thing out. The treasure was either there or it wasn't. If it wasn't, all speculation would be over. Back to Monday morning, as usual. Finished. But if it was there...well, there would be plenty of time to think about that if the time came.

That Pandora's "box" had not been disturbed for well over five years, so it certainly didn't need to be opened within the next five minutes. That's saying she could even open it at all. There was still every possibility that Nelson Peterson was the champion liar of the century, too.

But what if he wasn't?

She better leave tomorrow morning. She might even see if her friend, Marion, could come along to keep her company on the long drive. Not to mention there was safety in numbers. She needed a good excuse to get out of that dingy basement apartment of hers anyway.

Brooding was not good for anybody, no matter what kind of terrible experiences they had gone through. As a matter of fact, a "mission" like this might be just the ticket to snap her out of that despondency that moved in on her like a cloud this time of year, since her husband had died of a heart attack on the first day of an anniversary cruise.

And maybe Dee just wouldn't take no for an answer. She'd pack some things and show up on Marion's doorstep tomorrow morning ready for a drive to the coast.

By the time she pulled into the narrow garage next to her condo, she had made up her mind. She went in through the back entrance as the garage door was closing behind her and was met by the soothing strains of a Mozart concerto. The kitchen lights and stereo were hooked up to a switch that coincided with her garage door opener. Having been raised in a constant crowd of people, she found it so much more pleasant to come home to lights and music rather than dark emptiness. One had to make the best of living alone.

Kicking off the fancy heels she had bought expressly for visiting days at Wyngate (if one was going to play the role of a charity-minded member of the upper class, they should at least dress the part), she breezed through the kitchen and automatically turned the burner on under a shiny copper teakettle as she passed it. Then she went straight for the hall closet on the other side of the living room to get a duffel bag off the top shelf. Too high to reach without standing on a chair, though. So back she went to drag one over from the dining area.

All before she noticed the man in the room.

"Hello, Dee," he said sheepishly from the doorway of her study. "I'm afraid you caught me snooping."

"Why—Scotty! What on earth?"

Her friend and co-worker who seldom had a black curl out of place (or came to work in anything less than some expensive name-brand suit) looked unusually rumpled at the moment. No tie or jacket. His yellow shirt was unbuttoned at the collar and the sleeves rolled up. He avoided her accusing glare and sat down heavily on her suede couch.

"Well? This better be good!" She watched him take a folded handkerchief from his pocket and dab at a few beads of sweat on his forehead.

"It isn't." He still didn't look at her. "I know you've been onto something bigger than Peterson's legendary fortune, that's all. I wanted to find out what." He returned the handkerchief to his pocket. "Simple as that."

"So why couldn't you just ask me?" Dee moved over to the stereo and turned it down.

He sat forward to pick up a copy of *National Geographic* that was lying on the coffee table in front of him and then thumped it down again. "I put you onto the biggest scoop of the year and you don't even confide in me! Why can't you confide in me?"

"Confide in you...on the basis of what? You can't confide in someone who has no scruples about doing something illegal just to get information from people. You broke and entered, for heaven's sake! Of all the unethical—"

"Well, it's hardly breaking and entering when someone gives you their key." The look he turned on her then reminded her of a whining child, accentuated by the too perfect black curls above luminous eyes and the boyishly smooth skin. "I thought we had an understanding."

"What, because I let you stay here when you were having your house painted while I was on vacation last summer? I was just being polite." She would have laughed at the absurdity except that he looked dead serious. "I distinctly remember you giving the key back."

"I got a duplicate."

Dee felt a flush of anger at the admission and turned away to keep it to herself.

"Ahhh," he crooned. "Tchaikovsky on a Friday afternoon. How appropriate."

"It isn't Tchaikovsky. That was a sneaking, disrespectful thing to do, Scotty—I won't have it! And I want my key back."

"I don't blame you." He reached into his pocket and tossed it onto the coffee table. "I'm ashamed of myself, and I apologize."

The teakettle began to whistle, and as she started toward the kitchen, Dee could feel his eyes following. "You're just sorry I came back early and found you here." She shuffled through a basket of tea bags and dropped one into a cup without bothering to read what kind it was. "You want to know why I came back early, Scott?"

"A minute ago it was Scotty. I already told you I was ashamed of myself. Doesn't that merit me at least a little of that soul-cleansing forgiveness you dole out to everyone else?" Now his tone was sarcastic. "We all go a little crazy over the yearly office competitions. You won it two years in a row. Maybe I want another turn at one of those travel cruises they hand out."

She returned to the kitchen doorway and stared at him. "I thought you didn't like boats," she said carefully. "Besides, you tossed me Wyngate because...how did you put it? You were too busy with that high-profile criminal trial to take time for any local human interest story. Or did you expect me to do all the footwork, so you could—"

"I couldn't get close enough to that old man to do any footwork!" he snapped suddenly. "Did he tell you anything or didn't he? He's fallen under that spell of yours, I know that much. What are you waiting for? Just ask him to—"

"He died a couple hours ago, Scott. And let me tell you something, I—"

For the briefest moment he looked utterly stricken. But he recovered so quick, Dee thought she must have misread the response.

"Do you know what that means? These are dangerous people you're fooling with! You can't waltz in and take down the whole lot of them with one old man's confession and a desperate prayer!"

"Scott Evans, you've been reading my files!"

"It was an act, don't you see that? He was desperate, and the coward was trying to use you to get him out of that asylum."

"It is not cowardly to want out of a desperate situation. Just wait till it happens to you someday."

"I don't let things like that happen to me. I look out for myself."

"Nobody can take care of themselves all the time, that's the point."

"You can if you look far enough ahead. And what I see ahead now..." He rose to pace the floor. "Is you've got to kill that story."

"I can't do that."

"Yes, you can. It's too risky to turn any of that stuff in."

"I already did."

He stopped suddenly, swore, and turned around to glare at her. "Why couldn't you just mind your own business and stick with the missing fortune angle?"

"Maybe because I was raised to speak up whenever I see things going on that aren't right. We're reporters, Scott, remember? And, like you've been telling me for the last five years, investigation is part of the job.'"

"You were supposed to investigate diamonds! Not some farfetched allegations of a smuggling ring for donor organs!"

"They aren't farfetched."

"Your only way out now, is to say it was just some old man's demented delusion. Better yet, don't say anything. When did you turn it in?"

"This afternoon before I left the office. Devlin hasn't read it yet, or I'd have heard from him by now.'

"Maybe there's still time to go get it back, then."

"I doubt it." Dee didn't mention she had already told everything to the police. "Devlin said he was going to run the first segment Friday and the other two the following weekends."

"Well, if he does, you've killed us both!"

"What?' She closed her eyes and shook her head at this new absurdity.

"I hate it when you do that." It was a chilling tone, and in all the years they had worked together, she had never heard him talk like that.

"Then you mind your business for a change. Nobody knows you gave me the lead, I didn't mention it to anybody. If there's trouble, it'll be my trouble. This is the first significant story I've covered since I came to the *Columbia Herald*! I can't kill it. It's too important. A lot more important than just entertaining the public with a speculative account of where some lonely old man hid some jewels."

"Not just jewels. Stolen off some Russian royalty and they're worth millions now. Anyone who could legally claim them is dead." He returned to the couch and picked up the suit jacket he must have folded neatly and laid over the arm earlier.

Dee watched him put it on. "A man's entitled to do what he wants with what belongs to him, Scott. No matter how old he is or where it is in the world."

"Is that what he told you? That they belonged to him? You probably fell for that 'get me out of here and I'll share it with you' stuff, too."

"Obviously not, or I wouldn't have turned the story in."

Scott walked to the door. "In my opinion?" He opened it and turned back to her for a moment.

"That's exactly what the self-righteous, uncompromising, D.J. Parker would do." He started across the porch.

In my opinion. She had already heard that phrase once today. "Don't you dare try to talk Devlin out of this!" she warned. "Do you hear me, Scott? Because you don't know half what I'd do if—"

"Yeah, my mistake was in only knowing half." He crossed her short stretch of lawn. His car was parked nearly a block away. "Last thing I need to worry about, right now, is you sticking my neck out for me."

"You should be worried, breaking into people's houses!" She stepped onto the porch in her bare feet and yelled to his retreating back. "Which I will tell somebody about if you lay so much as a finger on that story!"

4
Drawn Away

*"It is only after one is in trouble that one realizes
how little sympathy and kindness there are
in the world." ~ Nellie Bly*

Dee stayed on the porch until Scott was out of sight. The nerve of him going through her private files! The duplicate key had to have been made last summer. Months before he even told her about Peterson's diamonds.

And what about this uncharacteristic fear at toppling the Wyngate Hospital corruption? Why, he was always digging up dirt on some public official down at the courthouse or delving into cold cases. A story like this should have been right up his alley. The kind they handed out Pulitzers for. They were constantly bantering about chasing that elusive prize. It had become a well-known competition between them down at the office. So even if it was Peterson's diamonds he was really interested in, why should he care that she had taken on the Wyngate Hospital scandal instead?

Stories where corruption was exposed to the

public in a local region could spark changes nationwide. Isn't that what Nellie Bly had done on her historic infiltration of Blackwell Island? Why, infiltration and exposure was her regular mode of operation. It's what got the most accurate (not to mention dramatic) results. The very thing that had first drawn Dee to investigative reporting in the first place. And while times and technology had changed since Nellie's time, human interest had not. Done well, a fantastic infiltration and discovery story could still garner interest and effect changes, today.

The very reason why she had jumped at the opportunity when Nelson Peterson reached out to her for help after personally experiencing the horrific illegal things that were going on at that mental hospital. Dee knew what she had to do the very moment he told her about it. This went far beyond investigative reporting. It had become a matter of her own personal integrity. Her editor, Ronald Devlin, had made the same choice for the same reasons and had even gone one step further by initiating the police investigation they were both cooperating with.

But what about Scott Evans?

He couldn't have known any of that information before reading her files today. Not without bumping into it the same way she had. By befriending Peterson, himself. Or at least someone like him. And in order to do that, he would have to be...friendly. Scott Evans might be Devlin's star reporter, but he was not much of a friendly person. No, that wasn't exactly true. He did have a way of making people laugh by poking fun at his own oddities. Like insisting he was allergic to paint fumes, and, on his salary, it would practically break him to have to stay in a hotel for two weeks.

Now, Dee wondered if he really did have his house painted, last summer. He had organized a charity booth for wounded war veterans at the Fourth of July picnic once, too. It was entirely manned by beautiful young girls handing out chocolate kisses, but it had brought in some substantial donations. People skills of a sort, but not really the friendly kind.

What did she actually know about Scott Evans?

Except that he had been in the newspaper business a long time, looked twenty-something instead of forty, and had contacts in every dark hole of the city. He told her he heard about Peterson's diamonds after dating one of the nurses who worked over at Wyngate. Probably somebody like that Jennifer, who had given her Peterson's note today. His last note.

Hadn't Scott admitted he already tried talking to the old man but never got anywhere?

She wasn't surprised. Peterson was way too sharp for that. A master manipulator, he could have anyone who struck up a conversation with him either bristling or cooing within minutes. An expert in human nature. Proven by the way he had so ingeniously set up the list system. He did not have a weakness for expensive whiskey and cigars. Those items were strategically placed on the lists to hide the things he was really bringing into the institution: all the items needed for his coming "great escape."

And while most members of the staff would never help him with that, there were more than a few who had no scruples about covering up, or even smuggling in, a few forbidden pleasures. No one knew what he was really up to.

No one but Dee.

Suddenly, she wondered just how much of her research notes Scott had actually read. Why...they were her personal notes, tucked away safely in her own home, and she had written down everything! Dee stepped back inside and leaned against the closed door in a moment of utter dread.

"Lord, what am I missing here?" she whispered. "How am I supposed to tell if this opportunity is a gift from you or some kind of trap from the devil?" Then, a terrible thought occurred to her. "How far into the files did he get? Enough to find out where the key to the deposit box is?"

It was at the very moment she spoke those words out loud that she was struck by such a sudden sense of urgency, she could hardly stand it. Next thing she knew, she was rushing around as if a fire alarm had gone off. No way could she wait till tomorrow to make that drive! Why, if he knew about that box, he might even...

She had to go, right now.

She called Marion to tell her to be ready by the time she got there, but there was no answer. Obviously she had gone somewhere for the afternoon and forgotten her phone. She was always forgetting her phone. It was still early, and even though Dee knew her friend would probably be home by dinnertime, she didn't dare wait that long. No telling what could happen by then. So, she changed into jeans and a black sweater (the closest outfit she could come up with for someone wandering around fishing boats), tucked her hair up into a black French cap with a narrow bill on the front, and literally threw a few things into her duffel bag.

By the time she left, it had been less than an hour since she first walked in.

While she filled up at the nearest gas station, the smell of spicy, deep-fried something made her realize she was half starved. She bought a large coffee, a piece of chicken, and an egg roll from inside the quick mart. But even with all her rushing around, the first stars of evening were already twinkling through dusky skies by the time she finally picked up Interstate Five to head south.

Five long hours later, she found the little fishing town Peterson had talked about. She pulled to the side of the road, just before a bridge that spanned a river near the end of town, then rolled down her window, as if removing the transparent barrier would help her see better.

Instead, an intoxicating breath of salt air wafted in. Along with the long, soulful dole of a buoy whistle somewhere on the water. A road wound its way down to the shore, and she could see twinkling lights illuminating a small marina at the end. Right in the spot where he said it would be. Dee remembered Peterson had marked it in the atlas last week. That was the starting place, he had told her.

Everything began from here.

She had taken that part of the story with a grain of salt, at first. Because, at that point, she was still having a hard time believing she could even get him out of the building safely. But the plan he had devised was so clever (almost as if he had done things like this before), he finally convinced her it might work.

All she had to do was steal him a set of scrubs from the hospital laundry (which she had no intention of doing and had purchased a set from a local thrift store, instead) and he would simply walk out through the housekeeping entrance during visiting hours. Ten minutes before they were over, so that most of the staff would be busy cleaning up after visitors and getting ready for the weekend.

Then she was supposed to drive him here to this little town, where he had money and a passport waiting for him in a safety deposit box at one of the local banks.

For this help he offered to donate a thousand dollars to any charity of her choice (he knew she wouldn't take a bribe).

However, if she agreed to act as a sort of temporary manager and help him with the business end of hiring a team to recover his diamonds, she could earn even more.

Keep that money—or give it away—that would be up to her own discretion. Her part of the entire project would only take a couple of weeks, here, in this little town. And she was scheduled for a two week vacation during that same time anyway. Oh, he had thought of everything!

She had looked into that project from every angle and could find nothing illegal about it.

Even though Peterson had told her, himself, what he had done during the war and why he had felt it necessary to hide the jewelry in the first place. Europe was in chaos after it was over. People were desperate. And desperate means called for desperate measures, he said.

Nazis were stealing heirloom jewelry everywhere they went, and that particular jewelry had been in the Strassgaard family for over two-hundred years. They were well documented and could easily be traced through the inlaid coat of arms. Which she could look up for herself, if she wanted to take the time.

Well she had, and they were. They were listed as stolen (like so many others) during the Nazi occupation of Holland. And, just as Scott Evans had said, the jewelry was worth a fortune, now, with not one family member left to make a claim.

Nels had told her exactly what happened to them. During a very brief cruise off the coast of Holland, in the middle of the war, the famous Hermann Göring had hired a boat on which Peterson occasionally served as a deck hand. It was there that he had first seen the Strassgaard jewels. Göring was well-known for traveling with his own personal hoard of stolen jewels. How Peterson had actually come into possession of them he had never elaborated on, but it certainly wasn't hard to guess.

It was a crime, lost among thousands suppressed for so long; the Strassgaard jewels were fair game to any treasure hunter that could find them now. Nelson Peterson just happened to be the wayward, desperate youth who had committed it and bore the brunt of guilt all these years. It was the reason he had asked Dee to pray for him in the first place. He wanted some measure of forgiveness before he died, even if he had to spend a good portion of his fortune to buy it.

So what was so different between Peterson and any other troubled young man of today? Sin was sin, and God never said he only forgave the small stuff. And if somebody—anybody—asked for it, they got it.

Only that familiar sense of peace that usually settled on new Christians never seemed to come over

Nelson Peterson. Instead, he became obsessed with the thought that there was some kind of curse riding on those diamonds that would take more than a five-minute prayer to get free from. That's when he declared he would make a pilgrimage back to the place he had hidden them and turn most of the proceeds over to charity.

He would even cooperate with the Wyngate investigation, if Dee could give him a guarantee that she could get him out of the place before the story was published.

Some place safe.

Dee agreed.

Not because of the diamonds (she wasn't sure they even existed) but because he had been an innocent victim of the corruption going on there even more than most of the patients. He had been committed there illegally. By some drug-running nephew, he told her, who was trying to blackmail him into disclosing the whereabouts of the jewels.

Everyone in authority stood by the falsified records that had landed Peterson in the asylum. His wild accusations were simply too bizarre to get past all the proper channels it took to get anyone un-committed. For five years Peterson tried to bribe anyone who might help him get out of the place. But his extravagant promises to share the wealth only seemed to prove his insanity even more.

Until one lone doctor finally responded.

That was four months before Dee came along to interview him for a human interest piece about recovering treasure that had been hidden during World War II. She and Peterson hit it off right away. It seemed he had been quite the adventurer in his day and had more stories about globe-trotting in the post-war era than anyone she had ever met. So she decided to stretch the piece into a series. Except that somewhere between interviews, something terrible happened.

Peterson lost a perfectly good eye.

It was punishment, he said. And that's how she got her big story. The one that began an investigation that would shortly topple this sordid little black- market ring for donor organs that had been going on there for years.

She should have felt good about it all, considering it was the biggest, most important and far-reaching story she had ever worked on. One that could affect some important changes in the entire system of state-run psychiatric hospitals. Except she didn't.

Something was off somewhere. Something just didn't add up. Now, she only had one week to sort everything out before the first installment would be published. Devlin hadn't read the last one, yet. The one she had turned in this afternoon. When he finally did read it, he was going to be in for one big surprise.

So, she hadn't exactly lied to Scott Evans.

She just hadn't told him all the truth.

And she certainly wasn't going to admit her plans for getting Peterson out of the place to anyone now. The poor man had been offered protective custody, but he wouldn't take it. Because their idea of protection was to place him in a similar institution under an assumed name. It seemed the District Attorney believed what was written on the commitment papers, too.

Nelson Peterson was eighty-two years old and had

been of sound mind and body when he first went into Wyngate. And four weeks ago, he lost a perfectly good eye to their donor program.

Which was why Dee Parker had taken it upon herself to get him out of there and deliver him to a "safe house" until his unique case could be brought before the proper authorities.

Just because a person committed a theft (many years ago), didn't mean they no longer deserved to be treated humanely. Especially if they were trying to make amends for it.

So, she took it upon herself to get him out and to take him to the safest house she knew of. It was her youngest brother's church in a small rural community, high up in the Cascade Mountains of Washington state.

As for the "treasure hunting" part of the proposition, she had promised they would all talk more about that after they got there. After all, there was no law against treasure hunting.

At any rate, the old man had been so overwhelmed at the generosity and commitment of her family to help him during his most desperate hours that he promised a sizable donation to whatever charity they chose. Something that would prove to be a miracle for the struggling orphanage her oldest brother Dan and his wife, Myra, ran in Somalia. One they had all been praying a long time for, simply because there were not enough buildings for the amount of kids who kept pouring in. Happy ending for everybody if Peterson came through with even a little of his promise.

And now... his entire fortune belonged to her.

Why, she could accomplish more good with that kind of money in a year, than a lifetime of investigative reporting! Her career had not turned out to be all she expected anyway. There weren't many reporters like Nellie Bly anymore. Champions of the poor and underprivileged who actually managed to change the world with their words. The world itself had changed.

Today's newspapers were big business. Now, they were governed by ratings and influenced by advertisers in much the same way the entertainment industry was. Besides that, the common people didn't feel as responsible for society as they used to. Didn't seem like it anyway. The truth was, other than her scandal piece for the editor's yearly human interest award, the rest of her year was filled mostly with covering social events and community projects.

One more reason why Peterson's legacy felt like such a temptation right now.

But she must not forget that old man had been tantalizing people with this crazy story for years. Still, the last missing piece of information... the item that would prove everything... rested in her hands, alone. "Lord, what should I do with it?" she murmured half-aloud as she continued to stare down into the dark, sleeping harbor.

What should she do if *Pandora's* box was exactly where he said it would be and actually had a key in it? The key to safety deposit box 127. According to Peterson, he had paid the rent in advance with plans of returning for it, himself, when he got out of Wyngate.

What he hadn't planned was that no one ever returned anywhere after Wyngate.

5
Enticed

*"But not once did I think of shirking my mission.
Calmly, outwardly at least, I went out to
my crazy business."* ~ Nellie Bly

Well, there certainly wasn't much she could do
this late at night. So she backtracked through the
center of town and stopped for a few hours' sleep at
one of the beach-side hotels. But early the next
morning, when her car finally wound its way down
that little road toward the waterfront... the very
moment she caught her first clear view of all the
fishing boats gently bobbing at the docks they were so
neatly tied to...

She actually felt like she had been there before.

Nels had described the picturesque place that
well. Steep green hills rose up on either side of a long
lazy river that widened where it emptied out into the
sea. The marina was tucked away on the south bank,
behind a man-made jetty that formed a straight placid
channel which led out into the river.

The first thing Dee noticed when she got out (besides the tang of salt in an early morning fog that was just lifting), was a large flock of seagulls circling overhead, calling and squawking to one another as if it were feeding time at the zoo. The object of their interest seemed to be a fishing boat pulled alongside a dock at a building farther down where a sign read, *Pacific Seafoods*. The nearest building to the parking lot was a restaurant.

She decided to have breakfast there but not before she took a walk down on the docks to see if her "inheritance" was actually there. If there really was an inheritance. *"The wealth of the wicked is laid up for the just..."* that phase was running through her mind again. Like a song she didn't know all the words for, it had been running through her mind all night long.

She was still checking things out. If there was even the slightest hint that it wasn't legal, she wouldn't take any of it. But at the very least, it would make a good follow-up story for the Wyngate articles. Something with a headline like: **Dying Wyngate Whistle-blower Leaves Fortune to Charity**.

That was it! If there really was a fortune, she could establish something called the Peterson Foundation. It would dole out money to various charities. She would merely be the executer of it all. It would be a sort of tribute to Nelson Peterson for thinking of her in this way, when he realized things weren't going to work out the way they had originally planned. Because it should have been the two of them coming down here next week instead of just Dee.

Oh, how could things have gone this wrong when she was trying so hard to help him?

A sudden memory of Scott Evans's warning that "these people aren't amateurs" flashed through her mind. But having begun her decent down the ramp to the docks at that moment, it left about as fast as it came. The time of reckoning was here, and she was about to find out if the wild story was true or simply one old man's very elaborate fantasy.

She felt a sudden fluttering sensation deep inside. According to Peterson, his fifty-six foot ketch *Pandora* should still be resting languidly in slip number forty-three, sorely rundown and neglected after the nearly five years he had been away from it. And in that boat, in a small box built into the back underside of a bookcase, was the key to safety deposit box 127.

Most of the docks were rickety and in need of repair. The slips were crowded to capacity with more than just fishing boats. There were other types down there along the docks, too. The bigger ones were farthest down, so they could come and go in deep water. Slip number forty-three would be nearly at the end of C dock.

Dee's inner butterflies increased just walking all the way out there. But when she actually caught sight of the back end of an old-time, classic wooden ketch with the letters *Pandora* fanned across the stern, she had to stop, take a deep breath, and will herself to calm down. Flashing neon couldn't have shocked her more.

Up close, it looked anything but run down or neglected. Instead of weathered gray, the teak deck and rails shown with the dark hue of fresh oil. The brass ports were polished and gleaming and even the sail covers looked new. But that couldn't be. According to Nels, the boat hadn't been touched by anyone for years.

Dee grabbed a stanchion and pulled herself aboard. The square cockpit was wide and roomy with an old fashioned pilot's wheel. The deck barely swayed as she crossed to the hatch, where louvered doors swung open as easily as if they were used every day.

After the bright light of outside, it was dark in there and she climbed down the ladder more by feeling than sight. The only boats she had ever been on—other than small boats at the lake—were two cruise ships that sailed to the Caribbean. Dee had never seen anything like this. Her foot bumped into something halfway down and a teakettle clattered to the floor.

By the time she picked it up her eyes had adjusted enough to reveal that she was standing in the center of a tiny kitchen. Everything one needed to cook was there; a stove, a small refrigerator, and even a deep stainless steel sink that gleamed at her from a smooth wooden counter. Why, a person could actually live down here!

All at once, there was a thump and muffled curse from somewhere close by and Dee jumped as if someone had pinched her. She hardly had time to turn around when a bare-chested man in a pair of cut-off jeans walked in from some sort of hallway behind her.

"What's the deal, lady—" he grumbled as he ran a hand through wavy, sun-bleached hair. "You ever heard of knocking?"

"For heaven's sake, who are you?" she asked as if

he had been caught in her kitchen instead of the other way around.

His hand stopped midway in the act of smoothing down an equally sun-bleached mustache, and he looked at her as if he hadn't heard right. "Wayne Hawkins," he finally replied. "What can I do for you?"

"You can tell me what you're doing on this boat, for one thing," she suggested. "Do you..." Her attention was suddenly riveted on an elaborately-carved, built-in bookshelf behind the maroon-upholstered dining area he was standing next to.

He sat down casually in front of it. "What are you? Some kind of private investigator?"

"Maybe." She looked him over carefully and tried to access his type.

Although she had obviously got him out of bed, he was not unkempt. His mustache was neatly trimmed and his hair, though curly, was not overly long. His hazel eyes looked peaceful and seemed to hold more curiosity than contempt. He also made no effort to conceal the fact that he was looking her over as equally as she was him.

She better get straight to the point.

"Have you ever heard of Nelson Peterson?" she asked. "Colonel Nelson Peterson?"

There were a few moments silence. "I sure have," he finally admitted. "He's the guy who used to own this yacht."

"Excuse me?" She spoke the words with emphasis, closed her eyes for a moment and tried to maintain some control. "I was under the impression that he still did."

"No one's heard from him in years." He crossed

muscular arms across his tanned chest. "The only reason it's still here is because it's some relic left over from World War II. There's a rumor it was used to entertain high up Nazi officials during the occupation of Europe. What was that famous guy's name...Göring or something.'

"So?"

"So, two years, ago, the slip fees stopped getting paid and the port authorities finally had to put a lien on it. Couldn't find Peterson anywhere. All the bills came back."

"You mean they just sold it?"

"Not exactly. It's going up for auction at the end of the month. I've been getting her ready. On account of, up until now, I've been the only one interested in making a bid."

"Oh."

"Did Peterson send you?"

"In a way, yes."

"He's dead, isn't he?"

The man had eyes one could not look into and lie at the same time. Not that Dee was the lying type. But she was certainly not ready to let go of the only leverage she had in the situation, either. Her connection with Peterson.

"Do you know how much this boat is worth?" she parried.

"A hundred thousand, if it's worth a penny." He seemed unruffled at the evasion. "If you count all the repairs and two years worth of unpaid dock fees."

"Is it...seaworthy?"

"Very."

"But it's over eighty years old. Doesn't that make

it less?"

"Pandora's one of the finest Holland-made yachts ever built," he insisted. "Outside of a little neglect, she's as sound as ever. But before we get down to talking business, I need some coffee."

"What makes you think I have any intention of—"

"Let's quit all the cat and mouse stuff." He got up from the table in a manner that made her feel like she had been pulling pranks in grade school and the principal just walked in. "You're the new owner, obviously. Swooping down just in time to put a wrench in the works."

"And obviously…" Dee stepped out of his way as he moved past her. "You have more interest here than just restoring an old boat that isn't even yours, yet. A pretty good guarantee since you're already living on it."

"I admit I've got a vested interest."

The aroma of fresh coffee wafted out of the can he was opening.

"Meaning?" Dee took his place at the table and could not help reaching a tentative hand under a certain carving in the bookcase behind it while his back was turned.

"Meaning I've put a lot of time and money into this old girl and I don't mind saying I—" He turned around in time to see her withdraw the little wooden box from its hiding place, slide back the top and stare transfixed at the small brass key inside. "I'll be a son of a…"

His voice startled her back to the problems of the moment and the fact that he was as much a "wrench in the works" as she was.

Their eyes locked and held.

In that moment, without words or explanation, they understood each other. It was a strange experience. Not even her best friend, Marion Bates, who could practically predict her next sentence, had ever penetrated her psyche the way Wayne Hawkins was doing right now. It might have felt like an invasion if she hadn't at the same instant, been able to read his.

He knew about the diamonds.

Not only did he know, he probably had some plan of his own to go after them. And he was at this very moment wondering how he should handle Dee Parker.

Well, Dee wasn't about to let him come to any conclusions. Having worked in the newspaper business long enough to know an offense was the best defense, her professional manner clicked in.

"I'll be by with the paperwork on Monday." She got to her feet and started for the ladder. "I'll pay for any repairs and all the other expenses then, too. Nice meeting you, Mr. Hawkins. I probably won't—"

"Hold it." He reached out one arm and blocked her way.

"I beg your..."

"You're not going anywhere until we talk, sweetheart, so you might as well sit back down."

6
Hooked

"Silently I marveled at my boldness to attempt such a feat...unused, as I was, to sea-voyages" ~Nellie Bly

There was the sound of a cheery whistle outside and a slight swaying of the deck as somebody came aboard.

"Hey, Hawk!" boomed a baritone voice from the cockpit. "I got eggs and bacon. They robbed me on the bacon, but—" A large bearded face that Dee thought bore a striking resemblance to Popeye's classic nemesis, Bluto, peered down through the open hatchway. "Oh, say. Didn't know you had company, boy. Want me to come back later?"

"Come on down, Starr." Hawkins took his arm away from in front of Dee but kept her nailed where she was standing with his eyes. "And meet the new owner."

"What?"

"Lady, here, says she's *Pandora*'s new owner and has the papers to prove it."

"Holy smokes." Starr eased his large bulk down the ladder without taking his eyes off her. "How'd that happen?"

"We're just about to find out," Hawkins replied. "Have a seat Miss..."

"Parker," she filled in for him. "Dee Parker."

"Miss Dee Parker." He turned back to the coffeepot. "Let's start at the beginning."

"It's simple enough." Dee sat across from the table this time, on the comfortable couch in matching maroon that spanned the salon. "Peterson left it to me. Free and clear. Except for the repairs you mentioned and the dock fees. That's all there is to it. Of course, there'll probably be an exorbitant inheritance tax if it's worth as much as you say it is. I wasn't expecting that."

"Meaning you'll sell?" Starr sank into a wide comfortable chair that belonged to a desk area across from the little kitchen. He turned on its swivel to face her.

"I hadn't planned on selling."

"What would someone like you want a yacht like *Pandora* for?" His laugh was deep and rolling. "You're obviously no sailor, and a gal like this costs a lot of money every year just to keep up."

"Because she knows about the diamonds." Hawkins poured coffee into three mugs and carried them to the table.

"Diamonds!" Starr exclaimed in horror. Who the devil said anything about diamonds?"

"Starr, she walked right over and picked up the key without so much as batting an eye. So let's all quit being so evasive and get down to business." He turned to Dee. ,"Now, what's your plan?"

"Well, to...go and get them, of course," she heard herself say, as if it had been her intention all along. The truth was she was still reeling at the fact that the yacht was even real. Much less such an expensive one. To actually be sitting on it was having a spellbinding effect on her. If the yacht was real (and exactly where Peterson said it would be) then the diamonds must be where he said they were, too. Wasn't it part of the original plan that she hire someone to help go get them?

At that moment, the old man's detailed plan suddenly sprung to life inside her with much the same force as a gambler who had just broke the bank. She never knew she was even susceptible to such feelings.

It was the most thrilling prospect she had ever experienced.

"We can take her in as a partner and split three ways," Starr thoughtlessly pushed up the white sleeves of his long underwear shirt that were drooping below the rolled-up cuffs of his plaid flannel one.

"A partner!" Dee set her coffee down before she had even tasted it. "It's my boat, remember? And you're forgetting I'm the one with the key. You obviously didn't know what it was for, or you would have used it already."

"We knew it was for *Pandora*'s box," Hawk countered. "We just didn't know where the box was. We do have the coordinates, though. And the know-how. Like Starr said, sugar...you're no sailor. You're going to need someone to sail it for you."

"Don't..." Dee closed her eyes momentarily for emphasis, "call me sugar. Maybe I already have the coordinates, gentlemen. And for all either of you know, maybe I am a sailor.'"

"We have the logbook," Hawkins pointed out. "If you do have the coordinates, then you must have the journal. And if that's true, you know you can't get the exact location of the diamonds without the logbook to go with it. That's how Peterson set it up. As for being a sailor, don't make me laugh. You came down the companionway backwards and..."

"How would you know how I came down?"

"You knocked over the tea kettle. If you'd have come down right, you'd have seen it."

"Whoever heard of a kitchen being right under a ladder anyway?"

"It's not a kitchen and it's not a ladder." Starr heaped three spoons of sugar into his cup and stirred with the same spoon before returning it to the sugar jar. "Case dismissed."

"Look." Dee tried a new tack. "You might have the logbook but you got it off the boat and it's my boat. Therefore...it is legally my logbook."

"The yacht's been abandoned for five years, sweetheart," Hawkins reminded her. "Legally, it's the property of the port."

He was fixing her with those penetrating hazel eyes again, and the effect was somewhat unnerving. Dee felt like he was looking right through her, and the constant use of words that were usually reserved for intimacy made her feel vulnerable somehow. All at once, a sensation she hadn't experienced in years washed over her. She was transported suddenly back to childhood days when the frustrations of being bested by older brothers were acutely stinging. Her crisp, well-practiced calm exterior started to crumble.

"I guess we'll just have to...talk this out in court." She got to her feet, feeling the need to make a quick exit before the tangled tumult of so many intense emotions betrayed her.

"Just a minute, now." Starr's tone was apologetic. "Back off, Hawk, will you? Can't you see you've got her flustered? Let's try and—"

"I am not flustered," Dee took a deep breath and sat down again. "I just didn't expect all this."

"You didn't expect it?" Hawk seemed dangerously close to the edge himself. "This is a bear of a situation to wake up to! What did you expect?"

"Like I said," Starr's voice was like a calming hand on the rising turbulence between them—" a partnership is the only logical answer. We don't need courts to settle this when we can do the same thing ourselves if we'll just sit down and be reasonable."

He cast a warning glance at Hawk, and then continued. "We all want the same thing, don't we? And we all have something the rest needs in order to pull it off. We're talking fifty million dollars here. I think that's enough reason to put our differences aside and cooperate."

Dee tried to determine Hawk's nature. He was leaning against the counter with one hand in the pocket of his jeans and the other holding the mug around its sides instead of by the handle, looking back at her with equal scrutiny. He didn't seem like the swindler type. But then, how many of them ever did? He gave her a certain feeling...almost as if they had met before...but of course, that was ridiculous.

"Let's have breakfast," Starr suggested. "I'm starved."

7

Pandora's Box

An hour later, Dee caught sight of her own reflection thrown back at her from the double glass doors of the First Interstate Bank. She hardly recognized herself. Yellow sundress, large floppy hat and sunglasses, all bought at a local tourist shop. She looked like something out of an old Alfred Hitchcock movie. The young assistant manager, who was accompanied by the effects of overindulgence in aftershave, had a rude glint in his eye when he looked at her.

And he stared at her for entirely too long.

"Well?" Dee lowered the dark glasses and gave him a firm glance. "Did I forget something?"

"Sorry." He held open the swinging wooden gate that led to the private viewing room. "Have a seat and I'll bring it in to you. There's a buzzer on the wall you can ring when you're done."

Dee sat down on the smooth oak chair at an equally smooth oak table and did not comment. Young people these days. Entirely too cocky. If she wasn't trying to keep such a low profile at the moment, she'd—

The door opened, and he stepped back inside to set box number 127 in front of her.

Then he left without a word.

Not until she heard the click of the completely closed door did she dare insert the key. Her heart suddenly began to pound. She lifted the lid to look inside.

There were the ownership papers to *Pandora,* neatly folded and official-looking and already signed over to...nobody. Only a blank line. How could that be? One certainly couldn't bequeath something to ‚the bearer,‘ and any self-respecting notary would never even sign such a document. Not if they valued their license, they wouldn't. Yet...if she did put her own name in there... At that point, Dee's eyes fell on what had been laying underneath that document. She knew immediately what it was and couldn't help a sudden gasp when she recognized the timeworn journal that held the exact location of the diamonds...in code.

Every page was filled with the neat, distinctive handwriting she had already come to recognize as his. There would be plenty of time to examine it more carefully, later. Right now, she could hardly believe she was actually holding these missing pieces of the famous puzzle.

"Thank you, Nels," she whispered. "I'll make sure it's used in the best possible ways, just like you wanted it to be." An almost physical sense of power swept through her.

At the bottom of the box, she found another large

envelope containing five thousand dollars in cash. A stab of guilt penetrated, but she couldn't think why. Hadn't the note said it was all hers? Money was not good or bad; it was how one used it that determined that and being a philanthropist was held in very high regard, these days. In fact, hadn't Nellie Bly herself taken over fifteen years off from reporting to do just this sort of thing after she married her wealthy husband?

That was the logical thing to do with such large sums of money. Besides, Dee felt sure that if she wasn't that kind of person at the moment, she could easily become one.

Meanwhile, she stashed the envelope into her bulky canvas bag that said *American Originals, Inc.* on it. That left only an old passport dated 1959, made out in the name of David Nelson. But the picture was Peterson. A much younger, almost rakish version of the old man, but definitely him. She got goose pimples. Beneath that, there was a black velvet box— the kind that held rings. Opening it, she found herself staring at the most beautiful setting of rubies and diamonds she had ever seen in her life.

They were exactly the way they looked in the research photos she had studied. The gold-work was done with amazing perfection in filigrees and fancy scrolls, on an unusual coat of arms. She recognized that, too. This was part of the collection! An exquisite piece of the Strassgaard family jewels. Just holding it in her hands was...absolutely breathtaking.

If there had been any doubt in her mind that the rest of the infamous collection was truly hidden somewhere along the Russian coast, it left her at that precise moment. She closed the empty deposit box with a decisive click and pushed the buzzer.

This time, it was not the cocky assistant manager who came but a very distinguished-looking older man with long gray sideburns. "All finished, Ms. Parker?" he asked.

"Yes, thank you." She had signed in, just as Mr. Peterson had instructed. How he put her name on that signature card she didn't know. But the old man was ingenious. Dee got to her feet and tried not to walk ahead of him too quickly. She nearly forgot to sign out again, but remembered at the last moment. The man seemed to be scrutinizing her signature as she scribbled it out. Her own nerves playing tricks on her, no doubt.

"Everything all right with Mr. Peterson?"

"As...well as can be expected...considering his condition." Dee took the sunglasses she had thoughtlessly hooked in the V-neck of her dress and put them back on.

"Good to have family around during trying times."

"Yes, it is."

"Give my regards to your sister when you see her again."

Dee never remembered exactly what she answered to that startling request because it hit her like another deluge of icy water. She didn't have a sister. And, as far as she knew, Nelson Peterson had no children. It suddenly felt hard to breathe. So she mumbled something non-committal and tried not to rush as she left. Once outside, she practically collided with the assistant manager who seemed to be enjoying a casual smoke next to her car.

"Nice hat." He dropped the nearly whole cigarette onto the pavement and ground it out with a perfectly polished shoe.

Dee put the car in gear and zipped out of the parking lot.

Once back on the interstate, she let out a long, slow breath. Activities like this were definitely hard on the nerves. But there was a long, five-hour drive ahead to calm down. Which she would need every minute of. Because obviously, she was also going to need every rational thought she could come up with from here on out. For heaven's sake, her heart was still pounding.

It was nearly midnight by the time she pulled into the alley that fronted Marion's basement apartment, back in downtown Portland. The lights were out, but she descended the few steps below street-level and rang the bell anyway.

After two more rings, Marion appeared in a hastily-donned bathrobe. Her short, gray-flecked brown hair was already askew from several hours of sleep.

"Well, thank heavens!" The older woman dragged her in. "You know I've been trying to call you all day? Why didn't you answer?"

"I took off without my phone. Must still be sitting on the kitchen counter from the last time I tried to call you."

"That just proves my point, Dee Parker, there's more reasons than grief for people to forget things."

"Well, maybe there is. Except I'm feeling sort of grief-stricken, myself. You wouldn't believe what happened, Marion." She sank into the easy chair in the one room studio: the couch having already been unfolded into the bed.

"Out with it, girl. Did you have any trouble springing him?" Marion headed for the kitchenette, filled an electric kettle and plugged it in for tea. "I wonder if it was a good idea to leave him all by himself in a hotel. What if he really does have dementia?"

"I didn't leave him by himself. Because he...he died yesterday."

"What?"

"And I have the most awful feeling it wasn't of natural causes. They had him in the violent ward." Dee leaned her head back. She had long since removed the floppy beach hat, and her curls were twisted haphazardly up into a clip which she realized was drooping. She unclipped it and twisted it up tight again.

"What happened?"

"Whatever it was, he saw it coming, and— She kicked her sandals off to prop her feet up on the corner of the bed. "He managed to slip me a note through one of the aides."

"What did it say...help? And you didn't get there in time?"

"He said it was all mine. Everything." She sat up straight. "Inside was a deed to a hundred thousand dollar yacht, and..."

"Are you kidding?"

"Fifty million in diamonds."

"I don't believe it!" Marion's mouth dropped open.

"Remember that wild story about those famous

jewels that were stolen by Nazis from some wealthy Russian-Jewish family?"

"I remember you said they were inaccessible. Hid on an island off some frozen Russian coast, that's what I remember. Dee, old people are always shocking anyone that will listen with whoppers like that. Is that the fifty million you're talking about? Well, I'm surprised at you. You're a very sensible woman, as a rule."

"I'm going."

She gasped. "What—to Russia?"

"Next week, to be exact. And I...I need you to

come with me, Mare. Because...well, there's safety in numbers."

"Dee Parker! What are you saying?"

"It wouldn't be much different than the cruise we went on, last year. A real adventure and it wouldn't even take..."

"But you know I'm not the adventuring kind! I wouldn't call visiting foreign countries on a huge cruise ship with hundreds of other people around the height of adventure anyway."

"You loved it."

"Of course I did. Because it got my mind off Bill, and it was wonderful of you to invite me. Only that's not the same thing. Why—" The kettle began to whistle, and she went back to the kitchenette to turn it off. "Russia! The Union of Soviet Socialist Republics! The KGB! It's dangerous over there, don't you know that? They're having some kind of—revolution or something. The whole country's falling apart from what I hear."

"Mare, listen to me." Dee breathed in the scent of

orange spice tea as it began to waft over the little room. "This could be the adventure of a lifetime. Not to mention the money part. I can't even imagine fifty million dollars. Can you?'

"Fifty million for a single set of jewelry? He had to be exaggerating!"

"It would be worth it even if it was a million, wouldn't you say?"

"But he could have dreamed the whole thing up. In the violent ward? He was probably as crazy as they said he was. The whole story was just some figment of his imagination."

"I checked it out already."

"Dee, you couldn't have been to Russia and back in a weekend. Look how long it took us just to get our passports last year."

"His yacht. Not only is it real, it's worth a hundred thousand dollars! I actually sat on it this morning. I even have a signed title for it already, five thousand dollars in cash, and—"

"Five thousand dollars!" Marion gasped.

"A pittance compared to what we're talking about, here."

"Pittance to you, maybe."

"I also have a ring that looks like a real czarina could have worn on her finger. Right now, right here in my purse." Dee snatched up the shoulder bag and fished around for the little velvet box. "There, take a look at that." Dee flipped open the spring lid and shoved it off to her.

Marion took it and moved over beneath the light in the kitchen corner as if she were in a daze. "Why, it's the most...fantastic...beautiful thing I've ever seen!" She let her breath out slowly. "You better give it back!"

"Who would I give it to? They're all dead, now, Marion. And Peterson gave it to me."

"I heard getting arrested in Mexico doesn't hold a candle to getting arrested in Russia." She murmured, almost to herself.

"Who said anything about getting arrested?"

"Believe me, it could happen." Marion finally tore her gaze away from the glittering jewels and handed the ring back. Then she got their tea. She put a heaping spoon of sugar into her own cup, stirred briskly, and then carried Dee's (without sugar) over to her. She sat down on the edge of the bed. All without saying a single word.

Dee could see her mind was already racing.

"It's not like vacationing in Hawaii, you know," Marion was still on the same track. "They say that whole country's run by the mafia now."

"Who says?"

"I think I heard it on the BBC. That's the only news I trust any more. Anyway, you can't just—" she blew warm steam away from her cup and sipped. "Get off the plane with a suitcase full of picks and shovels and start digging."

"We're not going by plane."

"We'd still have to go through customs."

"Not necessarily. We're taking the boat, Marion. My yacht!"

Marion looked up from her contemplation as if she hadn't heard right. "By ourselves? We could both be killed!"

Dee set her tea on the coffee table. "Have you ever

known me to jump into an assignment without figuring things out to the last detail? Look at the lengths I went to just to meet Peterson in the first place."

"This is way beyond pilfering information for a three-part scandal piece for the *Columbia Herald,* Dee. I'm telling you, we could both be killed!"

"Not if we hire professionals to run the yacht for us. That was Peterson's original plan, in the first place, and he wrote everything down to the last detail. I know I could follow that plan! It will be a bona fide treasure hunt. And, you'd get a share—that goes without saying. Everybody would. It would be listed under expenses. Professional boat handlers, Mare. I wouldn't do it any other way."

"There's professionals and...professionals. If you know what I mean. Why, it would cost a fortune to get somebody to take that kind of risk. Who in the world would do such a thing?"

"Why would we?" Dee countered.

"Well, for the money, I guess. Adventure you can find anywhere. But..." Now, she got a dreamy, faraway look in her eyes. "Just imagine not having to worry if you could pay all your bills next month. Why, I could write full time." She set her cup aside and began to pace. Her blue robe billowed with every turn she made between the door and the couch.

Dee had seen that fidgety concentration before and took it as a good sign. "What are you thinking?"

"I'm just wondering how we could be sure that anyone who would risk such a thing would even be trustworthy." She pushed a thatch of hair behind one ear. "That's what I'm thinking."

"You always said I'm a good judge of character."

"In the news media, maybe," Marion huffed. "How are you with the Russian mafia?"

8

Leaving Home

"I wondered if I should be able to pass over the river to the goal of my strange ambition." ~ Nellie Bly

Marion was in. Less than an hour later, she had packed her nearly-finished novel and a laptop computer into one suitcase and some clothing into another. Mostly ski clothes, because Marion heard it was cold in Russia, even at this time of year.

Dee put perishables from the refrigerator into a picnic basket, and by one-thirty in the morning, they were racing toward her place on the other side of town.

"Go on in. There's a backpack and some hiking boots I want to get down from the rafters while I'm out here." Dee said, as she pulled into the garage. She was halfway up an aluminum ladder when she heard Marion scream from somewhere near the vicinity of the kitchen.

The entire place had been ransacked.

Under any other circumstances, Dee would have called the police. But considering the only thing missing was a particular chart of the Russian coast that Nels had specially marked for her last week, she knew at once who to suspect.

Scott Evans was either trying to scare her…or get to those diamonds before she did.

There were no rules for treasure hunting.

With Nelson Peterson frantically seeking out accomplices over the last couple years, there could even be more than Scott who were involved. Who knew how much information he doled out to anyone who would listen? He had been so desperate to get out of Wyngate, there was every possibility he had handed out enough clues to send treasure hunters clamoring toward the *Pandora* from Canada all the way to Mexico. So she and Marion would have to be doubly careful.

People did strange things when large amounts of money were at stake.

That thought made any shred of caution that was left in her vanish.

Within hours, the two women were winging their way to the southern Oregon coast. Morning found them on the outskirts of Eugene.

Dee pulled off the interstate in a seedy section of downtown and began cruising slowly up and down the boulevards.

"Gads!" Marion woke out of a sound sleep and peered through the window at their surroundings. "We'll get food poisoning if we stop to eat in an area like this. What are we doing so far off the highway?"

"I need to check something out. Without the whole world knowing about it. That little town has eyes and ears all over and I wouldn't want word to get back to our partners. Or anyone else, if you know what I mean."

"Good grief, Dee, you're talking like some spy right out of the movies. Where did you get that crazy beach hat? I think you have more hats than most people have shoes." Marion gave a slight gasp when she caught sight of someone lying in front of the doorway to a shop. "Did you see that? There was somebody—there's another one! Dee, you've driven us right into the middle of some slum! Hang a U-turn and let's get out of here!"

"Marion." Dee took off the floppy hat she had bought yesterday and tossed it onto the back seat. Her hair was still a mess; the light brown curls still pulled up into the clip instead of combed. "There's something I haven't told you, yet." She spoke in a hushed tone, as if they weren't the only two people in the car.

"I knew it."

"There's a possibility...actually, it's just a feeling I have..." Dee parked in front of a block of run-down buildings.

"Will you say it, already? You're making me nervous. Possibility for what?"

"That Peterson wasn't exactly who he said he was."

"I could have told you that. Didn't I tell you that the very first time he..." Her gaze went to another odd-looking lump in front of a shop entrance. "Oh, my...Lord...I..." She leaned forward until her nose was practically touching the front windshield. "There's a dead man over there."

Dee's stomach did a flip-flop at the pronounce-ment but she forced herself under control and looked over to where Marion was pointing. "Probably just a..." She reached for her purse on the seat between them and opened the door. "A drunk who hasn't woken up, yet."

"Dee, get back in this car! I say you've driven us into a lowlife, dangerous..."

"I'm just going to make sure he's all right."

"He could be an axe murderer! It's none of our business!"

"Of course it's our business. We saw him, didn't we? Are we Good Samaritans or aren't we?" She pulled the strap of her bag over her shoulder and put her hat back on. "I'll be back in a few. I need something from this pawn shop right here."

"Then, I'm going to turn the car around and keep the motor running." Marion fumbled in her purse for a moment and came up with a cell phone. "I'll dial nine, one. And if you aren't back in five minutes, I'll hit another one."

"You hit someone with that cell phone, Mare, and it would only make them mad."

"The number one." She raised her voice as Dee shut the door. "If you're not back in five minutes, I'm calling 911!"

****

Marion slid over to the driver seat and watched Dee walk in front of the car, step up onto the sidewalk, and then cross over to the recessed doorway beneath faded red lettering on the side of the building that spelled out the words *Pappy's Pawn*. She leaned down to gently shake a shoulder... and the dead suddenly sprang to life.

It was an old man with leathery brown skin and a surprised but tolerant grin.

Marion couldn't hear what they were saying, but

the way he quickly got to his feet and opened the door for Dee, she was fairly certain he wasn't an axe murderer. So she hung up the phone and lowered the window, to sit there and wait.

It took closer to fifteen minutes by the time Dee came out again.

Meanwhile, Marion had turned the car around, parallel parked, watched a young woman several doors down roll a rack of used clothing onto the sidewalk, and kept the engine running, ready to start off at a moment's notice. Just in case.

So that when Dee climbed back in and closed the door, all Marion had to do was ease the little red Geo out onto the road and head toward the Interstate highway, again.

"Well, it cost me a pretty penny just to have them look, but that was the only kind of place I could think where they can at least tell me if it's real." Dee put her sunglasses on. "Those places are notorious for cheating people, though. I found out what I needed to, anyway. I made up my mind before I even went in, I wasn't going to take any offers."

"Believe me, if it was Cleopatra's wedding ring, they still wouldn't offer more than fifty dollars." Marion checked the rearview mirror before changing lanes. "That's the way those kind of people operate."

"They offered eight thousand."

"Eight thousand!" Marion jerked the wheel as she looked over at her and the car swerved slightly into the next lane before she corrected it. "What did you do? Sell it to pay for the trip? Eight thousand dollars!"

"Heavens, no! That ring is worth fifty thousand if it's worth a penny. I wouldn't even auction it off at

Christie's now. It's the best insurance we can get for what we're going to be doing."

"Fifty thousand dollars! Do you hear what you're saying?"

"It's a pittance compared to everything all together, Mare. Think about it."

"I'm thinking your pittance quotient just went from five thousand to fifty thousand in less than twenty-four hours. Are you sure all this is legal? What if it belongs to some long-lost relative or something and we're stealing somebody's inheritance?"

"According to my research, all the Strassgaards died in the war. I was very careful about that. There were some Kellermans that may have been distant relations...but I couldn't find any of them, either."

"They all died? The whole family just vanished off the face of the earth? Kellerman sounds like a pretty common name, if you ask me."

"Well, I'm not exactly sure. But believe me, Mare, we'll get the whole thing sorted out right, as soon as we get back. I wouldn't have it any other way."

"So, why don't we save the trouble of maybe getting ourselves killed and sort it out first? That ring all by itself is worth a fortune. Besides that, a bird in the hand is worth two in the bush, you know."

"But what if the whole collection, together, really is worth fifty million? The partners knew that before I ever even met them, yesterday. And what if, while we're fumbling around trying to do everything proper, Scott Evans gets there, first? Peterson gave them to me, Marion. Personally. Practically with his last dying breath!"

"I thought you said that old man might not even be

Peterson. What if he's the very thief that had to murder somebody to get them? A lot of those crimes went on in that war."

"Murdered somebody?" Dee looked out her window for a few moments, thinking. "Oh, you're...probably right. I wonder if we could get in trouble digging up stolen treasure sixty years after the fact? Even though it no longer belongs to anyone and we had nothing to do with the original crime."

"Beats me. But I know one thing." She clicked on the blinkers and turned onto the Interstate highway onramp, headed south. "Going to jail at my age would kill me."

Dee pursed her lips together and looked out her window again. "If it was a national treasure, I think the worst they could do is want it all back. Otherwise, it's fair game. All treasure can be traced back to some original owner, so that fact can't be relevant."

"Could be a finders-keepers sort of a thing!" Marion brightened at the thought.

"That's the way I was looking at it, too. But maybe we should go to the police anyway. Just to be sure."

Neither of them said another word for the next ten miles. On the outskirts of the city, Marion pulled into a fast food place.

"Listen. Bill and I used to have this rule when we were married. Never—never—make an important decision without sleeping on it for a night. Because the next day a person almost always regains their common sense."

"Marion, this isn't exactly a vacuum cleaner or a new car."

"But it's the same principle. Want an ice cream?"

****

It was nearly four o'clock in the afternoon when they drove into the marina parking lot. It's just that they kept thinking of little extra things they might need—a book on the basics of seamanship, extra batteries for their computers, and a few food items that were personal favorites.

When they gathered their things for the long walk out onto the docks, Dee suddenly realized how exhausted she was. She set her duffel bag and a suitcase down at space forty-three and knocked this time (as well as a person could knock on the side of a boat), but there was no one aboard the *Pandora*.

Marion came up behind her, panting under the load of both her suitcases. "This is it? Looks like something out of the eighteenth century. Where's the motor?"

"Inside somewhere, I guess." Dee climbed up over the rail, which was a little more difficult to do in her yellow dress than it had been in her jeans.

"Shouldn't we wait for the captain, or something?"

"I'm the captain, or something," she said more to herself than to Marion. "So we're moving aboard. Toss me the stuff, and I'll give you a hand up."

Once aboard, she didn't even take time to change. Instead, she left Marion to settle in and headed for the port office so that she could pay the outstanding bill before it closed. The partners had such a know-it-all attitude, she wanted nothing in the way of proving herself absolute owner of *Pandora*. She had to find out just exactly how far she could trust them. Until then, she would carry her canvas bag, with everything from the safety deposit box inside, wherever she went. She wasn't born yesterday.

As practical and business-like as Wayne Hawkins and his friend Henry Starr had seemed, she had no intentions of letting the journal (much less a fifty thousand dollar heirloom ring) fall into their hands.

She had made the deal with them because they already knew most of what she did and planned heading out on the expedition on their own anyway.

Now, she would not have to worry about them working against her if they were working for her, and a partnership seemed to be the only logical answer. Large sums of money did strange things to people.

The port office was small, but cheery. It had a bank of windows overlooking the marina and was attached on one side to a bustling bait and tackle shop.

Dee had to wait while the only person in attendance—a middle-aged woman with flaming red hair, who dressed like a teenager—filled out a fishing license for an elderly gentleman. According to several posters tacked between the docks and the bait shop, there was a salmon derby going on.

"What can I do for you?" the woman asked as the gentleman left.

"I'm here to pay a bill," Dee replied. "Quite a big one, I understand. For the *Pandora,* in slip number forty-three?"

"*Pandora*? That's Hawk's boat. There's no money owing on that one. As a matter of fact..." she flipped through a desk file a few feet away. "He's paid up for next year, too."

"That's funny. Yesterday, he told me the dock fees hadn't been paid for two years and next month it was going up for auction."

"Well," the woman hesitated as if she had to decide whether or not to confide in Dee. "Formally…" she drew the word out long, as if what was going to follow was a good piece of gossip. "It is going up for auction next month. But he's got an in with the Harbor Master and the whole thing's already decided. Know what I mean?"

"I'm beginning to. You wouldn't happen to know where Hawk is right now, would you? He wasn't on the boat."

"Oh, if I was going to guess, I'd say he's probably over at the *Seahorse Lounge*."

"Next to the restaurant?"

"That's the one. His party came in about an hour ago with the biggest catch of the day. Thirty-seven and a half pounds. If nobody brings in anything bigger before midnight, you can chalk up another twenty-five bucks for Starr's Charters."

"He works for Starr's Charters?"

"They're partners."

"I thought he worked here at the port. On boats or something."

"Only when you can talk him into it. My computer's been down for three days and can I get him over here? But," she sighed wistfully, "if I had the kind of money he does, I'd only work whenever I felt like it, too."

"I should probably head over and talk to him, then. How late will you be open?"

"Oh, I'll be out of here by five but we open at eight every morning. Thinking about buying *Pandora*?"

"Something like that."

"Hawk must want to sell pretty bad. You're the second person to ask me about it this week." She laughed and shook her head. "That boat's changed hands more times than a fickle woman! People always show up out of nowhere, put a bunch of money into her, then get scared and take off. Been watching it happen for years."

"Sounds like you know something nobody else does," Dee prompted.

"I do indeed." She smiled and pointed a bright nail-polished finger toward one of the bay windows. "Been working here fifteen years and know all there is to know about every boat in this harbor."

"Mind sharing what you know about *Pandora*?"

"Not a bit. Like I say to everybody. Don't tell me any secrets because I never keep them. And the secret on that boat is..." She leaned her forearms on the smooth wooden counter and looked Dee straight in the eye. "There's a curse on it."

9
Small Craft Warning

"Can you start around the world day after tomorrow?"
"I can start this minute," I answered, quickly trying to
stop the rapid beating of my heart. ~ Nellie Bly

The *Seahorse Lounge* was fairly quiet. There were a few obvious regulars seated at the bar, a man with a table to himself in one corner and a noisy party of eight beneath the windows that looked out onto the water. The dance floor and stage were empty but a glimpse of the current band's poster on the wall told Dee the place was of the honky-tonk variety.

Wayne Hawkins was sitting with his back to her at a crowded table with a woman next to him.

Starr gave her a friendly wave.

There were several tanned beauties among the group, as well as a few fishermen.

"Pull up a chair, Dee," Starr boomed. "We just ordered the best steaks in the house."

"Well, that's awfully nice of you." Dee smiled her most enchanting smile as she came up behind Hawkins. "Actually..." She laid a deceptively friendly hand on Hawk's shoulder but pressed it with much the same firmness as a teacher who had caught one of her pupils cheating on a test. "I was hoping I could steal Hawk, here, away for a few moments?"

Hawk reached for her hand with an equally firm grip as he stood. He tossed three quarters on the table, without letting go of Dee's hand. "Pick out something good on the juke box honey, and I'll be back before it's over."

"Is there someplace we could talk?" Dee snatched her hand away as they walked off.

"Sure. How 'bout my office?"

"Fine. Where is it?"

He pointed to a table in one of the darkened corners of the room.

"That's not —" Dee protested.

"We can talk here." He waved at the bartender as they sat down. "What happened?" He eyed her hat and the sunglasses hooked over the first closed button of the yellow dress. "You look like you came straight from work yesterday. I didn't expect you back before Thursday."

"Well, for one thing..."

A cocktail waitress came to the table with a glass of beer and set it on a napkin in front of him. "Thanks, Terry." He smiled at the young woman.

He had a charming smile, if one were to look at him that way. There was a sparkle, the kind that made people smile back without realizing it.

"Anything else?"

"Nothing for me, thanks," Dee answered crisply. "I'm fine."

"I think Dee Parker looks like..." He scrutinized

her. He must have had several drinks already. "The strawberry daiquiri type," he finally pronounced.

"I am not here on a social call, Hawkins," she spoke quietly, "And I don't drink."

"I don't like to drink alone."

"Obviously. Why did you pay the outstanding bill on *Pandora*?"

"Because I always pay my bills."

"But *Pandora* is mine. And I want everything done right and legal before we leave. Since you had an in with the harbor-master and are already registered as the current owner, I'm going to need your signature before they'll change it down at the DMV. Honestly, is there anyone in this town that doesn't know who you are?"

"Small towns are like that."

"Then you'll come with me to get it straightened out?"

"I didn't say that."

"But you agreed to cooperate. Something like this could hold us up for days." She ran a thumb over a smooth edge of the wooden table. "Do you want to get going, or don't you?"

"What happened, Dee? Yesterday, you could barely agree to leave in a week and now you're acting like you want to untie and take off tonight."

"Could we?"

His air of playfulness vanished and he suddenly looked deadly serious. "You told somebody."

"Not exactly. It's just that..."

The girl returned with a strawberry daiquiris and Dee smiled at her. "Could I return this for one that's heavy on the strawberries and no on the daiquiri?" Not that she was so inclined to order anything at all in a place like this. It's just that she had to do something to avoid that penetrating gaze as Hawk paid for the drink. He didn't take his eyes off her.

"Go on," he prompted when they were alone again.

"I just have a bad feeling about it, that's all. And I would just as soon—"

"Listen, sweetheart..."

"Don't call me that."

"No games. Understand? This is a dangerous enough venture we're in all by itself. So if you gave someone—anyone—the least little inkling something was up, you better tell me. People do crazy things for this kind of money. Secrecy, you got it? Secrecy is our best ally, sugar. Now, what happened?"

"When I got home, someone had gone through my apartment."

"Sure it wasn't just a routine burglary?"

"They only took one thing." The waitress returned and set down a glass of blended strawberries. Dee thanked her and then took a sip. "A chart of the Russian coast Nels marked for me," she finally admitted.

Hawk muttered under his breath and got to his feet. He walked a few paces away and then back, giving her the distinct impression he was about to lose his temper. But he didn't. Instead, he sat down and leveled his gaze on her. "You have a passport?" he asked.

"Yes."

"With you?"

"Yes."

"The papers on *Pandora*?"

She nodded.

"Let me see them."

Dee reached into her canvas bag and handed them over. Better to confront things between them here and now instead of run into problems later on. Especially if he might contest the validity and force her into doing anything legal, just to prove it.

"Looks official enough," he pronounced after a moment.

"They're official. Signed by Nelson Peterson." She reached across to tap an insistent finger on the old man's signature. "Notarized and everything down there on the bottom, see?"

"I see."

"Here come the steaks, Hawk," some woman called across the room.

"Be right there, doll." He got to his feet and handed her the papers. "I'm going to finish eating with these folks so nothing will look hasty. But I want you to go ahead and—where's your car?"

"In the parking lot."

"You can't leave it there until we get back. Anybody could trace it."

"You mean the police?"

"I mean anybody. Let me have the keys, and I'll park it in Starr's garage."

Dee hesitated.

"Listen, sugar, if you're having second thoughts, you better quit right now."

"Don't"—she reached for her keys—"call me sugar!" She handed them over.

"Just settle in on *Pandora* and get some rest," he

offered with a congenial smile. "You look like you need it. Take any cabin you want."

"Maybe I'll take the captain's quarters," she snapped, "as long as you're feeling so generous." She expected a complaint, knowing he had already claimed the luxurious main cabin at the back of the yacht as his own.

Instead, he flashed another one of his winning smiles. "Nicest offer I've had all day."

****

Back on *Pandora*, Marion had already moved into the forward cabin. "I hope you don't mind,"—she called when she heard Dee come in—"but this one has a little desk that's perfect for my laptop."

"I don't mind. Remember what the book said though." They had been drilling each other from the new seamanship book on the long drive down. "Forward cabins tend to toss more when under way."

"I don't get seasick," she replied. "Besides, those cabins in the back are already taken. So I put your things in that one on the right, just across from the bathroom. That's the cutest little bathroom. It even has a shower!"

"All the comforts of home."

"Speaking of home, where is everybody?"

Dee stretched out on the wide, comfortable bunk and leaned back on the pillow. "They're over at the local bar getting totally smashed. After which we are going to"—she fished for the right phrase— "set sail."

"What?" Marion stopped laying her papers out on the desk and gave Dee an astonished stare. "It's getting dark outside. And remember the two red flags we saw hoisted up on the pole when we drove in? Small craft warning. Some kind of a—storm at sea!"

"Well, we better mention that when they get here because I don't think they'll notice. I'm bushed. I think I'll change into some jeans and try to catch a nap before all the festivities start."

"I thought you said Friday was the big day." Marion snatched a few tissues from the top of a built-in dresser and swathed cold cream off her face. "I was thinking we were done for the night. But I better get decent again and run out for some Dramamine."

"He took the car."

"Oh, gads. Well, I'll try that little bait shop if they're still open."

"I thought you didn't get seasick."

"Not since they invented Dramamine, I don't." Though nearly twenty years older, Marion was the most spur-of-the-moment, enthusiastic, anything-for-fun person she knew. They had met three years ago, when Dee took over Marion's cooking column at the *Columbia Herald,* so that she could retire to work on her novel. And even though they came from opposite ends of life's spectrum (Marion was a widow with two grown children, while Dee had never married), they were kindred spirits.

"Well, don't be too long, Mare," she warned. "I wouldn't put it past these guys to take off without us. Or maybe even dump us somewhere."

"Dump us!" Marion gasped.

"Figure of speech. I mean, try to get us to quit or get off in some local port before we ever really get started."

"But you said they seemed decent! Now you're talking like they're pirates right out of the movies!"

"Maybe the only people who go after treasures are pirates of some kind."

"And just what does that make us?"

Dee pulled the clip out of her hair so she could rest more comfortably against the pillow. "I think if we were any better, we would have called the police this afternoon."

"We haven't not called them," Marion reasoned. "We're still deciding. It hasn't been twenty-four hours yet."

"A lot can happen in twenty-four hours, Mare."

10
Down to the Sea

*"Never having taken a sea voyage before, I could
expect nothing else than a lively tussle with
the disease of the wave."* ~ *Nellie Bly*

By the time their partners returned, it was nearing
two o'clock in the morning. Dee came awake
suddenly to the sound of voices and the thump and
crunch of things being tossed rapidly into the cockpit.
She fumbled in the dark for shoes and made her way
up on deck, still trying to blink sleep from her eyes.

The whole world had changed. The wind hit with
an eerily steady strength as she climbed out of the
hatchway, and there was constant flapping and
clanging of rigging from boats all over the harbor.

She zipped her lavender windbreaker snugly up
under her chin, but it had no hood to keep her loose
hair from whipping around her face.

"Hey, cutie, did we wake you up?" Hawk handed
her a box and reached for another as if she had come
up to help.

"Will you quit with the Casanova stuff?" Dee fell

85

into the rhythm of passing and stacking the supplies as he handed them up over the rail.

"Uh-oh. Looks like we've got the wake-up-grouchy type. Probably going to be like this every time it's her turn to stand watch. What do you think, Starr?"

"I can't think with a headache," Starr grumbled from the dock where he was unloading the supplies from a cart. "You could've at least told me we were leaving tonight before I drank six beers."

"Two grouches," Hawk pronounced.

"Are we leaving already?" Marion emerged from the companionway, wearing her blue-flowered bathrobe and curlers in her hair.

There was a dead silence as the two men stared at her.

Hawk cast Dee a questioning glance.

"This is my friend Marion Bates. Marion, this is Wayne Hawkins and Henry Starr. Better known as—"

"Will you step into my office for a minute?" Hawk took Dee by the arm and pulled her over the rail of the boat and down onto the dock.

She might have stumbled if he hadn't had a firm hold on her, which he did not let up on until they were two boats away.

"Hey!" Dee pulled her arm free and stood still. "What do you think—"

"You have any more surprises you haven't told me about?"

"Listen, I didn't sign on for one of your charters, you know," she objected. "I signed you on for mine!"

"Wrong. This trip was planned a long time before you got here, sweetheart, and if you were three weeks later, you'd have missed it."

"It's my boat, Hawkins. Legally, I could hire someone else to run it for me."

"Legally, I could hold things up in court long enough to keep you from going at all, Miss Dee Parker. I've got papers on it, too."

"According to the lady up at the office, not good for three weeks!"

"Will you two shut up?" Starr complained. "While you're standing there arguing over something we already settled, that bar we gotta cross is kicking up like the devil out there. Partners, remember? That's what we decided. So we got four now instead of three. So what. Just get your butts over here and get busy."

There was nothing but silence for a minute.

"Welcome aboard, Marion," Starr added and handed the last box up to her.

"No more secrets," Hawk said as they started back. "Got that?"

"Oh, sure. You tell me yours...partner... then I'll tell you mine.'

Getting under way was quite a project. Which led Dee to believe that getting a fifty-six-foot yacht out of a crowded harbor was a lot more complicated than pulling a bus out of a garage. It would have been a nightmare if she and Marion tried doing it alone, in spite of their newfound sailing knowledge.

Pandora's classic beauty came to life in a confusion of lines and rigging, each of which had a specific purpose vital to her operation. There were ropes to untie and others to tie down, while some needed to be untied and tied all over again. The engine was turned on and rumbling so far in advance Dee had become accustomed to the rhythmic drone of the diesel and only realized they were moving when the dock seemed to slip away of its own accord.

By that time, nearly an hour had gone by.

After stowing all personal effects that had been unpacked back into secure status again, the *Pandora* finally eased out and pointed her bow toward the sea. Outside the sheltered harbor, there were whitecaps on the crests of waves breaking at ten to fifteen feet in a brisk wind. But the sleek, gracefully-built yacht only shook the breakers off her gleaming decks and plowed with a steady, determined effort away from land. As if she remembered and was grateful for being let loose into her element again.

Hawk, who up until now had been preoccupied with the details of getting under way, was suddenly spellbound. "Starr, look at her! Even in this weather she handles like an angel."

"Yeah, yeah. But if you don't dump at least some of this wind, boy, I'm gonna have the pukes all the way to Frisco."

Dee clung to one of the support bars that the safety lines were strung through all around the rails and was glad she had given in to Marion's promptings to take a Dramamine. The trip over the bar resembled one of those fast moving carnival rides.

Marion sat next to her, clinging onto another support bar. She had traded her bathrobe for a sweat suit and bright orange life preserver—bought from the bait and tackle shop along with the Dramamine—and had fastened it over one of the navy blue cockpit jackets they had each been given.

The jackets were made with a special clip at the side which attached to a safety line. The lines ran through the support bars.

Looking at the frightening rise and churn of

impending waves, Dee could see little help the clips would be, outside of being a means to haul one's body back aboard after it was already drowned. She wished she had swallowed her pride and put on a life preserver like Marion.

The waves loomed up like dark giants and began to break over the decks with unnerving regularity. Everyone got soaked beneath the frequent cascades of cold, shocking water. The decks, as well as lurching, were slanted at a steep angle and made a person constantly feel as if they were falling off.

Dee began to get truly scared.

Two grueling hours later, the situation had not changed. If anything, it was growing worse. Starr could do little more than hang over the lee rail and curse between retching, and Marion, who had lost several of her curlers in the breaking waves, looked pale as a ghost in the moonlight.

"Captain Hawk!" she cried. "Shouldn't we pull into—into land somewhere and—and wait this thing out?"

"We pull into land in weather like this," he called back, "and they'll be picking us off the beach in bits and pieces. We're coming up on Cape Mendocino. Worst cape on the whole West Coast. Ready to take the helm, Marion?"

"What?"

"Take the helm. It's time to change the watch."

"But I don't know how!"

"Have to learn sometime. Starr's half dead, and the prima-donna over there looks too scared to move. Come on over."

Dee would have liked to give him a smart reply, only she was too miserable. Common sense told her he must know something they didn't, because he was far too casual. At the same time, she could not conquer the natural fear that had her rooted to her spot and could do little more than watch the five minute lesson he gave Marion before he went below.

"Hey!" Dee managed to call before he disappeared. "Are you just going to leave us out here by ourselves? What if something happens?"

"Between the three of you, I think you can handle it. I'm tired and it's almost dawn."

"Tired," she murmured after he was gone. "What does he think the rest of us—"

"It really isn't that hard, Dee," Marion said. "I'm actually getting the hang of it. All I have to do is keep it on course, and I do that by just watching this—"

At that moment, a deluge of frothing ocean thundered down on top of everything. The dark water had approached unseen from behind.

Pandora shuddered and shook her way free, but the force of receding waters was so strong, Marion could barely hang onto the wheel, much less keep it on course. The bow swerved, and too much wind against the giant spread of canvas created more pressure above water than below, threatening to roll the yacht completely onto its beam-ends.

Dee jumped up to help Marion regain control, but it was like trying to pull against centrifugal force and the boat didn't seem to respond.

"Help us, Starr!" Marion yelled at the slouched and silent figure as *Pandora* began to roll. "Help!"

11
Abducted

*"The commander of the ship set an example
for rudeness." ~ Nellie Bly*

The two women pulled with their combined strength against the wheel, and as the water receded from the cockpit, *Pandora* slowly began to regain herself.

"It's—too much for me!" Marion panted. "Go get Captain Hawk! That Starr man's either passed out, or he's dead!"

Reality hit Dee like a revelation. Her fear left. In its place, welling up like the storm around them was a seething, righteous anger at the realization they were being tricked. She stumbled across the cockpit, now only ankle deep in water, and shook Starr's massive shoulders. "Get up and help you no good—"

"Holy fright, Dee!" he bawled, "haven't you got any respect for a dead man?"

"Partners, you said!" What kind of partner would try to cheat the first night out? You're nothing but a—"

"All right, all right." He got to his feet and brushed

her off. "Tell it to Hawk, it was his idea. Here, Marion, let me show you how to dump some of the wind out of those sails and use the self-steering gear."

Dee headed for the companionway, angry enough to burst into the captain's quarters and yank Hawk out of bed. She brought a deluge of water down the ladder and barely succeeded in keeping her balance when her foot slipped off the wet steps and sent her in one long leap to the galley floor.

"Better learn to use the handholds, babe," Hawk said quietly. "Unless you want to spend most of the trip on your backside."

"No thanks to you!" She moved toward the sink, knowing instinctively he was there, but unwilling to run into him in the dark. She stopped at the edge of the counter. "Where's the light? I want to talk."

There was the click of a switch and the faint red glow of a navigational light spread over them. Hawk leaned against the counter with his feet braced squarely on a two-inch high brass rail that ran the length of the galley floor and seemed to be specially for the purpose of allowing one to keep their footing on a slanted deck. He was leisurely sipping from a mug of coffee.

She had noticed the rich, inviting aroma the minute she came in, but it only served to irritate her more because he was enjoying the small comfort alone while the rest of them stood wet and shivering outside.

"You have your nerve!" She wiped dripping saltwater from the side of her face. "If you're going to war, you ought to at least have the decency to declare it! Just how far were you planning to carry this charade? Until we rolled over completely? Or sank, maybe?"

"*Pandora* can handle a knock down without sinking. She's a good boat."

"You mean you were just going to stand down here and let it happen? What kind of—"

"This isn't some pleasure cruise, Dee. If you're going to give out on me, I need to know now. Not after we get ourselves in a fix somewhere off the coast of Russia."

"So," her voice trembled with outrage. "You have absolutely no faith in me!"

"Baby, I don't even know you. Two days ago, you walked into my life and turned everything upside down. In one slick move you ruined what I've been working at for six months! I'm supposed to be happy about that? Come on."

"Well, it was a shock for me, too! I wasn't expecting to find you here."

"No, it was an inconvenience for you. I'm the one that got the shock. You pulled my own boat out from under me!"

"That's not fair, Hawkins. I agreed to sell it back after this was over. Under the circumstances, that's pretty reasonable. If you thought different, you should have come right out and said so instead of...instead of acting like..."

Dee realized she was shaking. From anger or cold, she couldn't tell, but her teeth began to chatter, and she suddenly felt like she was going to slip into a dead faint.

"Here, drink some of this." He handed her his mug. "Then get out of those wet clothes and try to get some sleep."

"No, I'm—I'm going to stick it out till Frisco!"

"It's two more days until Frisco."

"Until my turn at the—helm, then."

"You've got two hours until your turn. I'll wake you up."

"What about Marion? If you're mean to her for one minute, Hawk, I'll—"

"Marion's a peach, that's easy enough to see. Anyone that'll take the helm for the first time under these conditions is all right by me. You're the only one I'm having trouble with, honey."

"Don't call me that."

"Go to bed."

"And don't boss me!" She handed the empty mug back to him and started toward her cabin. It was the first time she could remember not finishing an argument. But at the moment, she didn't care.

It took some time and ingenuity to get out of her cold, clinging clothes in the dark cabin. Her light didn't work. The floor was slanted and constantly moving. She let her wet things lay where they fell and was satisfied to find a dry T-shirt to replace them with. Whether it was inside out or backward, she hadn't the time or inclination to bother with. She was freezing.

It took more time and ingenuity to figure out how to stay in a bed that was practically vertical. Just as she was contemplating a move to the floor, she discovered a hammock-like nylon mesh attached to the bedrail that fastened to little brass cleats on the ceiling above her. The result was that one could sleep level and comfortable while the boat was at any angle. By that time, she was as exhausted as if she had just run a marathon instead of sitting immobile on a wet, cold deck for three hours.

She hit the pillow and that was the last thing she remembered.

****

Although there was gray daylight filtering through her porthole when she woke, Dee could have sworn she had been asleep only a few minutes. She could smell bacon and coffee, but didn't have the energy to do any more than roll over and close her eyes again.

The door opened and Hawk leaned his wind-tossed blond head inside. "Hey. On deck, sugar. It's your turn on watch."

"You could at least knock," she grumbled. "Go away. I'll be up in a minute."

"That's what you said last time. This isn't the *Queen Mary*. If you're late, someone else loses sleep."

"I said I'm coming."

"Five minutes before I haul you up there in your pajamas."

The door closed.

"Hawk!" she called. When he leaned in again, she threw her pillow at him.

He caught it and tossed it back. "I'm not kidding."

"Neither am I."

It was Starr who was bustling around in the galley when she finally made an appearance a few minutes later. Breakfast had obviously come and gone. He was scrubbing the frying pan, banging and clanging, looking as if he had been on a three-day vacation instead of awake and on deck all night.

"Here." He handed her a fried egg sandwich

wrapped in a napkin. "There's fresh coffee in the thermos on deck to go with it."

"Thanks. I thought after last night, you'd be giving me the bread and water treatment."

"Like I said, that was Hawk's idea. Better head up there. Though, he's in a lousy mood this morning."

"So I noticed. Where's Marion?"

"Went to bed a little while ago, exhausted. I'm about ready to do the same."

"You mean I have to be by myself?"

"Hawk's up there."

"Great."

"You know, if you two can't iron out your differences by the time we get to Frisco," he suggested. "Maybe we should go to plan B."

"Such as?"

"Such as..." He kept wiping the counter without looking at her, as if it had suddenly become important to make it shine. "You and Marion fly out. Meet us in Japan or something."

"Oh, right. The way he's acting he wouldn't bother to pick us up. He was starting out alone in the first place, remember? Which means he thinks he could do it without me."

"You walked in with the exact location. That changes things."

"He doesn't trust me, Starr."

"Do you trust him?"

Their eyes met.

"Thanks for the sandwich." She headed up on deck.

Everything had changed, even though it was still stormy and the seas were nearly as high as before.

Only now, *Pandora* was plowing steadily through them with less jostling and very little water breaking over her decks.

Hawk was stretched out on one of the red cushioned seats, reading.

"What happened?" she asked. "The weather looks the same but the boat feels a hundred percent better. You can even walk across the deck without hanging on."

"We reefed the sails and fell off the wind a little. Where's your jacket?"

"Still wet, so I had to wear my own."

"The one I gave you has a built-in flotation system, that's why we use them. There's a dry locker next to the engine room. If you hang it there every time you go down, it'll at least stay wearable."

"I'll remember that. But please don't play the big brother with me. I already have four. Besides, I've been taking care of myself for a long time, and I'm sort of used to it."

"There's no room for mistakes out here."

"So I absolve you of the responsibility if I happen to make one."

"You're my responsibility as long as you sail with me, sweets, so clip the safety line on and wear your flotation jacket next time."

"Hawkins?" She pocketed her sandwich and reached for one of the safety cords, which were fastened to the lines that now held up squares of maroon-colored canvas and formed a windbreak around the cockpit. "Let's be honest with each other here."

"It's too early to get serious yet."

"Oh, all right. But at least tell me what I'm supposed to be doing. Don't I have to take my turn at the helm?"

"She's steering herself." He turned a page and replied without looking over at her. "All you have to do is watch. Check the compass now and again to see if we're on course, scan the horizon frequently to make sure no ships are bearing down on us. We're in the middle of a shipping lane. Otherwise, just let me know if there's a change in the wind so I can adjust the sails. In the meantime, you can read, walk around, or do whatever you want."

"What are you going to do?"

"Watch you until you get the hang of it."

"Hawk, look. We've got to come to some sort of truce, here, or... "

"Have some coffee, Dee."

"I can't ignore when something's bothering me."

Her black French hat began to slip, and she pulled it off before she lost it. But when loose hair flew in all directions, she had to fumble to get it back on again. Must have lost her hair clip sometime during the night. If the wind got any stronger, she would have to tie something under her chin just to keep her hat on. Dee closed her eyes with a frustrated sigh and moved over to sit in the more sheltered corner of the seat against the cabin to block the wind.

When she looked up, she caught Hawk watching her frustrations with a satisfied twinkle in his eye but she decided to ignore it. "Can you at least tell if you're with me or against me, for heaven's sake?"

"I'm here, aren't I?" He closed the book, tossed it aside, and sat up. "Business partners. I'm not going to sabotage my own investment, Dee."

"I just don't want to be our own worst enemies; that's all." Dee took her sandwich out of her pocket and began to unwrap it. "Partners should at least trust each other."

"Trust is something you earn, sugar." Hawk reached for the thermos and poured coffee into his mug and another nearby. "A back and forth sort of thing. So, how about I tell you something you should know and then you do likewise? That would be a good start on us both being trustworthy."

"As long as it's something we could prove." Dee stopped eating for a moment as she contemplated the thought. "After last night, that's the only way I'd believe it."

He handed a coffee cup to her. "Your papers on *Pandora* are worthless."

"Not good enough, Hawkins. That's just a matter of opinion. One I am perfectly willing to bring up for scrutiny in any court. You said they looked official, so why would you even mention that now?"

"Because I have a set of papers on *Pandora*, too. Exactly the same as yours."

Dee stared him in disbelief. "Not signed over, like mine," she said.

"Identical."

"But you said you got *Pandora* through the marina auction as an abandoned vessel."

"I went ahead with that because it's simple, it's legal, and there are no strings attached. When I tried to register with the original papers, I was told they were forged. Probably a stolen vessel."

"Stolen..." A stab of guilt infiltrated the craziness

that had practically blinded her the last two days, and her conscience kicked into gear. No matter what the situation or how long ago the original crime, she would not have anything to do with anything that rightfully belonged to someone else. Boats or otherwise.

"The name had obviously been changed," Hawk went on, "but the case was so old, they said it wouldn't be worth the expense to track down. Especially since, by that time, it came under the jurisdiction of being legally abandoned."

"So mine's no good either?"

"Probably not."

"Then what's going on? What's all this 'I pulled your boat out from under you' stuff? And why didn't you tell me this in the first place if you were so worried about..." Dee looked at him as if for the first time and it occurred to her that she and Marion were miles from nowhere in the company of a couple of possible crooks.

"Because you have the journal, sweetheart." He watched her. "The log tells where the island is. But the journal...well, that tells just where on the island those jewels are actually hidden."

"Then you lied to me." She looked away from him, her eyes fastening, instead, on the curling white wake trailing behind *Pandora*'s stern as she tried to control churning emotions. "You let me believe *Pandora* was mine! How could you do that?"

"Would you have come otherwise?"

12
At Odds

*"He did everything that was rude and
unmannerly, I thought..." ~ Nellie Bly*

The shock that she had been so easily manipulated struck her momentarily speechless.

"I figured you weren't naive enough to just hand over the journal," Hawk explained, "or leave a hundred-thousand-dollar asset in the hands of total strangers, either. And—" A twinkle came into his eyes. "You seemed gutsy enough to go after the big money, one way or another."

"What a marvel you are at figuring things out!" she snapped. "I happen to have enough evidence to prove Peterson left the boat to me. For your information, Wayne Hawkins, a last will negates all previous ones. Besides, I have witnesses, the aide at Wyngate who delivered it for him and the head nurse on the floor who was there that day. I think I would have a pretty good case in court.'

"No one's taking anybody to court."

"I wouldn't be so sure if I were you. So if you're cooking up anymore schemes to scare us or dump us off somewhere, I'd—"

"You're in no position to make threats sugar, you got that? You wanted honesty, now how about giving some back? We both know we're not going to quibble over a hundred thousand when we could split millions, if we stick together. Let's admit it."

"Of course, I admit it. In reality, it's impossible to work with someone you can't trust. Just—" She closed her eyes and slowly shook her head. "What do you suggest we do about that?"

"Let me see the journal, that's what I suggest."

"Are you kidding? After what you and Starr tried to pull last night I'm not giving up that journal until I'm convinced we won't be murdered in our sleep afterward."

"If that's what you really thought, you wouldn't be here." He looked at the sky as if someone had tapped him on the shoulder and then stood to adjust one of the lines. A barely detectable fluttering sound disappeared, and he came back again, stepping off the upper deck as if it were as stable as a front porch on land.

Dee couldn't help admire the easy grace and wished she didn't have to hold onto something just to cross the cockpit.

"We need more time to get to know each other, that's all." He continued, as if there had been no interruption. "Listen. After Frisco, we're going to make a straight run for the Sea of Japan. It'll take about a month."

"A whole month?" How was she going to explain to Devlin that she needed a two week extension on her vacation? Maybe even more.

"Sure a whole month. Even under the best conditions, you can't make much more than a hundred, hundred fifty, miles per day in boat like this. Do the math. It's a long, tough trip any way you look at it. Plenty enough time for all of us to get to know each other, though, I can guarantee that. No outside interference from anything or anybody. We're just going to disappear off the grid for a while."

"Well, believe me, it's going to take a lot more than the four of us getting along before I give up the whereabouts of fifty million dollars. Just because I'm ignorant of sailing things doesn't mean I'm naive in others. And let me tell you something, Mr. Wayne Hawkins. By the time this is all over, I'm going to be a darn good sailor, too."

"What do you want, then?"

Dee could sense his frustration and decided to press. "When we get to Frisco, you add my name to the documentation papers, so everything's fifty-fifty."

The suggestion touched an obvious nerve. "Why would you insist on that when you don't really want her?"

"Because you do."

He muttered under his breath, obviously disturbed that she had put her finger on the thing that mattered most to him. He smoothed down his mustache. "How about a promissory note for what she's worth?"

"Not good enough. If you can't trust me to sell my half back to you when all this is over, then don't expect me to trust you not to double-cross us somewhere along the way."

"And the journal?"

"I show you the journal when—and only when—I

feel sure you aren't conning or sweet talking or otherwise tricking it away from me. That will take equal trust from both of us, Hawkins." Their gazes locked and held. "Deal?"

"Deal," he finally relented. "As long as you promise to turn over the whole thing and not share it out in bits and pieces. I don't like to be teased, Dee."

"Neither do I."

"Or used or made a fool of."

"Then that makes two of us. Which is why I resent the way you treated us last night."

"It seemed like a good way to find out who you were."

"So next time, ask for a resume. I'm D. J. Parker. I work for the Columbia Herald. I—"

"D. J. Parker?" He looked at her and the realization dawned. "Well, no wonder the word's out on this thing. D.J. Parker! You've probably got people tailing you already, no matter what we actually know about anything."

"The *Pandora* thing had nothing to do with the paper," she explained. "It was strictly personal. Between Peterson and me."

"Strictly personal, huh?" His eyes shown with amusement.

"Not that kind of personal. The man was eighty-seven years old, and they had him in a psychiatric hospital under false pretenses. He needed help, and I helped him."

"Was that before or after he gave you the diamonds?"

"I had no idea he was going to do that until he actually died. He was just a cooperative information source while I investigated Wyngate. That's a state hospital just outside of Portland, in case you didn't know."

"No, I didn't know."

She lowered her gaze to the coffee cup she had tucked between the cushion and the rail. "He needed someone to get him out of there. He was being blackmailed."

"For fifty million, I'm not surprised."

"Well, I didn't believe the whole diamond story, then. It was just too fantastic. My goal was to get him out and expose the hospital corruption. He wanted to come back to this boat but I had my doubts there even was a boat. I just wanted the story." She sighed and looked towards the water. "Maybe help out an unhappy old man along the way."

"But here you are," Hawk pronounced. "Caught up in *Pandora*'s curse whether you believed in it or not. It is what it is. Here we all are. Tearing across the ocean in one mad, long race to see who gets there first."

"Somebody could beat us, you know," she warned. "While we're taking a whole month to get across this ocean, whoever stole the chart might decide to fly."

Like Scott Evans, who didn't like boats.

She could just see the headline: **Oregon Reporter Recovers Legendary Jewels**, and it would not be D.J. Parker.

"Sailboat's the only way to get in there without official permission." Hawkins broke into her rampant thoughts. "You'll get boarded for customs when they spot you. But according to Peterson's logbook, the Siberian coast is so vast and isolated; there aren't much but fisherman out there. One small sailboat could slip through. Especially if they knew where they were going."

"You sound just like Peterson."

"I thought you didn't believe him."

"We still spent a lot of hours talking and going over his plan. Trading the things he needed for things I needed. That's how I got my story.' She nestled her coffee cup against the cushion again. "But it's like I told him. What about all the modern equipment they have these days? Radar that allows air traffic controllers to work the entire West Coast from one tower in San Diego. You know they can pinpoint every plane in the sky?"

"That's air traffic. Not boat traffic. And definitely not something as small as a sailboat on something as big as the Pacific Ocean. Crazy as it seems, a sailboat is still a free-moving entity unto itself. Able to get in and out of places without being noticed at all." He glanced at the sky again and then stood. "Hire a plane and there'd be papers to file and permission to get just to veer off regular tourist routes. Could end up in months of red tape. Russia's open, but it's not that open."

"Maybe they don't know that."

"If they stole the chart, honey, they know." He reached into the locker beneath the seat he had been sitting on and tossed a set of the traditional, yellow foul weather gear over to Dee, then took another out for himself.

She felt a smattering of raindrops against her hand.

"Better get into that gear before it really lets loose."

"You mean we could have been wearing these last

night instead of getting wet to the skin and freezing for hours?" she accused.

"I told you I had to see what you were made of." He donned the jacket and stashed his book in the locker.

"Well, I'm beginning to see what you're made of." She placed a yellow hat over the top of her cap and turned the wide brim up to see out from under it. "Can we at least agree to no more tricks?"

"Don't expect me to believe you haven't got a few tricks lined up yourself, D. J. Parker. Something tells me you're probably an expert on tricks."

"I haven't been out-and-out deceptive like you have."

"You look deceptively vulnerable. Does that count?"

"I can't help how I look."

"You look pretty cute in that outfit."

"Let's stick to business, OK?"

"You got something against making friends?"

"No, but—"

"Then lighten up. A month is a long time to be formal, especially under the circumstances."

"Well..." She tightened the straps on the overalls she had just climbed into and reached for the jacket. "How would you like to be called all sorts of pet names by someone you hardly knew?"

"Anytime, baby." He flashed a winning smile. "Anytime."

"You're incorrigible, Hawkins."

13
Under the Bridge

"I know everybody was experiencing a slight weariness, though we should all have stoutly denied such a reflection on our constant companions...and gladly welcomed the change of a few hours on shore." ~ Nellie Bly

Other than wind-tossed rain and a few periods of choppy seas, the *Pandora* sailed past Cape Mendocino with no trouble.

Dee found it amazing how four people squeezed into such small quarters could have so much order and solitary time on their hands. Three hour watches around the clock meant that, other than the ten or fifteen minutes one lingered in handing over their watch to the next person, everyone was either sleeping or working away at private projects during their off-watches.

In her own free time, Dee pored over the journal and compared notes from her talks with Peterson to maps and references that indicated the location where the diamonds had been hidden. She could only generalize distances when looking at nautical charts that she came across in the navigation locker.

Meanwhile, the steady whir and click of Marion's laptop from within her little cabin proved that the solitude and fresh sea air was having a significant effect on the advancement of her friend's novel. She didn't talk much about it but the satisfied glow in her gray eyes as she took over Dee's watch spoke volumes for the effect of the sea on her creativity.

Starr was forever tinkering in the engine room or down in the bilges or simply lounging on deck with a fishing line rigged up for trolling as they skimmed along. Which almost always resulted in something delectable, like a yellow fin tuna that was barbecued off the fantail for their dinner.

Other than an occasional sail repair or rigging change, Dee wasn't exactly sure what Hawk did in his cabin during the off-watch. But the enthusiasm and vigor he often brought back on deck proved he was not always sleeping.

Which made her wonder if he wasn't poring over Peterson's charts and logbook as avidly as she was deciphering the journal. But she wasn't about to ask him.

Things were fairly smooth and casual between them and after such a horrendous beginning, neither of them seemed eager to rock the boat.

They were all on their best behavior.

By the time they reached San Francisco Bay, Dee and Marion had become familiar with the routines of sailing and being at sea and were even learning to adjust the sails.

They were now linked like a chain to the enormous prospects of their expedition. An electric excitement ran like an undercurrent just below the surface of everything they did.

When they finally sailed under the Golden Gate Bridge and into the city of San Francisco, it was a sunny, blustery afternoon. They tied *Pandora* at the transient docks set aside for visitors at the Berkley Marina. along Market Street.

Even though the women put on light, festive blouses in contrast to their jeans and were ready for a shopping spree, they agreed to meet back aboard in the evening for a dinner and night of sightseeing in the famous city.

After two days on a slanted deck, Dee felt good walking on solid ground again. About four o'clock, when they were enjoying coffee in a little espresso stand along the boardwalk, Dee leaned close to Marion. "Don't look, Mare, but that guy over at that corner table...the tall one with reddish hair and dark suit...I think he followed us here."

"Oh, gads, Dee, you're not going to get paranoid again, are you? He's probably sightseeing just like us."

Dee shot another look over at him. Her freshly washed curls were twisted up into a new tortoise-shell clip she had bought and it was a relief to finally stash the black knit cap into her shoulder bag and not worry about the wind, which was blowing steadily against the back of her neck even in this sheltered nook of the little sidewalk cafe.

"He looks suspicious," she continued to whisper. "Like he works for the Mafia or the CIA or something. He keeps watching us, too."

He glanced in their direction and she made a

pretense of studying the menu card, even though they already had their coffee.

"What if someone turned us in and there's an APB out on us?" she asked over the top of the coffee-colored menu card.

A momentary alarm flashed over Marion's face. "Who would turn us in? Listen, even if they did put out an APB, we've only been here a couple of hours. Right? This is a huge city, Dee. How would anyone even know where to look? Believe me, it would be some lucky guess if they thought to look in San Francisco. It's not even in the same state. You didn't see any police boats following us, did you?'

You're right. It's carrying this stolen ring around with me: that's what's doing it. Probably as cursed as everybody says it is. Worse yet, it probably has the same curse as Achen's stuff.' She gave an exaggerated shudder and set the card back in its holder.

"I've never heard of a pharaoh named Achen,' Marion's gaze fell on the menu-card. She took it from the holder and pointed at a delectable photo of a fudge brownie a la mode. "Wonder how much that costs? But I don't know how much of that curse stuff I believe anyway."

"Achen wasn't a pharaoh, and curses are definitely real," said Dee. "I thought you used to teach Sunday school."

"Six-fifty! Can you believe it? You want to split one?"

"Sure."

"I didn't teach the kind of Sunday school you grew up in, Dee."

"Achen's story has no gray lines of controversy,

Mare. It's in both our Bibles. Guaranteed."

"That's what you always say. Next thing you know, we're arguing differences. But all right, I'll take the bait. What sort of curse did Achen have on his stuff?"

"Enemy loot!" Dee's face took on the animation of her enjoyment of storytelling, and she spoke the words like a reporter describing a hot lead. "He thought he could get a good price for it on the gold market, I guess. Even though the Lord said everything those people made was evil, and He didn't want anyone to have any of it. Can you believe that?"

"Well, I don't know. I guess maybe he..."

"Achen kept some anyway and buried it under the floor of his tent. Can't hide from God, though. That's why it's the only place in history you'll ever hear anything about Achen and his family."

"What chapter and verse is it in?"

"Off the top of my head? Joshua, maybe. Or one of the early prophets."

"You see, that's the beauty of memorizing chapter and verse. It's like an address. With the exact address, anyone can find their way to it, no matter what church they were raised in. You're talking about this guy like he was down at the New York Stock Exchange just last week. Here comes the waitress."

"Go ahead and order that dessert." Dee slid her chair back and got to her feet. "I'm going to take a few more pictures for my column."

"Aren't you supposed to be on vacation?"

"A working vacation if I can talk Devlin into it. Like a travel log or something. Because he still thinks I'm coming back in two weeks."

"How are we going to keep any secrets if you leave a trail in your column publishing everywhere we've been?"

"Not until way after we've been there. I can't just disappear for a whole month without telling him something, I'll get fired. Here..." She took her camera out of her shoulder bag before shoving it toward Marion. "Why don't you carry the goods around for a while? I'm telling you, they're giving me the creeps."

"All right, I'll do it. But only if you promise not to rope me into an all-night discussion on whether inanimate objects can be good or evil."

"OK, I promise. Back in a minute."

****

Marion had become engrossed in the brownie a la mode. By the time she got concerned about Dee, the coffee was cold, and the man at the corner table had left. She left her brownie and searched. She couldn't find Dee anywhere.

She screamed. Which brought the owner of the cafe out on a run, as if someone was having a heart attack. He told the waitress to call 911 and darted toward Marion, through the labyrinth of tables and into the little knot of onlookers that now surrounded her. Looking relieved there was no body and he would not have to perform CPR, he listened with sympathy as she wailed that her friend had been kidnapped by one of his patrons.

The police arrived. They gave the routine excuses: complaints of missing persons could not be filed until after forty-eight hours unless the missing person was a child, or there was hard evidence that foul play was involved. Because most of the time adult missing persons tended to be missing of their own accord.

"No woman," Marion insisted, "ever leaves her purse in a cafe of her own accord! Especially one who is on vacation and only stepped out on the street to snap a picture!"

The two officers conferred together for a moment, after which one went back to the patrol car, only to return a few minutes later and whisper something to his partner.

"Mrs. Bates…" The officer in charge studied the notes he had just taken. "It looks like we have something of a coincidence here. Did you and Miss Parker arrive in San Francisco today, aboard a sailing vessel named *Pandora*?"

Marion blinked her gray eyes in a moment of surprise, thought of being evasive and then thought better of it. "Why, yes, we did," she finally admitted. "But I can tell you right now, we had every intention of—"

"Just a minute, ma'am." He turned to his partner again. "Steve, who's handling that?"

"Dispatch said it was a federal case. Couple guys named Eddington and Reynolds were sent out with a couple of ours this morning to check on the marina. No reports yet, though."

"Okay. Get them on the radio and have them meet us at the station. Mrs. Bates, we're going to have to take a ride downtown."

"Am I under arrest?"

"Not at the moment. But there are some pretty hefty charges here, so I suggest you cooperate."

"What about, Dee?"

"Every officer in the city has their eye out for her, ma'am. She'll turn up."

14
Against the Law

"There are so many murders committed, and the police never catch the murderers..." ~ Nellie Bly

"Excuse me," Dee said automatically when she backed into someone. She lowered the camera, only to realize she was surrounded by strange men who began to force her backwards into a waiting car.

"Hey—what do you think—" In seconds, she was squeezed into the back seat with two men beside her and two more in front.

A moment more and they were speeding away, leaving the crowded little cafe in their wake, where no one even noticed what had happened.

"Dorothy Jane Parker?" Dee recognized the reddish hair of the man in the front passenger seat.

"Oh, no..." she moaned. "Am I under arrest?"

"Let's see some identification, first." He grinned a wide toothy smile, as if he had just won a prize. "Then I'll let you know."

"I...well, it's back at the cafe. In my purse. But I have my social security number engraved on my camera. What sort of arrest is this anyway? Don't you need a warrant or something?"

"Miss Parker." He flashed a badge and then put it away before Dee had time to scrutinize it. "Does the name Heinrich Keller mean anything to you?"

"It seems to me…" Dee tried to sound firm and irate while her heart was pounding hard enough for the men next to her to hear. "That I have the right to remain silent."

"It's up to you," he said in what she detected as a slight southern drawl. "You can either talk to us here or we can take you downtown." Then he winked at her.

Dee looked at the man on her left but he just sat stoic and silent, the thin lines of his mouth pressed together.

"Why couldn't you just talk to me in the cafe?" She addressed the redhead again. "This is pretty unorthodox, if you ask me."

"Because the information here is classified. You're in some trouble. So I suggest you cooperate."

"I don't know any Heinrich Keller."

"Then what were you doing in his safety deposit box?"

Now Dee's heart began to pound as if it might leave her body entirely. "But that was Nelson Peterson's box. He's an old man I befriended at the Wyngate State Hospital. He left those things to me and—"

"How about the Strassgaard ring? Did he leave that to you, too?"

"Yes, as a matter of fact, he did. Because the Strassgaard family was gone before he ever came into possession of those things. Which only happened because he was a deckhand on a boat Göring chartered. He told me he won it gambling with one of his aides, who lifted it from Göring's personal stash. The guy hid the other jewels in Russia until he could go back for them. Only he never got back."

"Why was that?"

"Russia isolated itself after the war, maybe. "How should I know? Peterson's mother was Russian, and his father was Austrian, but I don't know much about him."

"Peterson was Dutch, Miss Dee. And he wasn't any deckhand, he owned that boat you came in on this afternoon. He also had a lot of gambling debts he never paid to Göring's aide, Heinrich Keller. We have reason to believe those two people were one and the same."

Dee was stunned.

Peterson an aide to Göring...a Nazi war criminal! Someone who would have been tried right along with the worst of them if he had been caught. No wonder he'd changed his name so many times. And to think she had almost aided and abetted his escape. How could she have been so gullible as to believe such a story? She could be in some serious trouble, here.

She looked into eyes that were nearly as blue as her own and decided the man didn't look half as shocked as she felt.

"I thought he was Swedish...Dutch, or something," she murmured more to herself than her interrogator. "His medical records said his name was Nelson Peterson. He was at Wyngate for nearly five years."

"He used that name on occasion, that's how we

knew about the box. Hasn't been any activity on it for years, though. So. Why did you leave Oregon in such an all-fired hurry, Miss Parker?'

"Because I..." Dee took a deep breath and felt the force of a fast and sudden turn into back streets. "Where are we going?"

"Just answer the question, please.'

They passed an industrial warehouse and bumped over railroad tracks.

"I think I'd rather talk at the police station," she said. "How come none of you are in uniform?"

"We're not those kind of officers. Now, try to calm down a little, Dee, and think carefully before you answer the questions. Because everything you say—"

"Can and will be used against me in a court of law?" She tried to look past the man on her right (another zombie) and caught a glimpse of a street sign zipping by. "I'm familiar with the rules, Mr...Mr..."

"Eddington," he supplied. "Why did you leave Oregon so fast?"

"I don't know what you mean by fast. I always take a vacation after I turn in my yearly scandal piece. You can even ask my editor."

"Dee." He shook his head slowly in mock admonition. "Mind if I call you Dee?"

"Really, I'd rather you wouldn't."

"Don't get so hasty, now. Answer each question carefully. Let me rephrase that last one for you. Your editor said you were scheduled for Mexico in two weeks and he couldn't figure why—"

"You talked to Devlin?"

"Yes, ma'am. We ran your license plates and talked to a lot of people."

"My license plates?"

"Courtesy of the assistant bank manager back in Oregon. We've been watching that box ever since we lost track of Keller four and a half years ago. Now your editor, he couldn't figure out why you left so sudden. Truth is, he didn't even know you were gone."

"But—"

"Just a minute." He held up his hand to stop the flow of words. "We already know the only commercial cruises out of that little town are fishing charters. So considering the yacht you came in on today, that's some exclusive fishing trip, Dee."

"All right," she relented. "I had no idea accepting that ring was going to implicate me like this. What is it, the missing piece to the Austrian crown jewels or something? If it's that important, I'll be happy to give it back. I'm not a crook, you know."

"Interesting choice of words, the Austrian crown jewels. The Crown Jewels are English."

"English Crown Jewels, then."

"But you said, Austrian, Dee. Which proves you know more than you're letting on."

"I said I was willing to give it back!" she snapped. "Did you hear that part? Honestly! I think you're all just trying to scare me!"

They pulled into a deserted factory parking lot and stopped next to a side door.

Dee felt a wave of sudden panic. "All right, I'm scared—you've succeeded. I'm not interested in keeping stolen goods. Do they belong to someone else? Is that it? If they do, I'll just give them back."

They all got out in unison, as if some signal had

been given. Dee was pushed toward the door.

"I want to make a statement!" She could not wrench her arms free or keep from being propelled inside. "I'm ready to go downtown! Mr. Eddington!"

"You can call me, Ed." He switched on a light. "Most people do."

The little room had no windows. But the single bulb that hung from the ceiling revealed a table, several chairs, and an old metal file cabinet.

The men escorted Dee to a seat, after which the driver and one of the others went back outside. One of the men who had ridden next to her took off his sunglasses and sat down while Eddington remained standing.

"I could write a letter of apology to the Strassgaard family," Dee suggested.

"The Strassgaard family no longer exists," Eddington replied. "They were wiped out in the war. The significance here is that the Strassgaard jewels— and we're talking a collection that would run something in the vicinity of fifty million on today's market—was last noted to be in the possession of a certain Heinrich Keller. A Nazi war criminal who was never apprehended. And, I might add, who is now known to have also been a Soviet agent.'

A Soviet agent! Well, I...I never..." Dee looked from one face to another and then back to Eddington, again. "Honestly, I didn't know any of this about the ring, and I...I certainly didn't know any of this about Peterson!"

"So, where is he?"

"He died. Several days ago. In Wyngate."

"Maybe he did, and maybe he didn't. We'll have

to check that out. Keller is what you might call a master at double identities. As an aide to Göring, he was a member of that elite circle and known to have the ring in his possession. Along with other things the old guy liked to bring along when he traveled. I don't think I need to tell you, Dee, that your involvement with this fugitive puts you in the position of an accomplice."

Dee gasped at the thought and was about to object. Eddington suddenly looked deadly serious.

"Withholding information," he warned, "any information that might lead to his arrest or apprehension, is a crime against your country."

He took a package of gum from the pocket of his black jacket and began to peel the green wrapper off as he talked. "Why did you leave Oregon so quick?"

"Well..." Dee faltered, "maybe I eloped."

Eddington popped a piece of gum in his mouth, shook his head in disappointment and sighed before looking her in the eye again. "What do you think we are here, stupid? If you're just on some honeymoon cruise, then what are you doing on Göring's boat?"

"I was under the impression that it was my boat, Mr. Eddington, because Peterson gave it to me." Dee realized she was way out of her element and trying to match wits with someone who had started ten steps ahead of her.

"Göring once chartered that boat to entertain some high-up Nazi officials." Eddington rolled the gum wrapper into a little ball and tossed it into a nearby wastebasket. "It's one of that town's most popular rumors. Any history book will tell you he was a fanatic about fine jewels. Wore expensive rings. Was known to travel with a vase full of diamonds wherever he went. His aides would bring them to him for amusement on long journeys. He flaunted them everywhere. Heinrich Keller was one of those aides to Göring."

"Peterson did say it had been chartered by wealthy Nazis, and he admitted taking the diamonds the last time they were there. Something he regretted most of his life, because he was always worried someone would catch up with him."

No one spoke as she went on. "I don't think he's had any home but that boat for the last fifty years. If he was this Keller person you're talking about, would he have drawn so much attention to himself as a sportsman and adventurer? Arctic expeditions, mountain climbing... hardly the sort of recognition someone in hiding would pursue."

"Or a very brilliant one." He pulled out a chair and sat down across from her. "Do you always accept such expensive presents from wealthy gentlemen? You're not saying you became so infatuated with this eighty-some-year-old man that you eloped with him?"

"Good heavens, no!"

"I didn't think so. What you became infatuated with, Dee, was fifty million dollars in diamonds. But who could blame you?"

"There's no law against treasure hunting, Mr. Eddington."

"No, there sure isn't. And as long as you and your party stay within the law...well, shoot, I guess you're as free to treasure hunt as the next person."

"That's all I thought I was doing, so, what's your point?"

"The point is, we'd like to make a little deal with you."

"On the fifty million?" she gasped.

"No, ma'am. Making that kind of deal under the pretenses of an arrest, now that would be a felony, wouldn't it?"

"I should think so."

"Sure it is. And I might remind you that it is also a felony to bribe a federal officer with that kind of offer, too."

"But I didn't make any offers! You were the one who—"

"I'm willing to overlook it this time. You willing to overlook it, Ren?" His partner nodded slightly to signify approval.

"See," Eddington went on, "we're all in agreement. Now, let's get down to business."

"Business about what?" Dee began to feel panicked again. "You're putting words in my mouth and I won't have it! I'm not going to say anything else without a lawyer present. I believe that's one of those rights you didn't tell me about. I'm allowed to have a lawyer, aren't I?"

He gave a wide smile. "You're a smart enough woman to figure out this little interrogation is unofficial, aren't you?"

"Lord help me." She closed her eyes for a moment and took a deep breath. "Are you police officers or aren't you?"

"You saw our identification."

"Not very well, I didn't."

"Then we'll show it to you again. Get your badge out, Ren, we're making the lady nervous. I can see that right now."

Dee scrutinized their badges a little longer than necessary since she wasn't sure she could tell a real one from a fake. "Federal Bureau of Investigation. You expect me to believe this is your downtown office?"

"It's just a convenient place to talk, Dee. As I said before, this meeting here is unofficial. You surfaced with a notorious piece of evidence that has been linked with an international criminal, known to have been operating within our jurisdiction. Now, we can either take you downtown and arrest you on charges of grand theft and espionage, or..."

Dee went faint under the impact of the words.

"Or, you can agree to cooperate." He leaned his forearms on the table and brought his head so close that she could smell the mint in his chewing gum. "So, which is it going to be?"

15
Surveillance

"We stood...shivering in the damp, chilly air, and looking in the gray fog like uneasy spirits." ~ Nellie Bly

It was almost dark when Dee was dropped off at the Berkley Marina. By that time, the air was cool, with a heavy salt- scented fog that reduced all the boats to ghost-like shadows. Somewhere out on the bay, the long doleful moan of a buoy whistle made a sound that started a ripple of chill over her bare arms.

She wished she had a sweater for the long walk out to the transient dock where *Pandora* was tied. Instead, she folded her arms, bowed her head, and hurried down the ramp to the main dock, where she suddenly ran into Hawkins on his way up.

"Where the devil have you been?" he asked, unable to hide the edge of concern in his voice. "Marion came back so hysterical Starr had to force a double scotch down her. Are you all right?"

"I am now."

He looked her over intently, as if to make sure. Then he took his black windbreaker off and draped it over her shoulders as they continued down the ramp. "What happened?"

"I got picked up by the FBI."

He stopped suddenly.

"Listen." She turned back to him. "It's a long story, but—uh-oh, they're still up there."

"Who?"

Before he could turn to look, she threw her arms around his neck. "Oh, Hawk, act like you missed me! I let them think we..."

"Dee Parker," he spoke the name with such pent-up frustration, she thought he was going to yell. "Do not tell me you lied to the FBI!" But he circled her waist in an answering embrace and fairly lifted her off her feet in repressed anger. "Or I swear, I will—"

"They knew about the diamonds and the boat!"

"There's no law against what we're doing here. Why couldn't you just tell the truth?"

"Don't squeeze me so hard!" She pushed away from him, thought better of it, and linked her arm in his as they started walking again. "The evidence was so incriminating against me, and they had me in a corner."

"What evidence?"

"Something about grand theft and espionage."

He stopped abruptly again. "That's it, sweetheart. The deal's off. You can take your—"

"Hawk."

"I can't go anywhere with that kind of—"

"Hawkins! Do you want to hear what I have to say, or don't you?"

"You've obviously said enough already." He looked back at the dark car. "What are they waiting for?"

"They're watching us, probably." She coaxed him along once more. "To see if you're acting the way a concerned, overly distraught husband should be."

"Husband?"

"I let them think we eloped."

"How could that help anything?"

"Everything happened so fast, I—"

"You realize by doing that, you've linked me up with the same charges?" This time when he swore, it was not under his breath. "What were you thinking?"

"It was the only thing that came to my mind. I guess I was—"

"How come they let you off if they suspect you of something that serious?"

"I had to agree we'd work with them, or they wouldn't have."

The next swear word he breathed with such vehemence that she inwardly braced for a complete blow-up. But he managed to keep it intact for a few moments of determined silence while all the implications sank in. "You had no right to get the rest of us mixed up in something like that when—"

"Oh, what was I supposed to do?" She ducked in time to avoid an overly long bowsprit that stretched out over the dock. "I just spent two of the scariest hours of my life thinking I was going to end up as a statistic somewhere! They said I could either go to jail or cooperate. What would you have done?"

"I wouldn't have implicated my friends."

Now she was the one to stop and confront. "You're an American, aren't you? Are you saying if your government asked for your help with something, you'd have the audacity and the...the capacity, to say no?"

He looked at her for a moment and in the fading gray of evening, she thought she detected a sudden glimmer of distrust in his eyes.

He reached out a tentative hand before she realized what he was doing, ran a searching finger along the neckline of her blouse. "Are you wearing a wire?"

She pushed his hand away. "Of course not! How could you even think something like that?"

"Because that sounded like a textbook question for a commie rap, that's why. I spent twenty years of my life in the military and the wrong answer to a question like that could get me in some serious trouble."

Worry softened the rugged handsomeness of his features and made him look vulnerable, causing Dee's conscience a twinge of regret over the predicament. She sighed miserably.

"How was I supposed to know that? I was scared and that's all I could think of. Oh, I'll...do what I can to straighten things out tomorrow. But let's not argue anymore, Hawkins. I'm cold and I'm tired."

Her voice quavered and she realized she was on the verge of a good cry. She didn't dare say another word. Instead, she pulled the windbreaker more snuggly around her and began walking.

But he did notice. He hesitated only a moment, then put an arm around her. He drew her close up against him again as they walked the rest of the way in silence.

An odd sense of security swept through her and the reassuring strength of the protective gesture had a soothing effect. He couldn't mean it. She chided herself for being so impressionable. She was just having a delayed reaction to the trying experience. Perfectly natural. Still, she melted against the inviting shelter of his body, enjoying the warmth and the way he moved with an easy stride.

Dee felt even more secure in *Pandora*'s welcoming atmosphere. The spacious main cabin was warm from the stove fixed to the forward bulkhead that radiated a fine, even heat throughout the entire yacht.

As soon as Dee climbed down inside, Marion threw her arms around her and cried.

Even Starr was misty-eyed as he mixed her one of his own variations of a hot, buttered rum, which Dee insisted he leave the rum out of.

"Listening to this crazy woman for the last half hour," he shook his head, "almost had me convinced you were the latest victim of a serial killer."

"Well, I was worried!" Marion pulled a tissue from her pocket and dabbed at her nose. "Oh, Dee, I just didn't know what to think!"

"I was pretty scared myself," she admitted.

"Hawk's been pacing the docks out there for the last hour." Starr handed Dee a steaming mug brimming with all sorts of spicy aromas. "I thought he was going to hire a taxi and start combing the streets when Marion came back without you."

"Worried about my investment." Hawk closed the companionway doors.

Dee sank into the comfortable red upholstery and took a sip of the hot drink. "Mmmm. Thank you. I practically froze walking down here."

"There's been a change in plans," Hawk informed

them. "Instead of hitting the town tonight, I think we'd all feel better if we just barbecued some steaks right here. That way we can have a group conference."

"That suits me," said Marion. "I've had all the excitement I can take for one day."

There was a knock against the hull.

"Hello the boat...anybody aboard?" A man called.

Dee recognized Eddington's voice immediately, but she didn't say a word as Hawk turned and went back up on deck again.

"Your wife forgot her camera." The officer handed it over the rail. "Name's Eddington. I work for the Bureau."

Hawk took the camera. "I don't know whether to shake your hand or punch you in the nose," he admitted. "I haven't had time to hear the details."

"Well, it looks like you have a real adventure cut out for you. Good luck, Major Wayne Hawkins, US Army."

"Retired."

"Two years ago, honorable discharge, out of Honolulu, Hawaii. We did some checking on you, too."

"I didn't agree to anything."

"Better talk to that wife of yours, then. The trouble with hasty marriages, they sometimes conceal surprises. In case you haven't noticed, she has an odd mixture of guts and patriotism. Dangerous combination." He reached into an inside pocket of his jacket and took out a business card. "You can reach me at this number if you have any questions."

"I have plenty of questions, bud," Hawkins replied. "The first one is: what makes you think I'll go along with any of this?"

"Because according to your records, you're a pretty gutsy patriot yourself." As if that explained everything, he turned to leave. "See you around, Major."

16
The Round Table

"Nonsense! If you want to do it, you can do it. The question is, do you want to do it?" ~ Nellie Bly

Hawk returned without a word, placed the camera inside the engine room, and turned on the diesel. The motor came to life with a loud, steady hum.

"Holy fright," Starr complained. "Are we gonna make another midnight run? I'm not familiar with these waters."

"We're going out for dinner after all." He looked at Dee as he spoke. "It seems Miss Lois Lane here has fixed it so we can't do any real talking aboard the yacht. Not until we get out to sea about three days anyway."

"I'm sure I don't..." Dee defended.

"Let's save the explanations for the round table. You can fill us in on your little episode this afternoon and then we can all take a vote whether or not we want to go on."

"Why wouldn't we want to go on?" Starr asked.

"I want to go on," Marion said cheerily. "I haven't had this much excitement in years."

"You might change your mind when you hear what we've got ourselves into. For the record, no more talking about anything but cruising while we're here in port. Food, bargains, the weather...we're all on vacation. Got it?"

Dee exchanged her short-sleeve blouse for a white angora sweater and splashed on some cologne. The cheery fire and hot drink had warmed her and she was finally starting to feel halfway normal, again, as they made their way back up to Market Street.

Marion and Starr seemed to have developed a companionable rapport and were walking a little way ahead, enjoying the sights.

Dee and Hawkins were walking in a silence that was charged with volatile unspoken words. Halfway to the restaurant, she thought he was going to put his arm around her but he only steered her clear of an oncoming pedestrian whom she failed to notice because she was stealing a glance at Hawk.

Martinelli's was a cozy little Italian place overlooking the water, complete with red-checked cloths and candles on every table.

They picked a private far-off corner that was made further ideal by the soft background of Italian music and the pleasant hum and buzz of a popular restaurant. They listened to Dee's story of how she had been whisked off Market Street, pausing only to order large platters of scampi, manicotti, and linguini with clams.

"Let's get to the vital question." Hawk buttered another slice of warm sourdough bread before he looked across the table at Dee. "Why did you lie?"

"First of all," she explained, "I didn't lie. I just threw out a sort of what-if scenario because they had me backed into a corner. I said maybe I had done it, and they just naturally believed I had. They were trying to intimidate me. I needed a diversion, and that was the best I could come up with on the spur of the moment."

Marion and Starr looked at her.

She didn't continue.

Hawk jabbed at his salad as if he had a personal vendetta against it. After a few moments, he tossed his fork onto his plate with a decisive thump and took a drink of water.

"Well, Dee," Marion finally prompted, "what exactly was it that you maybe did?"

"When they asked me why I left Oregon so fast, I said maybe I eloped."

Hawk reached for his wine.

Marion's mouth fell open.

Star took another piece of warm bread from the basket. "What business is it of theirs anyway?" he asked before returning his attention to linguini with clams.

Dee pushed her barely touched scampi aside and put the red linen napkin from her lap back onto the table. "Quite a bit, actually. You see, they know about the boat and the diamonds."

Starr dropped the bread that was halfway to his mouth.

"They know everything. More than us, even, because I had no idea Peterson was some Nazi war criminal they've been following for years."

"Wait a minute," Hawk spoke. "Something doesn't make sense, here. If they were following him for years, how come they never arrested him?"

"Because by the time they did find him," Dee replied, "he was working as a Soviet agent in some spy ring that—"

Hawk swore so loud that the pleasant hum of voices around their table paused .

"We could be in some serious trouble, here." Starr moaned. "A no-good Nazi, Russian spy! Holy fright, we could be..."

Hawk shook his head and swore again.

"I think it's only me that's in trouble, at the moment," Dee tried to sound reassuring. "You would all just be considered innocent bystanders, since you've only known me for a few days. Especially if you quit right now."

Marion blinked. "What about me, I've known you for years! Dee Parker, this is worse than driving us into that slum—what am I going to tell my kids? I'll be a disgrace to Bill's memory!"

"Marion, I'm so sorry!" Dee felt as if a crushing weight were pressing down on her. "But I think as long as you go home right away, you'll be all right. I'm the one who actually took the ring from the safety deposit box. I guess they were watching it because they figured he'd come back for it sooner or later."

"What ring?" Hawk asked.

Dee felt a stab of guilt at the worry she saw in his eyes. "The Strassgaard ring. They knew all about it. That I could only get it from Peterson and then only if I were collaborating with him in some way."

Now, it was Starr who wore the mask of astonishment. "You mean you got the Strassgaard ring? Right now? That's a piece of the collection! By the hoagie—that's proof right there that this thing is no hoax! What do you think, Hawk—she's got the ring!"

"I think our...partner...was holding out on us, that's what I think." He answered without taking his gaze off Dee. "And if this hadn't happened, we might have—"

"Just out of curiosity," Starr turned back to Dee without waiting for him to finish, "what did they say it was worth?"

"All they told me was that it's listed on some international directory of stolen jewels and—"

"Oh, dear Lord!" Marion moaned.

"Whatever it's worth," Dee insisted, "it's not what the FBI is after. They want Heinrich Keller. Of course, I told them I never heard of Heinrich Keller. But they didn't believe me. I had the ring, I left town suddenly, and I left on Göring's boat. Which is what implicated me and linked me with Keller. You see? You really are just innocent bystanders, so the best thing to do is quit right now."

She sighed, picked up her fork and pushed at the unfinished scampi. "All I have going for me is the fatal blunder story. Which is the truth—even though nobody believes it."

"It was fatal, all right," Hawk accused. "Do you realize they investigated me?"

"They investigated all of us, but I was the only one they picked up. I told them I befriended a crazy old man who left me a boat and a map and a tantalizing piece of jewelry to prove there was more. Which is all true, it really is. The fatal part was letting them believe that during the course of planning the trip, I fell in love with Hawkins and...eloped."

Marion gasped. "Dee Parker—that wasn't fair to Hawk!'

"They investigated all of us?" Starr bawled. "Holy fright, I haven't filed my taxes for three years!"

"You should have asked the rest of us before you agreed to work with them," Hawk said.

"Hawkins," Dee finally felt her patience beginning to crumble. "I wasn't in any position to call a committee meeting. I agreed because being unwilling to cooperate with your government is dangerously close to subversion when you're being accused of...subversion!"

"People go to jail for tax evasion," Starr mumbled.

"Quit being so evasive, sugar, and let's have it. What kind of deal did you agree to?"

"Nothing we weren't doing in the first place. Just go after the diamonds. The same way before I knew any of this."

"So, what's the catch?" Hawk pressed. "You didn't agree to something crazy like taking this Eddington along, did you?"

Starr choked, belched, and then gasped. "Holy fright—a fed—right in the same boat with us?"

"No, of course not," Dee assured. "They just want us to keep on doing what we're doing. Like I said, they're not interested in the diamonds at all. They think whoever Keller was working with will be following us."

"Then I think we should all quit right now!" Marion declared.

"I can't quit. I look guilty. The only reason they didn't arrest me on the spot was because I agreed to cooperate. The rest of you can quit, though. I'll just hire someone else to—"

"Who said anything about quitting?" Starr shoved the sleeves of his flannel shirt up past his elbows and leaned his forearms on the table. "I, for one, need a break like this and that's good enough for me. If they're not going to interfere with us like Dee says then I say let's go on."

"Well, I'd worry myself to death wondering what was happening to all of you if I stayed behind," Marion relented. "So I guess I'll have to go, too. What about you, Hawk?"

"I'm not letting anyone else run my boat, I'll tell you that much." Hawk turned his gaze back to Dee. "And listen, sweetheart, you better start sharing more than just what you get caught red-handed with. Such as million dollar rings that are hot enough to get us all in trouble."

"A million dollars!" Starr whispered.

"We've got to straighten up and start pulling together," Hawk challenged. "That means sugar, here, lays everything out straight with us before somebody ends up in jail, or dead.'

A long, sobering silence descended, during which no one ate or drank.

"What exactly do you suggest?" Dee finally ventured.

"From now on, I make the decisions."

"All right by me," Starr said. "Somebody's gotta be responsible."

"I don't like it." Dee objected so fast it was more a response than an opinion.

The others looked at her as if she had suggested treason.

"Listen, sweetheart," Hawk warned, "your little

shenanigans over the last week have gotten us into more trouble than if you put a full page ad in the paper and let the whole country know what we're up to. Between you flashing million dollar rings around and Marion sending postcards home like we were on some cruise ship to—"

"How did you know about my postcards?" Marion's expression was indignant. "Did you go through my drawers?"

"I went through the boat from one end to the other while you women were out getting yourselves in trouble."

"That's unethical!" Dee accused. "I don't know how you can expect us all to put our faith in you if you continue to stoop to such—"

Wayne Hawkins crashed his fist against the table with an incriminating swear word that could be heard halfway across the room. "Where's the journal!"

There was another break in the hum of restaurant noise.

"It's in my purse," Dee replied quietly. "And if you say it any louder, Hawkins, we might as well auction it off right here."

"You mean you're carrying it around with you wherever you go like some tour brochure?" He swore again.

"Now, just a minute," Starr intervened. "Both of you settle down. Hawk's just worried you'll let it fall into the wrong hands, Dee."

"If only it wasn't so hard to figure out who the wrong hands were," she complained.

"Do you still have it, or don't you?" Hawk asked.

"Of course I have it."

"Then something is way wrong! Eddington should have confiscated it for evidence. The only reason he wouldn't was if—"

"He didn't take the ring."

"He didn't?"

Dee shook her head.

"He didn't!" Starr said ecstatically.

"He should have taken it." Hawk worried. "It's standard procedure in a case like this. I don't get it. Unless..."

"It was in my purse," Dee explained. "Marion had it."

"Didn't they go through all your things down at the station, Marion?"

"We never got to that part," Marion replied. "I hardly got in the door before they told me there had been a misunderstanding. That Dee had been found and I was free to go. But they wouldn't tell me where she was. For all I knew, she was dead somewhere. They put me in a taxi with no more explanation than that. And that's why I was so upset when I got back. I thought maybe they were notifying her family first."

"I'm so sorry, Marion." A wave of sympathy washed over Dee. "That had to be awful!"

Hawk got to his feet with a frustrated sigh. "I'll see you all back at the boat. I need some air."

"Sit down and keep your shirt on." Starr's tone carried a ring of authority and Hawk automatically sank back down again. "Now, all we need are two rules. Dee puts the valuables in the yacht's safe, and we form pairs. Nobody goes any place alone anymore." Starr glanced over at Marion. "Not even to snap a picture."

"The trouble with that," Dee objected, "is I can't trust Hawk not to..."

"Listen, sugar, the thought of you and Marion running off by yourselves again gives me the creeps."

"You two will have to pair up," Starr reasoned. "It's the only way both of you can be sure of what the other one is or isn't doing."

17
Amends

"I was the most surprised girl in the world."
~ *Nellie Bly*

Hawk stuck his head inside Dee's cabin as she sat propped up in bed with pillows, typing away intently on her laptop computer. The short-sleeved, khaki shirt, with its light sand color against his tanned skin made him seem more attractive than usual. Or maybe it was a pleasant hint of some spicy aftershave or the sparkle in that smile.

Caught off guard, Dee got butterflies and it startled her. "Would you mind not barging in without knocking?" She ran a frustrated hand through her uncombed hair. "At least while we're in port?"

"Come on, sugar, you've spent the whole morning in here and I need to run an errand."

"Don't call me sugar! And can't it wait? I've got to finish this and send it off before we get out of Internet range."

"Finish what? Let me see it."

She pushed the save button and folded down the

screen before he could look. "It's just some installments for one of my regular columns. Nothing related to what we're doing here."

"Then why all the secrecy?"

"It's not secrecy, Hawkins, just principle. Outside of *Columbia* staff, nobody sees what I write until it's in print. If we're leaving tonight, I have to get it finished and turned in today. I'm not retired like you. I still have to work for a living. I don't believe you're retired anyway. Nobody but millionaires retire before forty."

"Maybe I'm over forty."

"You're thirty-seven." She set her things aside and got up. "I looked at your driver's license."

"So, while you're criticizing me for reading Marion's postcards, you've been going through my wallet?"

"What do you expect when you leave it on the counter? Now, get out of here, will you? So I can change into something decent. I'm not going to walk around town in a jogging suit."

Actually it was powder blue, top of the line, and had cost her eighty-five dollars. The nights were cold on the water, and after the first few experiences of being wakened by Hawk at all hours, she wasn't about to be caught wearing pajamas. Being on this boat was giving her flashbacks of summer camp.

Once outside along the famous wharf, the smell of fresh-baked sourdough bread and boiled crab permeated the air.

Hawk flagged down a nearby cab. Dee, dressed in a rose-colored silk blouse, matching sandals, and a flower-print skirt, protested the confinement when it was such a lovely sunny day and the perfect time for a walk.

"County Courthouse," he said to the driver.

"County Courthouse? Oh, Hawk, don't tell me you're going to do it!" She rummaged through her bag looking for some lip gloss as she talked. "You're actually going to add me to the papers so everything's fifty-fifty?"

"Something like that. Do you have any identification in there?"

"Of course. I have everything in here."

"I'll bet. You don't have a gun in there, do you?"

"No, but I have a can of pepper spray on my key chain in case I run into any bad characters."

"Pretty useless. Most bad characters aren't polite enough to wait around for you to get out your keys. Yesterday was a good example."

"Yesterday, I left my purse in the cafe."

"Sheesh." He sighed and looked out the window. "Let's not bring that up again."

The tall courthouse could have been anywhere in the country. There was a directory not far from the entrance and men and women were coming and going within the routine of their own personal agendas. Very few of them acknowledged or even noticed anyone else.

"Fifty million dollars is a lot of money." Hawk scanned the directory while Dee waited.

"It certainly is," she agreed, "and it's making us all act despicable."

"What's it worth to you?"

"To quote what someone else said recently...I'm here, aren't I?"

He pointed down a hall and they started in that direction. "You never asked many questions about me."

"You're Captain Hawk. As for what type of person you are, you wear that right in the open. I knew the first time you talked to me. When you said: "What's the deal, lady, you ever heard of knocking?""

"I spent nineteen years with the government."

"You already told me that," she reminded him. Amused that he suddenly seemed nervous, she tried to lighten things up. "I can see the headline now: **Retired Army Major Discovers Famous Austrian Jewels.** And I'm going to write it. Might even put me in line for a Pulitzer."

"Gonna put you in line for something, I can guarantee that."

Knowing how hard giving up half the boat must be on him, Dee's heart softened. "Hey. You don't know how much I appreciate this, Hawkins. It's a real vote of confidence on your part, and believe me, I won't forget it."

"Well, before you get all sentimental, maybe you could look at things from my perspective for a minute."

"Don't worry. I'm a woman of my word. I said I'd sell my half back to you when this is all over, and I will."

"You willing to guarantee that? Legally?"

"For heaven's sake, what do you want me to do, sign in blood?"

"Something like that."

"Let's draw up a paper, then. Whatever we both agree on, then we can have it notarized while we're here. That way we'll both have more peace of mind."

"Peace of mind is important. I was up half the night trying to find some. I don't think you realize what an incriminating position you put me in here."

"Hawk, I already told you how sorry I am about that. If there was any way I could take it back, I would."

"You linked my name with espionage in some pretty important circles. I might be retired but..." He looked down at her and lowered his voice. "Once you've signed yourself over to him, Uncle Sam can haul you back and court martial you anytime. Especially for something as big as treason."

"They didn't officially bring any charges, once I agreed to cooperate."

"Well, it might not bother you to tell little white lies to the big boys but I can't afford to take chances. We've got to set everything straight. Right on down the line."

"So, what do you want me to do? Sign a notarized affidavit that I never consulted you prior to my subversive acts?"

"Something like that."

"Wayne Hawkins, that's the third time you've used that phrase this morning and it's making me nervous."

They stopped outside an office with a sign above it that said, Marriage Licenses.

Dee immediately started to back away. "Not on your life, Hawkins, are you kidding me?" She shook her head as she moved off. "Not even if you were—"

"Will you just listen a minute?"

"No."

"It solves everything."

"Solves everything for you, maybe. But I take things like this very seriously! Marriage is something you promise someone forever. Definitely not something to do for convenience, to keep yourself out of trouble."

"Look at it from a different angle."

"Looking at something from a different angle doesn't change what it is."

"It does if it's business, and that's all it would be. I promise." He smoothed his mustache down, sighed, and raised his voice in frustration. "I'm not asking you to spend the rest of your life with me."

Another couple on their way in looked over at the startling remark.

Hawk drew her away from the door and lowered his voice. "Listen. It lends integrity to your story. Just think about that for a minute."

Dee stared at a potted plant a few feet away, unable to look him in the eye as he talked. What's worse, her heart started to beat faster, as if she were some school girl being asked to a dance.

When he continued, his voice was low and cajoling. "It automatically puts *Pandora* in joint ownership status. That's what you wanted, isn't it? What's more, if anything goes wrong—and this is the important part, baby—if anything goes wrong, we wouldn't have to testify against each other in court. Because frankly, the thought of you telling your version of the truth about me in front of some—"

"Hawk!"

"It gives me chills. Now, like I said, it would be strictly business. Then when all this is over, we can get a quiet divorce somewhere and go our separate ways. Live the rest of our lives out any way we want, with no worries. What do you say?"

"I come from a family that doesn't believe in divorce, that's what I say."

"Annulment, then. Whatever you want to call it. Only this way, ten years from now, when I get picked up for being involved with you because you're still out being subversive somewhere—"

"I am not subversive!" She closed her eyes and shook her head for emphasis. "It was a fluke they even thought that about me."

"I have a feeling you were born subversive."

"Anyway, since you so flippantly used me as an alibi, I would like the option of being able to do the same with you. I'd like to say I had no idea you were involved in this kind of stuff and felt they were grounds for divorce. And, since you were so quick to marry us in the first place, everything would be true."

"But you don't realize what you're asking me."

"You don't realize what I've got on the line here. If I lose my honorable discharge, I lose my retirement pay and all my benefits. Not to mention my honor. First my boat and now my dreams. How much more of me are you going to take?" He turned and walked a few steps away, hooked a thumb subconsciously in the pocket of his jeans and walked back to her again. The hazel eyes revealed sincere turmoil and Dee felt a sudden pang at the thought of ruining his life.

"Don't take away my dreams, Dee."

"Oh, how was I supposed to know you worked for the government?"

"Will you do it?"

"But you don't know where I come from. I'm warning you, Hawkins, you'd regret it a whole lot more than I would."

"Where you come from has nothing to do with this deal."

"It has everything to do with it. You and I are on two different roads. And marriage can't change that. We'd be miserable."

"We're miserable anyway. The important thing is, it'll cover our backsides, and that's all we need for it to do. Walking away would only make things worse. For everybody. Not just us."

Dee was quiet for a few moments. He struck a chord inside her when he said for everybody. Because if there was one thing ingrained into her more than anything else was the necessity of living for others. Her whole life had been shaped around that philosophy, and she didn't know how to live any other way. Now, she had not only endangered other lives with her own personal zeal, one man was dead because of it. That would haunt her for the rest of her life. Even if Peterson had been an aide to Göring.

And now this band of unusual friends, who could have walked away from the mess she had gotten them into and been safe, had opted to stick with her in spite of the dangers.

Getting married would not only settle things for Hawk, they might actually all end up with what they started out for in the first place. A fortune. One that would let each of them do anything they wanted for the rest of their lives.

The whole group.

More than that she would be able to organize the Peterson Foundation. Well, maybe not the Peterson Foundation, now that she knew the whole story. But one with a different name that would promote peace and help some of the suffering in the world, nevertheless.

There was something else stirring, too. Something that only became perfectly clear to her this very moment.

As much as she hated to admit it, something undeniable was beginning to stir in her for Wayne Hawkins. He was not like her in any way. And even though she had argued more with him in the last five days than she had with anyone in the last five years, the thought of destroying his dreams (anyone's dreams) had struck to the depths of her heart. Even though being married to someone with a lifestyle like his would be almost unendurable, he was right about it being the most honorable thing to do.

How was it Wayne Hawkins had a sense of honor most Christians strived all their lives for?

Even so, actually being married to him would take a lot of getting used to. It would definitely take some new strategies. So, she opted to pin him down with his own set of rules for the time being, although going back on a sacred promise would never be an option for her.

"Strictly business?" she asked again.

"On my honor, sweets," he replied. "I'll even try to stop calling you names."

There was another long moment of silence before she sighed, closed her eyes and nodded her head ever so slightly, and then took a deep breath. "All right, Hawkins. But I hope, when you live to regret this, you remember how hard I tried to talk you out of it."

Her hand shook as she filled out the paperwork.

An hour after that, when they were standing in front of a clerk and the Justice of the Peace, Dee began to feel like she might even faint. What would her family say? One should not enter into a solemn oath if they did not mean it (she knew that in her heart of hearts), and this was getting more and more serious by the minute.

The words were familiar. Though she had never spoken them, she had seen it done enough times at church and in movies. For a moment, she was afraid she might not be able to go through with it.

But when the judge said, "Dorothy Jane Parker, do you take Wayne Edward Hawkins..."

Her voice was her own and everything went the way it was supposed to.

Except they didn't have a ring.

After that bit of confusion was past, they were pronounced man and wife and the judge informed Hawkins that he could kiss the bride.

The thought of kissing Wayne Hawkins in front of people when he had never kissed her in private gave Dee another incredible case of butterflies. But she dutifully turned her face up to his and prepared herself for the light, customary kiss that tradition demanded.

Instead, his arms came around her and to her surprise—almost tenderly—he drew her close and kissed her as if she were truly the love of his life.

It caught her off guard. She felt the quick, startled intake of her own breath and then his hand, firm but gentle against her hair, so that she wouldn't back away.

She melted against him as if she really loved him.

The clerk dabbed at her eyes. "This one's going to

last. I got goose bumps!" she said.

They were quiet when they left the office.

The bustling, sunny street that greeted them outside seemed to reassure Dee that none of it was real. She might have forgotten the incident entirely and gone on, except for the lingering telltale signs which proved that (in spite of their lesser intentions) a promise was a promise, and some kind of bond had been forged.

When they climbed into the taxi and their shoulders touched, neither moved away. When they emerged once again onto Market Street and he helped her out of the cab, there was a gentleness about him that hadn't been there before. Or, maybe she just imagined there was.

"You want to go to lunch somewhere before we go back?" Hawkins asked. "This whole thing's got me rattled."

"Me, too," Dee admitted.

"There's a little place a couple blocks down called *The Grotto*, where we can order all the crab we can eat, talk long enough to get in an argument and then we'll be back to normal."

But they had already been cast adrift from their separate worlds...and it was too late for that now.

18
Changing Course

*"A table, graced with a profusion of tropical blossoms—
a man, handsomer than an ideal hero, at its head—
a fine menu..." ~ Nellie Bly*

They sat at a large bay window that overlooked the waterfront and Hawk ordered champagne to go with their meal.

"I thought we were going to treat this strictly business." Dee waited until the waitress was gone to speak.

"People celebrate all the time over business deals," he replied. "I need a drink, that's all I know. We can drink to our coming divorce if it would make you feel better. Champagne just seemed fitting, all of a sudden."

"So, when do we leave, exactly?"

"There's a high tide coming in at four forty-seven this evening. I want to make it."

"Four forty-seven, that's awfully precise."

"Tide tables are accurate to the minute. A lot of people go by them, so they have to be."

"We leave the country just like that?" She snapped

her fingers for emphasis. "We don't have to fill out a travel plan, show our passports, check the weather or something?"

"That's the beauty of sailing. You can come and go as you want, with very little fanfare. One of the last remaining expressions of absolute independence. As for the weather, we're going to hit every kind there is on this trip, so it really doesn't matter what it's like. Outside of a hurricane she can handle anything."

"And I suppose we'll go back to having watches again."

"It's all part of the routine. You'll get used to it."

"I'm not much of a morning person, so I probably never will."

"You just haven't seen enough mornings. Honey, I could show you some mornings at sea that would make you break down and cry."

Their food arrived.

When they were alone again, he raised his glass in her direction to signify a silent tribute before he drank.

"I thought we came here to argue," she reminded him.

"We can argue after lunch."

"Hawk…" She leaned forward and spoke in a quiet, confidential whisper. "Did you ever notice how we keep seeing the same people everywhere we go? Like that couple over there for instance. I just know they were at *Martinelli's* last night."

"Tourists tend to hop around to the same places," he said with equal quiet. Then he leaned forward until their heads were nearly touching, as if he were going to share some similar observation.

Dee waited, expecting him to confide that they were being followed.

"Baby, you look pretty enough to—" he whispered.

"It's just the champagne." She sat up straight again. "Excuse me while I go freshen up."

Even the restrooms in these California tourist spots seemed luxurious to Dee. Polished wooden flooring, a potted palm in one corner that was really alive, and lighthouse and ocean paintings hung over a backdrop of real fish nets. She had very few experiences in places like this (crab for lunch), and couldn't help the feeling of pleasure that washed over her. Which abruptly vanished when she caught a sudden whiff of night-blooming jasmine.

Of course, lots of perfumes had that scent, especially in places like California or Hawaii. But hadn't her feeling of being followed, yesterday, been true? Then, as if she needed more proof, a pair of sandaled feet passed in front of her stall with lavender- painted toenails.

"Jennifer?" Dee snatched her bag off the door-hook and threw back the latch. "Wait a minute!" But by the time she stepped out, no one was there.

Back in the dining area, she did a scan over the room, but no one remotely resembled the young aide from Wyngate State Hospital who had escorted her out of the building last week. Still, the experience was unnerving and her heart was pounding when she sat down at the table.

"What's wrong, sugar? Delayed case of shock setting in?"

"I..." Dee reached for her glass of water. "Thought I saw someone I knew."

He made a reflexive scan of his own around the room as if he might spot them, himself. "Which one?"

"Nobody in here." She set her glass down. "And there wasn't enough time for anyone to leave without seeing them go out the door."

"Just nerves, then. Now you've got me feeling jumpy."

"I thought you were going to quit calling me names."

"I was. But quitting will be harder than I thought. I'll have to think of something else to call you. Like Mrs. Hawkins."

"Hawk, don't you dare! I don't want Marion and Starr to know. Marrying just to get us out of a fix...I'd never live it down."

He didn't answer but his eyes were fairly dancing with pleasure at the thought. "Seems I've reached a depth in your character that up to now was untapped. Might be you have flaws just like the rest of us. Such as money."

"For your information, a lot of people depend on my money. Very important ones, actually."

"Why am I not surprised?" He winked at her and she quickly looked down at her food. "In all fairness, I didn't expect you to be such a good sport about everything."

"Thank you."

"Thank you, Dee."

When they finally returned to the *Pandora*, Marion and Starr were back aboard, packing away fresh food and snack items that would see them through the long days ahead. Among these were six Louis L'Amour paperbacks and an equally tall stack of romance novels. Obviously Marion's contribution.

"I told Starr I'd be plenty busy finishing my own novel," Marion explained when she caught Dee eyeing them. "But he insists that's work and a person has to have a certain amount of escape reading in order to maintain one's perspective during a long voyage."

"Sounds reasonable," Dee replied. "Marion, do you still have my camera?"

"I put it on your bed. But you better hurry up and download those pictures if you want to get your assignment in before we leave."

"Going to do it right now."

Dee spent the next forty-five minutes getting her *Around Town* column finished and downloading the appropriate pictures to attach to the email. Her editor allowed her to choose her own subjects, as long as they were lively and local. She was hoping he'd now allow the next installments to follow her own travels for the summer with the title changed to *Around Towns*.

She was fairly certain he would go for it. Especially since—by now—he would have had time to read the Wyngate material she turned in last week. He was always an easy touch after she turned in a scandal piece because it sent the public opinion page soaring. Controversy, he said, is what really sold newspapers. The bare facts one could get on TV.

The first two installments highlighted that little Oregon fishing village as the hidden jewel of tourist spots and the other offered a glimpse into the famed bustle of San Francisco's Market Street. She sorted through snapshots, searching out the best to go with each story. There were several of the Berkley Marina, which she had taken early this morning, just for her own pleasure, and she downloaded those, too.

"All right, it's time to batten down." She heard Hawk's voice in the companionway. "Everything stowed away down here? We're about ready to head over the gas dock." Her door opened with no warning just as she was hitting the send button.

"You can take the first watch, sugar," he said. And then, "Hey, put this stuff away, now, or it'll be all over the place. Come on, it's four o'clock, already."

"Hawk, I have to run up to that corner drugstore and get another memory card for my camera. Something could happen to this one on a trip this long and it's better to have a backup. It won't take long it's just up the street. Go ahead without me and I'll meet you at the gas dock."

"I'm not going anywhere without you, not even to

the gas dock," he declared. "One disappearance is enough."

"Send Marion or Starr with me then and you won't have to—"

"What are you up to, Dee?"

"Hawkins, I have to call Devlin."

"Then why didn't you come right out and say so?"

"Because I don't feel like arguing about it. I have to touch bases with him at least once before we go. I can't just take off for a month with no explanations, I'll get fired."

"What are you going to tell him when he asks questions?"

"He won't ask questions."

"He's human, isn't he?"

"He's a newspaper editor. And no, they're not human. All I have to do is tell him I'm on the story of a lifetime and his lips are sealed. He'll put me on an expense account and run interference if anyone else comes around asking questions."

"You have that kind of pull?"

"So far. I still need the extra memory card, though."

"All right, but we'll have to make it fast. Starr can top us off on the fuel and we'll meet them over there."

Dee didn't mention the fast talking she would have to do to get Devlin to say, yes. Outside the drugstore, she pressed the work button on her cell phone, and hoped he would not be too busy to answer. He answered on the second ring, and it was nearly a minute before she got a word in.

"Dev, do you want me to come home and type up press releases or do you want pure, unadulterated, gut-wrenching controversy? Now, what I have here is a follow-up on Wyngate. You liked the Wyngate pieces, didn't you, Dev?"

There was a silence, a huge sigh, and then finally, "It's the best you've ever done. It's going to blow the top right off this town. Probably start an investigation of state hospitals from one end of Oregon to the other. And the way you broke it up into three parts, painting the whole picture, never dropping the bomb until you've got them right where you—I say it was brilliant! True to your form, kid."

"Thanks, Dev."

"The first part's coming out this week. But listen, you've got me worried running out after the old guy kicked off. I've had the law down here asking questions."

"What kind of questions?"

"The typical kind they ask about people who were

the last to see somebody alive."

"But, Dev, I wasn't."

"According to them, you were. Considering the cause of death was insulin overdose that doesn't look so good."

Dee gasped. "Insulin overdose!"

"Having cops in my office two days in a row doesn't look so good for me either."

"What did you tell them?"

"What I always say. You went on vacation, like usual. But the second guys were investigators or something. You'll have to answer to them when you get back. Don't worry. I already told them you left town two days before it even happened."

"Two days?"

"You said on the machine you left Sunday. Coroner's report said Peterson died on Tuesday. Looks like your source paid the band, kid. It's too bad, even if he was an old geezer."

"He was more of an old geezer than you think. But it was my fault and I feel horrible about the whole mess. How could it have leaked out? You wouldn't believe the lengths I went to just to keep this thing under wraps. One more day and I would have had him out of there!"

"You did great, don't worry about it. Peterson probably talked and they're trying to set the dogs on you. The article turned out to be hotter than we realized. Some pretty big jobs are about to topple. So you did the right thing. The best place for you is a thousand miles away from any member of the Wyngate staff."

Hawk, having been pacing the sidewalk a short

distance away, came up alongside her. "Hurry up, baby, we've got a tide to catch."

"Dee—" Devlin's voice rose. "Who was that—are you on a fling?"

"No, of course not. That was just...the captain. He talks like that to everybody. Sort of."

"Are you alone with him?"

"No, Dev, I'm not."

"Well, it's a good thing. Because if somebody like you can fall for that stuff, I'll lose my faith in humanity. By the way, what am I supposed to do with the Caribbean thing? It's all set.'

"Give it to Scotty. He was upset with me for beating him to Wyngate, anyway. Maybe it'll soothe some ruffled feathers."

"Maybe I'll have to use it for my own ruffled feathers. After nine years, that ungrateful bum walked out on me without even giving a notice."

"What?"

"That's right. I come in Monday morning and what do I get? A message from you that you went off on some cruise and my number one reporter packing up his desk. Had to have the carpenters in to patch the hole I punched in my own office wall. The guy really got to me."

"Did he say where he was going?"

"He was like the silent Buddha. Possessed or something."

"That doesn't sound like Scotty."

"Well, I got news for you, kid. That message you left on my machine? That didn't sound like you, either."

19
Overboard

"I am off," I thought sadly, "and shall I ever get back?"
~ Nellie Bly

"I think Scott Evans may be following us." Dee tightened the drag on her fishing line.

The afternoon sun was beating down and the wind was so light that *Pandora*'s usual six knots had slowed down to three over a smooth, glassy sea.

Dee had donned the nearest yellow rain hat to keep the glare off her face and it was an unusual accessory to the white, lace-trimmed, cotton undergarment she was wearing. It was a one-piece, sleeveless affair that might have passed for a set of long underwear if the material wasn't so light and the legs hadn't barely reached her knees.

"Scott Evans?" Marion lowered the book she was reading and made a quick scan around the horizon from where she was sitting on the other side of the cockpit. "Dee, there isn't another boat out there."

"Not literally. He's got the chart, so he doesn't have to. But he doesn't have the journal, so he won't be far behind."

"He certainly is the last person on earth I can picture doing something like this." Marion picked up her book again and did a double-take when she glanced over at Dee. "Good grief, if you take anything else off you're going to be indecent."

"It's blistering hot out here."

"Then go change into something cool."

"Hawk said if I left my watch one more time we were going to have a man overboard drill. And I wouldn't put it past him. Besides…" She carefully reeled in a few feet of line. "It covers more than a bathing suit."

"It's the way it covers. You don't want to be provocative do you? Suppose one of the guys woke up early?"

"Marion, for the last two nights of this heat spell, or whatever it is, I have been dragged up here in this very outfit because it's the only cool thing I have to sleep in that's decent."

"Well, no wonder Hawk's been showing more than a little interest. You can't complain if you're going to lead him on."

"Don't worry, I'm not his type."

"His type is anything female and I hope you realize that. In a situation like this you have to be doubly careful. Even if it means sleeping in your clothes."

"I have been. But it's been way too hot. Don't worry. Neither of them will be coming up here anyway. This late afternoon watch when they're both asleep is the only peace I get. I feel like I'm in the Navy."

"More like the fishing fleet, with that hat on."

"My nose is sunburned."

Marion, who had only recently come on deck, was well equipped with sunglasses, a visor and a Hawaiian print shorts outfit. She returned her attentions to the book. She read a line she had already read twice and then closed it, again. "I tell you, I just can't picture Scotty doing something like this. He's too much of a pansy. You know he used to ask for a copy of every recipe I collected for the coastal cooking column?"

"He still does. I figured he just likes to cook. A lot of men do, you know."

"I sort of miss writing about food. I wonder if Devlin would let me come back on a part-time basis when I finish my novel. Do you still have the cooking column?"

"Yes, but I'd be glad to give it back to you because I'm overloaded."

"I can't picture Scotty stealing anything either."

"Well, if you could have seen the way he acted when he found out I was going to blow the whistle on Wyngate you could picture it. He didn't seem the type to break into my house, go through my files, and steal the chart, either, but he did. Besides that, Devlin said he quit last Monday. Maybe he doesn't mind boats so much, after all."

"But remember the fuss he made about the fumes when they were painting his house? I think he'd get deadly sick on a sailboat." Marion reached for a nearby bottle of tanning oil and began to spread some more over her legs. "And all by himself? Definitely not."

"Maybe he isn't by himself." For the next few minutes there was only the steady click, click, click of Dee's reel as she brought in more line. "He was snooping around Wyngate when I—" There was a snag, a sudden forceful yank, and her pole bent into a crescent curve over the rail. "I got a bite!"

"Oh, gads," Marion replied with disgust. "I hope it isn't another one of those grouper things like you pulled up yesterday."

"No, this is bigger...it feels like...something really big!"

"That's what you said yesterday."

"Where's your enthusiasm, Mare? We could be eating like royalty tonight."

"Let me know when you pull up a tuna, then I'll be interested."

Dee couldn't reel any more line and the tip of her pole seemed fastened to something solid instead of a lively fish. She peered over the side. "Nuts, I think I'm just caught in the propeller or something." She reached over the rail and gave the line a tug "Yep. Stuck fast."

"I don't see how you could enjoy fishing so much when it's mostly just false starts and jerks and getting the line tangled up every few minutes. How could you enjoy that?"

"I guess I had to learn to enjoy it. Or I would have spent my whole childhood relegated to baiting hooks for my brothers. I was raised on a lake, remember?"

"Why, Dee..." Marion put the cap back on the tanning oil. "I've just figured out your whole problem in life!"

"Hey, that sounds pretty serious. Hand me those little pliers out of the tackle box, will you? I don't want to let go of this pole. It's one of Starr's expensive ones. He'd flip if I dropped it overboard."

"You've been competing with men all your life."

"That's an understatement."

"I mean, the reason you're thirty-one and never bothered to get married. You're too busy competing with men to ever fall for one."

"I haven't run into any worth falling for, Marion. That's the problem." The line went slack before she had time to snip it. "That's funny..."

"It's not funny it makes perfect sense." Marion sat down beside Dee at the rail. "Don't you see? Being raised in the country with four older brothers— brothers who had the chance to grow fit and strong and confident—It gave you too high a standard. Now that you live in the city, nobody has much of a chance at stacking up."

Dee set the pliers aside and tried reeling in the line again. "It gave me a double standard. Like the way my brothers used to rough and tumble and do all kinds of fun stuff. But let me jump into anything close to a brawl, and—thwack! My brother James would wop me across the backside and say, 'Dee-Dee!' like I had just committed some mortal sin."

"You've been on your own a long time and I don't notice you brawling with anybody. I'd say the opposite. The peacemaking type."

"That's the thing. By the time I got off by myself, it was too late to change. I tell you if my conscience had a face, it would look like James." Her line slowed, resisted, and pulled to a tight stop again as soon as she locked the reel. "Gosh—I still have something on here!"

For the next few minutes Dee was totally engrossed in pulling and tugging, and trying to reel in, inch by inch, whatever the heavy weight was, that was now practically doubling her pole in half. At first, she was on her knees on the seat, and then she was standing with one foot braced against the rail for better leverage. "Get the—the net, Marion! I can't hold him— up close for long—he's—he's too strong for me!"

Marion dutifully lifted the net out of a seat locker and took a position at the rail. But without any enthusiasm at all, since yesterday's experience with the grouper had given her a sudden, cold drenching that dried to a salty stiffness on her skin.

"Here he comes—he's coming! Are you ready, Mare?"

"Ready as I'll ever be, I guess."

"Head first—or he'll swim right out!"

"OK, OK. But try not to let it splash so much this time, for heaven's sake. I really don't—"

There was a jerk on the line and a tremendous thump. Dee lost her balance and toppled against the rail. Slowly, she felt the pole begin to slip from her grasp. "Oh, no!" Suddenly, her prize fish leapt through the water's surface only a few feet away.

In the brief seconds before it splashed down, again, in a deluge of cold spray over the entire cockpit, it revealed itself to be fourteen feet of ugly, writhing, jaw-snapping shark.

Marion screamed. The very thought of trying to wrestle that angry head into three feet of net was out of the question, and she tossed the offending tool aside as if it had suddenly become too hot to hold.

Starr came charging up the ladder wearing nothing but a pair of red boxer shorts.

Hawk was following close behind and emerged just as the shark leapt one more time before making a deep, last ditch dive for the sea.

"Dee—let go!" Marion screamed.

"A blasted shark on my salmon pole!" Starr found pliers to cut the line.

"Where's your safety line?" Hawk reached for Dee and missed, just as she was yanked—pole and all—over the side. "Grab the tow-line!" he called to her even as he snapped the jib sheets free of the winch locks to dump the sails at the same time. "It's right behind you—swim for it!"

"No—the shark!" She flailed in a panic away from the boat. "The shark!"

Hawk swore and stepped up on the transom. "Turn her around, Starr." And he dove over the stern.

"What do I do—what do I do?" Marion cried.

"Put the helm hard over while I get the rest of the sails down and start the motor." Starr's voice had the fear of death in it. "Don't let them out of your sight—don't take your eyes off them!"

If there had been more wind, the *Pandora* could have turned smartly and picked them up within minutes. Instead, she lumbered awkwardly, almost dead in the water, until Starr finally fired up the engine and maneuvered the yacht back around.

"I see Dee's hat." Marion pointed at the bit of yellow bobbing in the far-off distance. "But I can't see Hawk at all."

20
Honor Bound

"I commenced to review my life. How strange it all seems! One incident, if never so trifling, is but a link more to chain us to our unchangeable fate." ~ *Nellie Bly*

Dee thrashed through the water, feeling it tug and push at her, as if its very substance were something alive, pulsating and trying to swallow her down. She was swimming strong and steadily along the surface, yet twice she gulped water when she opened her mouth to breathe. Unlike the placid waters of a lake, the sea was undulating up and down with a constant rhythm, lapping against her face and head from every direction.

Linked with the image of those snapping jaws that had seared into her mind, she was in a state near hysteria and screamed at the sudden, terrifying feeling of being grabbed from behind. She kicked and struggled to get free.

"Hey, hold it—hold it!" Hawk swung her around to face him. "Where do you think you're going, back to Frisco?"

"Hawk—oh, Hawk, the shark!"

"Forget the shark." He hooked her around the waist with one arm and started to swim back toward *Pandora* with the other. "Just calm down and relax."

"But—"

"Relax," he said again. "Just lay back and float, or you'll wear us both out before the boat gets turned around."

"I can't, I'll sink!"

"No, you won't, sugar."

How could he sound so calm?

"Put your feet up and you'll stay right on top. There...like that. Hardly any effort, see?"

"Don't let go."

"I've got you. Now we're just going to move slow and easy. No hurries. We could do this all day if we had to."

"But what if they...what if..."

"Don't think about it. Just float."

An engine came to life even though Dee could no longer see *Pandora* anywhere. Ten minutes later the sleek dark hull was slipping up alongside them.

Marion put the boarding ladder over the side, dragging Dee into the cockpit as soon as she emerged from the sea.

Starr cut the engine and let out his breath as if he had been holding it since they went into the water. "That was too close! That was—" His mouth dropped open in an astonished stare when he was confronted by Dee's clinging underclothes. "What kind of a get-up is that?"

Dee gasped and reached for the pink sweatshirt lying on the cushion where she'd left it.

Hawk ran a hand over his face to wipe the saltwater away, paused halfway through, and sighed so deeply it was almost a shudder. Then he went below without a word.

Dee felt her cold wetness soak into the dry sweatshirt she had thrown over her shoulders. "He didn't say anything," she said to Marion. "He didn't even yell at me."

"You could have been killed!" Marion declared.

"For the second time in three days, Dee Parker, you could have been killed! What if that shark had decided to eat you instead of dive down? And, Hawk—was amazing! He jumped right after you like there was no choice for him at all. I never saw anything like it!"

"I better at least go say thanks." She untied the yellow southwester she had put on to shade her sunburnt nose, tossed it onto the seat, and headed down the companion-way after him.

Hawk was in the galley, leaning with one hand on the counter and the other on an open bottle of brandy. There were drops of seawater dripping from his glistening hair, trickling down his tanned back and shoulders, running in rivulets from his cut-off jeans.

"Are you all right, Hawk?" she ventured.

"I will be in a minute." He put the cap back on the bottle as if it took great effort to do so.

"I'd feel better if you'd yell at me."

"That was too close, Dee. Too close!" He ran a hand through his wet hair. "I lost a friend like that a few years ago. Only by the time we got the boat turned around, we just...we just couldn't find him. He waved to us as we drifted apart and we even tossed him a life ring to hold onto until we swung back around again.

Can you believe that? We looked for two days...but we couldn't find him."

"I'm sorry."

"Where was your safety line?"

"I forgot to put it back on after I took off my—"

"You don't take that safety line off for anything, baby—do you hear me? I don't care if it's a flat calm out there, you still—"

Dee reached out for him first.

The next minute she was in his arms, locked in an embrace that went beyond barriers and words. It was not contrived or pretend this time, but open and honest and incredibly intense. Suddenly, a dam had broken loose. All the tensions between them were converted into emotion so highly charged; she was startled by her own response. They held each other tight, as if the overwhelming need to hold could never be satisfied.

"Hawk..." she whispered longingly, moved by her impulses even before she realized them. And in response to that whisper, he lifted her off her feet until she could feel nothing but him.

She drew back suddenly, shocked, not only by her own strong feelings but also his open willingness to oblige them. It was a moment of such intimacy that she wondered how it could have happened in broad daylight, in the casual surroundings of the galley. Especially when it had been the last thing in the world on her mind.

Hawk let her go without a word, but he held her a moment longer with his gaze. In that moment she saw that he knew her deepest feelings, that he had somehow felt them go through her at the same time she was experiencing them. And while they were new and mysterious to Dee, they were as easy for him to read as an open book.

"I didn't mean to," she apologized as she backed off. "I only wanted to thank you for..." She pulled the sweatshirt more tightly around her, as if it could shield her from that penetrating gaze. "For saving my life, Hawkins."

"Well, I couldn't just stand by and watch my wife drown," he replied.

Dee murmured something about changing into dry clothes and tore herself away from the searing remark. But it followed her as intensely as if it had been Hawkins, himself. It echoed through her mind even as she stood alone in her cabin. It was an honest statement. But he had emphasized the word wife in such a way that she knew what he meant it to mean.

He was asking for more than a business arrangement.

She spent the rest of the afternoon having mental arguments with herself. Unable to sleep during her off- watch, she lay awake and tried to pray. She made decisions, changed her mind, then made them all over again.

Why on earth had she done such a foolish thing? Marrying a ladies' man! It wasn't the kind of life she had been looking for all these years. She had dreamed of finding someone like herself, who cared for the down-trodden and wanted to make a difference in the world. She wanted someone who loved God and others as much as she did. Someone who would go to the ends of the earth for a fantastic cause, no matter how dangerous.

She had wanted a hero.

But none ever turned up. Now in one crazy

moment of weakness (yes, it was a moment of weakness) she had let down the guard she had so carefully kept around her heart all these years and allowed herself to be influenced by someone who, by his own admission, was simply floating aimlessly around the world, living the high life. Someone whose dreams she had felt obligated to save at the expense of her own. Was God really that literal when He said we should put others before ourselves? Who were the others?

Whoever they were, one thought became crystal clear. She had not been caught in this trap, yesterday. She had been caught in it the day she had allowed herself to venture into those gray areas of integrity and enticed away by what she saw there. Money. Adventure. And (to be honest) an incredibly exciting man. Whether she would have personally gone on the expedition if Henry Starr (who was old enough to be her father) had been the only captain of this boat, she wasn't sure. What she was sure of, was that she was "unequally yoked" to a non-believer, now. Something that led to nothing but misery, as she had heard so often in her growing up days.

As if having a pastor for a father wasn't enough, she had four brothers who were following right along in his footsteps.

Why, if she hadn't felt such a driving force to use her talent for reporting to help fight some of the corruption that was so prevalent these days, she would have had a hard time believing she was even part of the family. Now, look at the fix she was in. Hadn't her own mother always warned that a person could find something appealing in a monster if they lived with one long enough? Much less someone as handsome and beguiling as Wayne Hawkins happened to be.

Now he had saved her life.

He must care at least something for her if he had so selflessly risked his own life for hers. That he had done such a thing made her feel incredibly close to him. Incredibly grateful. Incredibly blessed to have a second chance at getting things right. Suddenly, one of her father's sayings echoed in her mind. "People aren't judged as much by how they feel," he said, "as by how they make others feel. Always be careful with other's feelings, girlie."

She had become very vulnerable to Hawk's feelings, somewhere along the line.

At dinnertime, it was Dee's turn to cook. While she was frying hamburger and grating cheese for enchiladas, the others were on deck enjoying chips and cold drinks along with the pleasantries of idle conversation. Hawk came down for refills and she halfway expected him to make some advance. He lifted a portion of the counter top that was the door to the refrigerator and took inventory. "No more cokes, Mare, just cherry, ginger ale, or beer."

"Ginger ale, please," came the reply. "Want any help down there, Dee?"

"No thanks," Dee returned.

"Smells good." Hawk reached over her shoulder to snatch a bite of cheese before he left.

It wasn't until he was gone that Dee realized she was disappointed. What did she expect? That the first moment he caught her alone, he would sweep her up in his arms? The thought sent a shimmer of sweetness all through her. She remembered when they were passing in the narrow companionway, he put a momentary hand on her shoulder but, even though it sent shimmers through Dee, was nothing more than a casual politeness. Again, that night when the breeze brought a chill, he snapped the safety line onto her jacket as she put it on. He probably would have done the same thing for anybody.

Finally, Dee decided that she was over reacting, as well as over responding. Hawk's ways were naturally outgoing and flirtatious, and she (in spite of her original resistance) had finally been taken in by them. So much for her afternoon of soul-searching. There would probably never be a need for the little speech she had rehearsed in her mind because—at the moment—she was the only one who was feeling this way.

By the time her late watch came around at ten, she had finally managed to recover some sense of balance. She brought her i-Pod with all her favorite classical recordings on it, to absorb a little of its peace and remind herself who she was. And one of Marion's romances, too, in case she felt like trading that plan for a little out and out escape. So when she appeared on deck it was in much the same manner as she had taken over the watch every other night they had been at sea: friendly, talkative, but distinctly casual.

Only this time, Hawk was waiting for her.

21
Confessions

With four people, the watch was three and a half hours long. The last person stayed on a half hour to make coffee and conversation until the next was fully awake and alert enough to take over. During the day it was casual, and one could hardly tell who was on or off. But the underlying routine was there. Those who had late night or early morning watches often took a nap in the afternoon. Dee liked the night watch best because it meant no one had to wake her. But so did everyone else, so they rotated.

Tonight, she heard the steady clicking of Marion's laptop as she passed her cabin and Starr's rhythmic snoring as she passed by his before going outside. Up on deck, Hawk was reading one of Starr's Louis L'Amour novels beneath the red glow of the tiny cockpit light. It was just bright enough to read by but wouldn't affect night vision. He closed the book and set it aside when he saw her.

"Don't let me disturb you," Dee offered, "I'm wide awake.'"

"Honey, you've been disturbing me all day. Come

sit down and let's talk."

Considering the emotional roller coaster Dee had been on since the afternoon, she didn't trust herself to get that close. If he so much as brushed a hand against hers, her feelings would go careening all over the place, again.

She took refuge in being as casual as he had been all day. "If it's about the salmon pole," she began, "I already told Starr I'd replace it."

"Dee."

"If it's another lecture about the safety line, look..." She unhooked one of the neatly coiled lines from where it hung over a stanchion and clipped the free end onto a ring at the belt of her jacket. "I'm all set." Then, without waiting for a reply, she went over to look at the compass to note their course. She barely had a chance to glance at the green luminous numbers when he reached out for the safety line and pulled her toward him.

"Don't you think it's about time we made some adjustments in our arrangement, sugar?" He brought her down on the seat beside him. "Move into my cabin with me, Dee."

The directness startled her. She had expected him to make an advance, something smooth and flirtatious or a persuasive speech on the pleasures of romance. Nothing as serious as this. Long-term things like that resulted in the kind of entanglements men like him usually did their best to avoid. Now, what was he up to?

It didn't fit in with her image of him.

But the thought suddenly occurred to her that it might fit his image of her. Hadn't she told him how important a solemn oath was to her, that she was not one to take such things lightly? Maybe this was his way of appealing to her on her own terms. An honest, genuine marriage even though he had no intentions for it to last. Something pleasant to indulge in simply because there was time.

They were sitting along the low port rail, the seat nearest the water, and she held a hand out to it as she settled against the cushion. "What we've got here, Hawkins..." She could feel an occasional spray against her palm that managed to separate itself from the sea, "is a romantic situation."

"We sure do."

She turned her face into the wind, more to avoid his gaze than to keep hair back. As if he might somehow catch sight of those sweeping feelings she was hoping not to show. "Like when two co-workers fall for each other during a project," she went on, "or —"

He took her face in his hands and turned it back to his, and knowing he was going to kiss her, Dee put both of her hands on his in an effort to slow him down. "Or two actors that work too many hours together on the same— picture—it's just the situation, Hawk— it's—"

She didn't get any farther on her prepared speech. His mouth stopped the flow of words, gently at first, and then with an intensity that made her heart beat faster. Dee tried to pull back, surprised that he could convey such intimate messages without any words before she could even ward them off. It was as if she were an instrument he already knew how to play.

"What's wrong, sugar?" he whispered. "You can't say my intentions aren't honorable."

"No relationship, that's what we agreed, Hawkins." She pulled his hands away from her face but didn't let go of them in case he should catch and hold her again. "That's what we agreed."

"Dee, we have a relationship." He closed his hands over hers as if she had meant for him to hold them.

"This isn't a relationship, it's purely physical."

"You've been sending out some pretty strong signals, yourself, sweetheart. You're not going to turn and run, now, are you?"

"I'm not responsible for your uncanny ability to interpret feelings. You ought to be ashamed of yourself playing with people's feelings the way you do. It's...it's an invasion of privacy."

"You shared them with me."

"I didn't mean to."

"Why hold out? Did it ever occur to you we might actually enjoy ourselves, here? Friendly's better than bickering and we might even turn out to be real friends."

"You risked your life for mine, Hawkins. Friends don't come any better than that. But you know something? I think if it had been Marion or Starr out there, you would have done the same thing for them just as quick. That's a rare and amazing quality few people have and I'm... Awed by it, Hawk...I..."

"So, why the no?"

Startled by his directness once more, yet, this time when he pulled her into an embrace, she had no inclination to resist. How easy it was to put her arms around his neck and give into the wonderful feeling! Suddenly, it was not hard to reveal her deepest feelings and the discovery that he was as easy to talk to as he was to take shelter in, made her feel safe.

The simmering below the surface of her heart—that feeling she had been mulling over since this afternoon—was as much a revelation to herself when she replied, as it was to him.

"Because I don't want to be left in bits and pieces when you go. I don't want to love you, Hawkins! Because I'm a forever person, and losing someone I had given myself to would kill me. So if you care anything for me at all, don't ask anymore. Please."

He didn't answer but he didn't let go of her, either. Dee knew she struck a nerve and he was deciding.

"You don't know what you're passing up. How can you decide on something before you try it?"

"Because both of us already know who we are. My heart wouldn't handle devastation very well. And I have a feeling yours wouldn't, either." Dee pulled away from him.

"You're driving me crazy, Dee."

"I'm just being honest."

"Well, if you said anything else, I'd have had an answer for it."

"Meaning?"

"Meaning I hope you're good at saying, no, because it's not one of my strong points."

"I don't have another no left in me, Hawkins."

"I knew that before you came up here."

So, where does it leave us?"

"You on one side of the boat and me on the other." Then he smiled that beautiful smile. "Which I would trade in on a friend for life any day. You're quite a woman, sugar."

"You're not so bad yourself."

"Yeah, well, we're going to need some serious rules if this arrangement's going to work." He stood up and unclipped his own safety line. "No more enjoying how sweet and cuddly you are before you wake up, that's for sure."

"Wayne Hawkins! You mean you...why if that isn't the most underhanded way of taking advantage of a person, I don't know what is!"

He laughed. "I couldn't resist. But people only give what they want to, you know. Even in their sleep. Maybe if you'd trust me a little more you wouldn't have to carry the weight of so many secrets."

"I don't have many left."

"That's an understatement. We've got the whole country knowing what we're up to. What else could there be?"

He stopped the rhythmic motion of coiling the safety line up neatly and looked over at her. "There is something else, isn't there? Come on, baby, let's be straight with each other. You've got me wrapped around your finger, what else do you want?"

"There is something else, actually. One last thing before we can...oh, Hawk..." She sighed and looked away. "I'm afraid it's going to knock you for a loop."

"Then you better tell me straight out and get it over with."

"It's about the journal."

"I knew it!" He shook his head and swore under his breath before placing the coiled line over one of the nearest stanchions. "It didn't make sense keeping it to yourself this long. Has to be a hitch somewhere."

Dee felt a sudden stab of dread at the thought of

disappointing him.

"Well, come on, what is it?"

"Maybe we shouldn't talk about it. I mean, didn't you say we had to be far enough out so they couldn't pick up our conversations?"

"It's all right." He sat down on the seat. "I took the camera apart last night. Turned out it's only a small tracking device, not a bug.'

"You took my camera apart? Hawk, that's a thousand dollar camera. I do all my work with that!"

"I put it back together."

"You should have at least asked me. What if it doesn't work right?"

"I'll replace it. Now, what about the journal, sweets?"

"It's...what it is..." She readjusted the clip in her hair but even with the momentary delay the right words still didn't come. "Oh, I should probably just show you," she finally conceded.

"How about right now? You know where the key is. Might as well get it out of the safe."

"You mean, leave my watch? You said, if I ever—"

"The captain's on the bridge," he answered in a tone that sounded more ominous than permissive. "So go ahead."

22
The Last Secret

"I found it a great relief to be again on the sweet, blue sea, out of sight of land, and free. Only on the bounding blue, is one rocked into a peaceful rest at noon of day, at dusk of night, feeling that one is drifting, drifting, not seeing, or knowing, or caring, about fool mortals striving for life.' ~ Nellie Bly

Even Marion's laptop was quiet down below. The salon, bathed in its red glow of night lighting, looked like a crimson pen and ink drawing from an era gone by. The luxurious tufted seats and mahogany table, shining brass and glass fixtures, and even the small painting of an old schooner that hid the yacht's safe, spoke to Dee of another time. In this dark and quiet hour she could almost picture the famous Hermann Göring sitting at this table, his face flushed with drink, cigar smoke wafting up toward the ceiling, running thick ring-clad fingers through his notorious hoard of jewels. It almost gave her a chill.

But she was avoiding, again.

By the time she returned to the deck, she had a hollow feeling in the pit of her stomach. The journal was her last hold over Hawk for keeping the upper hand in a contest that was rapidly slipping to his favor. A week ago, she would have held out to her last breath to keep the controlling factor. But it didn't seem to matter so much anymore. What mattered to her now was not whether she could keep the reins on this whole expedition but that Wayne Hawkins would not lose whatever respect he had somehow built up for her.

He was not in the cockpit when she came out but adjusting a loose sail on the upper deck. She felt the slight increase in their slant as he pulled on a line, making the sail take more wind and pick up *Pandora*'s speed. When he returned, she was sitting at the lower rail, again. Dee quietly held out the journal to him as he stepped lightly down from the walkway to join her. He took it over beneath the red glow of the cockpit light and, unable to sit still, she got up to stand near the wheel. It only took a few minutes.

"This isn't Peterson's writing." And then a few moments later when the full realization struck him. "This is... it's not even...why, the whole thing is in German! Do you speak German?"

"No," she replied. "But Nels gave me a general idea of what was in it. And I brought a German/English dictionary."

"A German/English dictionary—it would take weeks to figure this thing out with all the colloquialisms, slang, and conjugated verbs! You know where this puts us? It puts us right back in—" He stopped as the full impact of their situation dawned on him.

He shook his head slowly. "You are one cool

manipulator." He set the journal aside and looked at her in utter amazement. "You bluffed your way right into the middle of this thing. You don't know any more than Starr and I do! If I'd have known this, last week, I would have left you in Oregon."

Dee's first inclination was to back off when he started toward her but she held her ground. He put a hand over one of hers, against the wheel so she couldn't move away even if she wanted to. Once again, she could see shadows of a temper only barely kept in check.

"You're like the eye of a hurricane, you know that? All beautiful and peaceful to look at but deadly dangerous to get tangled up in." He let go and moved back under the light to flip through the journal pages again as if he just couldn't believe it.

"You can still quit," she offered.

"It's too late to quit. You've got us in up to our necks with Eddington, now. But you sure enough better quit keeping things to yourself, I'll say that much. Start by telling me everything Peterson told you about this thing."

"Well, the important stuff is in code. Beginning with pages thirty-seven, forty-eight, and ninety."

"That sounds like location, latitude and longitude."

"It is. How did you know that?"

"Sailing around the world twice, I've plotted a lot of courses. Mind if I take it down and work out the exact position on the chart? I'd like to look it over more anyway."

"How could I say no?"

He tapped the journal thoughtlessly against his

palm for a moment. "You can't." Then he bent down long enough to brush the side of her face with a kiss. "Goodnight, Dee Hawkins."

"Shhh!" Now she looked toward the dark companionway as if one of the others might materialize at any moment.

"Don't worry, sugar, your secrets are safe with me." He tapped the top of her head with the journal before turning to leave. "All of them."

Dee sank back onto the nearest seat cushion as if she had barely averted a catastrophe. What had just happened? Once again, he had surprised her by behaving totally opposite to the kind of person she thought he was. What's more, that brief inkling of anger had rustled like a gust of blustery wind that was here one moment and gone the next.

As if that wasn't enough, she felt an incredible sense of relief that, not only had he kept his temper in check, their strong connection was still intact. She had confronted him with the one thing she had dreaded most to tell him and they were still friends.

Still married.

Married!

Her lawfully wedded husband. The man she had just poured her innermost feelings out to, when she had never in her life been that open with anyone else. It happened so easily. As if there were no walls, at all, between them. That he had even gone so far as to say her secrets were safe had actually intensified that odd sense of protection she felt in confiding them to him in the first place.

Or even being physically next to him. The truth was, she felt safe standing next to Wayne Hawkins, no matter what they thought of each other. But that he had understood her so perfectly—and obliged her—was the last thing in the world she would have expected from someone like him.

Dee pulled a pair of black knit gloves out of the pocket of her jacket and put them on as she thought about all this. She actually felt relieved at not having to keep her guard up anymore or be so careful of what she did, or didn't, reveal.

When a momentary drop in wind intensity came as *Pandora* glided down into the trough of a long, rolling swell and then snapped back into the sails with a sudden freshness and quickening speed as it rose up on the other side... a sense of thrill came over her. She was on the adventure of a lifetime. At this very moment. With the most dedicated, dearest (in spite of all their quirks), friends in the world. And she absolutely, loved sailing!

The very nature of it. The giant grandeur of the sea and the power of the wind. And the amazing experience of being able to control those two things to such a degree that something as small as *Pandora* could ride between them and make her feel as safe and content as a baby in a cradle. She liked the rhythmic rocking sensation that soothed one's nerves and had given her some of the deepest, most relaxing sleeps she had ever had in her life. Not since she was a kid, anyway. Then there was the complete and exquisite order of this little man-made world as it glided through all that was unpredictable in the natural world around it.

She even liked the deep peaceful privacy of the night watches, where one could actually hear themselves think and thought about things that hadn't surfaced in years or even decades. Where little shafts of understanding broke through with quiet whispers, until even the most confusing of issues gained new perspectives and began to make more sense. During this night watch, in such a state, Dee even began to contemplate what life like this might be like on a permanent basis. Frivolous daydreaming, really, because she would have no claims on any of it by the end of their journey. Not really.

For while she took a promise (a solemn oath) seriously, Hawk did not. In fact, he was probably at this very moment, below decks dreaming dreams of his own that did not include her. Something that she could do little about, no matter how she felt about him. They had married in California. In a day and age where a claim of incompatibility by either partner was enough to sever all ties. No one took solemn oaths seriously, anymore. One could become worse entangled in a business contract. So, her mother had been right, after all. A person could become enchanted by a monster, if they spent enough time with them.

But exactly what did one do about a mistake like that, after it had already been made?

23
The Journal

"How's the novel coming, Mare?" Dee asked the next morning at breakfast. "I heard you typing away last night like things were really rolling."

"Oh, they are!" Marion wiped up the counter as she talked. "I think the sea inspires me."

"More than a basement apartment downtown?"

"How right you were." She laughed at the thought. "If you had inherited a boat a year, ago, *The Ghost and Charlie Hooper* might be done by now."

"*The Ghost and Charlie Hooper*?" Starr sopped the last traces of golden yolk off his plate with a piece of toast. "That sounds more like a kid's book than a great American novel."

"It is," Marion replied.

"You mean all this time you've been working away in there, telling us it's the greatest work of your life, it's just some...some kinda kid's book?"

"Not a kind-of kid's book, Starr," she corrected. "A for sure one. Children are the hope of the future. Especially in this day and age. Why, childhood is the closest we come to perfect in this life. It's when today is forever and tomorrow never comes. Absolutely magic! Come on now, don't you look back on your own childhood as the most wonderful, life-inspired days you ever had?"

"I do," Dee agreed as she sipped her coffee.

"More like the most confusing, kick in the butt days I ever had, if you want my opinion," Starr intoned. "All that rat-a-tat I've been hearing in my sleep every night and it turns out to be a pop-up book!"

"The subject of ghosts would be highly inappropriate material for a pop-up book," Marion said defensively. "Why, I wouldn't dream of doing anything like that."

"Hey, sugar!" Hawk called down from the cockpit. "Come on up here a minute."

"Here." Marion handed her a thermos of fresh coffee. "Might as well take this up while you're at it. Tell him if he doesn't come down pretty soon, he's going to miss breakfast."

Dee reached for the thermos and started up the ladder. On deck, a brisk wind was blowing *Pandora* along at six and a half knots under an overcast sky. The sweltering heat and whisper breeze of the last two days had finally slipped behind them with the miles and she realized she was going to have to go back down and exchange her shorts for jeans, again. The deck was slanted at more than the usual angle so that she had to fairly pull herself up out of the hatchway.

Hawk had rigged for speed and was trying to make

up time.

He finished taking in the jib sheet and stepped down off the upper deck. His eyes softened when they met hers. "Go get the journal and logbook out of my cabin, will you, sweets? Then let's get everyone up on deck for a round table before Starr goes to bed."

"Sounds like you made a decision." She set the thermos in the wire holder attached to one of the seat lockers. "Several."

"Hawk, are you going to—"

"Let's wait until the others get up here. We should all be in on this. Unless you want to hear something personal like how I was up most of the night thinking about you."

"I think I'll go get the others." She pulled the hood of her lavender sweatshirt up over her hair to keep it from blowing in her face.

Suddenly and without warning, he took her by the waist, lifted her out of the open companionway to where the others couldn't see them and kissed her before she could resist. The sensation was too exhilarating for pretense. One moment she was grappling with a chilly wind on an uncertain deck and the next she was swept up in the contrasting warmth of an alluring kiss.

"The cake's good, too," He told her when she didn't resist. Then he placed her hand, almost subconsciously, on one of the mainstays so she would have something to hang onto before he let her go.

"What's that supposed to mean?" She clasped the supporting wire with both hands and looked away from him and out toward the sea. So much for avoiding any advances.

"It means, why be satisfied with just snatching a

taste of frosting when you're invited to stay for the whole dessert. That's what it means."

"Shhh!" She glanced toward the open hatchway and asked in a demanding whisper, "Are you going to act like this all the way to Russia?"

"If you keep wearing outfits like that, I am. Short cut-off jeans, bare feet, and colors that make your eyes look like violet...your skin look like honey..."

"Hawkins! Are you going to honor your agreement, or aren't you?"

"I've already done the honorable part. So did you, as I recall. I distinctly remember the judge asking you to solemnly swear—"

"Shhh!"

"To take me as your..." He leaned close and whispered each word slowly and distinctly, "lawful... wedded... husband."

"Wayne Hawkins, that's not fair! Are you telling me what you agreed to, last night, was nothing but a fickle promise?"

"A solemn oath overrides a fickle promise, every time."

"Well, I'm not listening to another word." She backed off and would have stumbled if he hadn't reached out a hand to steady her. Which she did not refuse until she reached the safety of the companionway.

"Hawk wants us all up on deck for a round table," she informed Marion and Starr on her way past. "I'll be along as soon as I change clothes. It got cold out there."

They watched her disappear down the narrow aft companionway, after which Starr observed, "That's not all it got out there. Those two are either gonna kill each other or move in together. I give them about a week."

"Dee wouldn't do that," Marion replied. "She's not the type."

"Yeah, I guess you're right." He got up to rinse his mug out and then put it back in the cupboard wet. "Definitely too much of a softie to commit murder."

Outside of a brief glance the first night they moved aboard, Dee had never really looked closely at the captain's cabin. In the daylight, the full impact of it was a little overwhelming. It confronted her in the same way the empty salon had the night before, like a stirring of lives past. A bank of windows against the stern drew in the lonely turbulence of a brooding sea. There was a long window seat beneath them, an almost hypnotic place that might keep one spellbound for hours.

Like the rest of the yacht, the room was luxurious with dark paneling. It even had an oriental carpet tacked to the floor. There was a small private bath and a desk with a leather-tufted chair beneath a row of bookshelves along one wall. The bed was large, with drawers underneath and covered by a beautiful woven throw of navy blue and red.

The journal and logbook were lying open on the desk, and as she reached out for them, her attention was drawn to a small, framed photograph on the wall above. It was of a robust handsome man in his early forties. He had light golden hair and eyes the color of the sky. All at once, a feeling as if someone were watching came over her so strongly she turned suddenly to check the doorway.

But no one was there.

A strange sense of heaviness flooded over her, then, and she hurried back through the slanting corridor, past Starr's unkempt cabin, through the galley, and up on deck. When she finally arrived in the center of the cockpit, amid the comfortable ordinary chatter of her friends, she was irritated at herself for having been so easily spooked.

She felt a sudden need to be occupied. "Would anyone mind if I fished during the meeting?"

"Oh, no," Marion moaned.

"I've only got one pole left," Starr replied, "but go ahead, I guess."

"Get your safety line on," Hawk said when she handed him the two books, then took the pole out of the seat locker and quietly began to busy herself with the gear, instead.

She reached for the last line and clipped it onto her jacket.

"Let's get on with the meeting," said Starr.

"Well, to begin with, there's a problem with the journal." Hawk poured himself another cup of coffee from the thermos and sat down next to where Dee was now totally involved in attaching one of the lures.

"You looked at the journal?" Starr asked.

"Last night. But Matta Hari, here, neglected to inform us that the whole thing was in German."

"I resent that implication," Dee objected without looking up from her project.

"Who's Matta Hari?" Starr questioned.

"Some famous lady spy you read about in history books," Marion explained. "Go on, Hawk, we're listening."

"According to Dee, Peterson gave her some sort of page numbered code to work out the exact location. But without speaking the language, the only information I could get was latitude and longitude."

"But we already had latitude and longitude,' Starr said.

"Exactly. So, the missing element we've all been making fools of ourselves over hasn't told us anymore than what we already knew."

"How was I supposed to know that?" Dee asked. "Peterson told me the exact location was there and that's what I told you. I did hand it over, and I did tell you the code. Which is why I resent the Matta Hari thing." She dropped her six-inch, three-pronged lure over the stern and began letting out line.

"Not that one," Starr whispered an aside to her. "You want to catch a blasted marlin or something? Stick to the small stuff."

"Oh, all right," she whispered back and reeled it up again. "But they're not as much fun."

"However," Hawk went on, "from what I could make out last night, the journal isn't Peterson's at all. I think it belonged to someone else."

A chorus of disbelief went up and Dee quit reeling in line to turn around in surprise.

"Look." Hawk opened both books before handing them across to Starr for inspection. "The handwriting is different. And the logbook—which is in English— is written by the captain of this boat, describing an expedition to recover the diamonds back in 1946. An expedition headed up by one...Heinrich Keller."

24
Peterson's Story

"We sat on deck talking or nervously walking about..."
~ *Nellie Bly*

"So even if the journal was Keller's," Dee pointed out, "everything still fits. Peterson said he got the jewels from a German officer, he just never mentioned his name or that he had been an aide to Goering. Probably knew I wouldn't have agreed to get him out, if I had known he hobnobbed around with war criminals for years on end."

"You tried to get a Nazi war criminal out of the loony bin?" Starr's expression was one of unveiled surprise.

"How was I supposed to know who he really was? He lied to me."

"Dee, you could have been killed!" Marion's voice carried the same tone as a death bell on an old church. "Why, he could have murdered you the minute you got him to the first—"

"Let's not even go there," Hawk interrupted. "The

point is, the log is full of the name, Heinrich Keller. It tells a story of how he switched sides during the invasion of Russia. He got away with it because he spoke perfect Russian. His mother was Russian, a wealthy aristocrat who married a German officer named Friedrich Keller before World War I, which is why Heinrich Keller spoke German, some Swedish that he and Peterson communicated in, and Russian. He didn't speak any English back then."

"But what difference does it make whose book is whose as long as they substantiate each other?" Marion asked.

"Peterson spoke English," Hawk replied. "He wrote the log in English to keep an account of the expedition that he didn't want Keller to know about. I think he suspected him right from the start. The moment Keller commissioned him and the *Pandora* to go get the diamonds. Both their countries were in post war pandemonium. Keller was probably just out to save his own hide. But..." He picked up his forgotten coffee cup and took a long thoughtful drink of the cold brew. "He never expected the new U.S.S.R to close itself off from the rest of the world indefinitely. Or the Cold War that followed after that."

"Maybe he started off trading sensitive information as a way of working himself back into the country." Dee's tone sounded almost hopeful. "It's just hard to believe he could have been so... so evil. He sure never seemed that way when I knew him. Crafty, yes. But you'd think I would have had warning bells going off all over the place, if he was such a horrible person. Wouldn't you think so, Marion?"

"All spies look ordinary," she said. "As a matter of

fact, that's one of the requirements."

"We even said a prayer together!"

"About what?" Hawk asked.

"He killed a lot of people during the war and he didn't want to go to hell. I thought he meant as a soldier. Fighting the enemy and all that. Which is not the same thing as murder, in my opinion. We had a lot of military people in our family that gave everything they had and then some. So, nobody can convince me otherwise."

"Probably meant killing Keller," said Starr. "Last entry in the log was nothing special. Position and weather conditions from somewhere in the Arctic Sea, about a week off from the island. Poor duffer never saw it coming."

There was a moment of silence as it all sank in, during which Hawk noticed a barely detectable flutter along the edge of the foresail and got up to take in the sheet a little. "I think the Feds are right." He adjusted the sail and returned to his seat. "I think what the old man told Dee happened the other way around. He really was Heinrich Keller. A war criminal who killed Nelson Peterson back in 1946."

"Some partner!" Starr mumbled in disgust. "Must have had it in mind all along. For the identity more than the diamonds. What people won't do for money!"

Then, he gave an embarrassed gasp, let his brown eyes roam self-consciously around the group and pointed out, "None of us have been acting like angels, around here, either. I think he wanted the *Pandora*. He needed a way out nobody would notice, and *Pandora* was it."

"That makes sense." Dee tugged back and forth on the fishing line as she talked. "Keller wasn't just a regular officer, he was an aide to Göring. With the Nuremberg Trials in full swing by then, the bloodhounds were out for anyone in that elite circle. They still are. Remember just last year, some radical crashed into an apartment in Europe and shot a ninety-some year old man who turned out to be another war criminal in hiding?"

"I do remember reading something about that," he replied. "And Keller was a survivor who had switched identities before. I say he just strung Peterson along enough to learn how to handle the boat on his own and then dumped him somewhere out at sea."

That's the most gruesome thing I ever heard." Marion declared. "On this very boat, too! No wonder I've been having nightmares. I thought it was just exhaustion."

"But if it's so easy to figure all this out by looking at these two books together..." Dee set the pole aside and finally turned to face the circle. "Why didn't Peterson—my Peterson—just destroy the evidence? I can't imagine he'd leave something as incriminating as the logbook floating around."

"It wasn't floating around," Hawk replied. "I found it in a hidden compartment behind the bookcase in the aft cabin, about four and a half months ago."

"Nels sailed this boat around for nearly thirty years, Hawk," she objected. "Why wouldn't he have found it, himself, in all that time?"

"The only reason I found it is because after five years of being abandoned, the yacht was deteriorating. There was a leak in that aft cabin behind the bookcase and when I pulled it apart to fix it, I found the logbook. It's one long, gripping narrative of the five months Keller and Peterson spent together. It's what got me caught up in this thing in the first place. I pulled into Oregon on my way south to Mexico and stayed almost six months before making a deal on *Pandora.*"

"I thought you said you didn't find that logbook until after you started renovations, though." Dee sounded skeptical. "What made you want *Pandora* in the first place?"

"I guess she haunted me," he replied. "Every time I walked by, some unearthly magnetism grabbed at me. When I started asking questions, the legend that had built up around it was just as intriguing. Became an obsession."

"It's an obsession, all right. He got me dreaming about diamonds right along with him." Starr reached for the pole Dee had set aside and cast the line out himself. "Look at me. I haven't put in a decent day's work since you started talking about this trip."

"How ironic," Dee marveled. "To think you started planning it around the same time I met up with Nels."

"I wouldn't be surprised if Divine forces were merging to absolve an unjust murder." Marion said. "A tortured soul, that's what it is."

"I don't believe in that junk," Starr objected. "There's always a logical explanation if you look hard enough."

"Cases of that nature have been very well documented," Marion argued. "Especially if foul play was involved. And as long as we're on the subject...well, I've been trying to think of a way to bring it up ever since we started. I haven't even told

Dee."

"Told me what, Marion?"

"My cabin," she replied in a tone of deadly earnest, "is haunted."

There was a tentative tug on the fishing line and Starr's attention was diverted. He adjusted the drag, reeled in a little, and then gave a sigh of vague disappointment. Then as if there had been no break in the conversation, he commented, "A boat this old has creaks and groans all over. Nothing supernatural about that."

"I don't just have creaks and groans," Marion clarified. "I have a wet spot."

"A wet spot—we're cruising—we got wet spots all over. Here, Dee, you want this back?"

"But you have a bite, don't you want to do it?"

"Just a lousy mackerel, go ahead."

"How can you tell?"

"Because it fights like one and I fish for a living." He handed her the pole and turned back to Marion. "So, what's a wet spot look like when it's haunted?"

"No different than any other, except it shows up for no reason. Right in the middle of my bed. If I didn't know better I'd think I had a bladder problem."

"For heaven's sake, Marion," Dee said over her shoulder, "that's the strangest thing I ever heard."

"Strange isn't the half of it. Listen to this. I dry everything out, remake the bed, and two hours later it's wet again. Downright eerie. It's getting so I can hardly sleep in there anymore."

"You should have said something." Dee pulled back on the pole and reeled in more line. "At least to me."

"It was too embarrassing. I thought maybe my

health was going."

"How could your health be going when you're barely fifty?" Starr objected.

"I'm fifty-one. And for all I knew it was the preliminary symptoms of some fatal disease. I've been totally depressed."

"Marion, that's just awful!"

"Well, it's a relief to know that's not what it was. But on the other hand, it's pretty unnerving to be sharing living quarters with some kind of poltergeist."

"It's not a poltergeist," Hawk said.

"Tell us what it is, Cap'n." Starr reached for the net as Dee's fish began to splash off the stern.

"It's a chain reaction from something you probably did when you first came aboard," he suggested. "Tell me if I'm right. The first night out when we were taking on all that water, I'll bet you went down there and sat on the bed with your wet things on."

"Fell on the bed is more accurate. I was so exhausted I fell on it, wet clothes and all. I couldn't have moved if you paid me. I think I slept eight hours straight before I even realized it. But I told you I dried everything out. How do you explain the fact that it keeps getting wet again?"

"The salt residue left over from sea water acts like a sponge. Absorbs moisture right out of the air. Result? The proverbial wet spot."

"Now how did you come up with that?" Starr deftly dipped in the net at the right moment and scooped up eighteen inches of flailing silvery mackerel.

"Just logical," Hawk replied.

"Logical—it's brilliant. A bloomin' scientist couldn't have figured it out better. How do you think up those things?"

"I spent my first fifty-eight days at sea soaking wet from one end of my boat to the other, that's how I figured it out. When I was in Tahiti, drying every mattress and cushion aboard, the white salt rings were a dead giveaway."

"Well..." Starr held the wiggling fish for a few seconds while he removed the hook and then threw it overboard.

"Hey!" Dee protested, "I was"going to—"

"They're not worth eating," Starr said. "Just a scavenger fish."

"That would explain things," Marion conceded. "I've sure had some eerie feelings over it, though."

"Which proves my theory that ghosts, and demons, and Bermuda Triangles, are nothing but a bunch of junk." Starr yawned, scratched lazily at his thick dark beard and sat down again. "Let's get back to the round table. I've been up since three, and I'm beat. We figured out a mystery here. I don't see what difference it makes whether Keller was Peterson or Peterson was Keller. What's that got to do with us? Can we make it on coordinates alone, or can't we?'

"We've got as much of a chance as we always had," Hawk said. "We just don't have the sure shot we would have had with landmark descriptions. One island looks as much like another and your guess would be as good as mine as to where Keller might have hid the stuff."

"I have landmark descriptions," Dee spoke up. "They're in a cave, halfway up a rock face on the north beach. You can't get to it from the beach. You have to come by way of the south and climb down. Besides, the beach is populated by sea lions and they don't like intruders. Anyway, it was fifty years ago." There was such a long silence that she stopped dabbling with the fishing line and turned around.

Everyone was staring at her.

"Why in the world didn't you say that before?" Hawk finally demanded. "You've known that all along and you only just now mentioned it?"

"It only just now came up," she answered.

He cast a warning glance. "This is the sort of stuff that makes me wonder who you're really working for, sweetheart."

"Oh, gads," Marion sighed. "No one's working for anybody. We're all just four regular, ordinary people with everyday lives, who happen to be going berserk at the thought of a share in fifty million dollars. I don't think any one of us is acting like our own decent selves, it's like we're possessed or something!"

"And you two are the worst," Starr agreed. "At each other like a couple of kids."

"We've all got to be more understanding when everyone's on edge like this," Marion soothed in a tone that only years of mothering could produce. "Hawk, you have been awfully harsh with Dee, sometimes. You don't realize how sensitive she is."

"I know what she is," he replied in a tone Dee recognized as a dam about to burst.

"And Dee," Marion went on, "you've got to quit being so mistrustful of Hawk and tell him everything. Everything! The best thing to do is go down right now, and bring up all your maps and notes and—"

"You've got maps and notes?" Hawk was out of his seat so fast Dee barely had time to scream, much less fend him off. He swept her up like a madman snatching a child and, in one swift motion, carried her kicking and hollering down the companionway ladder.

****

"Starr! For heaven's sakes, do something!" Marion thumped him on the shoulder. "You can't just sit there and let him—"

"What am I suppose to do, Marion, punch him in the nose? He'll deck me. I'm sixty-three, and overweight," he reasoned. "Nothing but an old fisherman and he just got out of the military. Besides, I think she can hold her own."

"Hold her own? You saw that blind rage—we've got to do something!"

"Leave them alone. Like I said, they'll either kill each other or come out friends."

"They still have their safety lines on..." She leaned over to see if she could hear anything alarming.

"They reach from one end of the boat to the other, so you don't have to unhook in heavy weather."

"If he lays one hand on her, I'll get a frying pan, and—"

"Leave them alone, Marion."

25
Torn Apart

"This dreadful exhibition made me feel that probably there was some justification in arming oneself with a club"

~ *Nellie Bly*

Although Dee was furious at such treatment, she was not afraid of brute strength. She knew from experience that it was almost always coupled with weakness. And after years of being bossed, pushed, and dragged around by four brothers, she had become a near-expert in pin-pointing the weaknesses. Hawk's weakness was women.

The surest thing that would stop Hawk in his tracks was a contrite, irresistibly upset female. It wasn't difficult. Since her youngest brother Dan had a similar nature, she was fairly well-practiced. It had been a few years, but it was a knack one never lost.

Only she didn't have time to use it.

He grabbed her by the lapels. "We agreed no more secrets! When are you going to be straight with me, Dee?" Then he swore and let go of her before imploring, "When are you—going to be straight?" His anger turned to the hurt of betrayal, which swept over his face like a breaking storm.

"Hawk, I'm sorry," she whispered. But it was a feeble effort against a wound that was already made.

"You're just like all the rest." He turned away from her.

"I wasn't keeping secrets, Hawk. I told you last night I had a general translation. You didn't give me a chance to share it."

"What kind of chance were you waiting for? You didn't bring any maps and notes to share with the group. You were fishing!" He turned with a look of pure astonishment. "I was fumbling around with vague coordinates, and you didn't see a chance? I think if Marion hadn't slipped up and mentioned it—"

"If you hadn't lost your temper like some rampaging bull, I would have come down here like she suggested and got them!"

"We'll never know."

"You know, Hawkins." She felt her own emotions start to churn at such a loss of faith in her. "You do know!"

"I thought I did. I thought there was something different about you. That you had some genuine concern for others that went beyond just what's in it for you. Like there might be something to the way you're always talking to God like He's right there next to you and I just never tried it, myself."

"There is! And if you'd only listen, I could—"

"All religions are garbage! It just takes some longer to rot than others."

She hadn't known he'd been watching her in this way or even thinking about God. He had passed judgment without the subject ever having come up between them. A realization that made her feel the heat of tears threatening to spill over at the very thought that her own unwillingness to be open was driving him away from the God she knew and loved.

"Don't." He pointed a warning finger at her. "Don't do that."

Tears began to course down her cheeks in a magnitude she hadn't experienced in years.

"I'm not going to fall for this, Dee, you hear me?"

"Go away!"

"Stop playing games with me! Give me the maps, notes, and whatever else you've got and I'll get out of here. I've had it with you!" ,

She opened one of the drawers beneath her bed with her foot and took out the canvas bag. She reached inside and found, more by feeling than sight, a medium-sized leather notebook with a zipper closure, and tossed it onto the bed in front of him.

"You sidestep me again, for any reason, I'm going to dump you off the first chance I get. I don't care whether it's another boat or a harbor. And I don't care what harbor—you got that, sugar?"

She opened her mouth to answer but a sob came out instead and it was all she could do to snatch up a pillow to hide her face in before she broke down completely.

"Very convincing." The tone held no trace of sympathy. "But since I've sat through this kind of act before, I think I'll skip the rest of the show. My instincts may be off, honey, but my memory's working just fine."

He slammed the door on his way out and Dee cried for nearly half an hour. Even when Marion came in to check on her, she was still too upset to communicate anything more than a nod or shake of the head to assure she was all right and, no, Hawk had not hit her.

"The nerve of him!" Marion fumed. "The absolute nerve! Why only a monster would treat a woman like that in this day and age! If it hadn't got quiet in here so fast I would have barged in with a frying pan! Are you sure you're all right?"

"Oh, Marion!"

"What is it, Dee? You can tell me."

"I—I feel just awful!"

"Oh, no..." Marion's face went pale. "Dee, he didn't... You didn't..."

"I hurt him so!" She sobbed with renewed remorse.

"Hurt him? Why, Dee Parker! Sometimes, I think I hardly know you at all. I better go make you a cup of tea."

But nothing was the same after that.

He switched the watches, and that night, it was Starr who woke Dee when it was her turn. Along with the next night, and the next.

And as the days slipped by, one after the other, a depressing cloud began to settle onto *Pandora*'s crew. There were no more gatherings of everyone together in the cockpit. Even the chatter of daily living dwindled to a mere trickle as each of them began spending more and more time to themselves.

The second time Dee failed to respond to a simple wake up call, leaving her new partner waiting on deck for half an hour, he developed a method of his own for getting her out of bed in the middle of the night.

Instead of a polite knock and an announcement

that it was her turn at the watch (which she always answered, but was never really awake when she did) he brought in a steaming cup of coffee.

"Sit up and drink this, Dee." Then he would place it in her hands after she spontaneously responded to the direct order. When he returned a few minutes later to refresh the dwindling supply, she was always agreeably ready to shuffle up on deck. He even made the concession of helping her into her jacket (though it went against his grain to pamper any crew member, male or female). He only did it because he felt sorry for the way Hawk was treating her.

He hadn't spoken a word to her for days.

Then, as if the very ocean were reflecting *Pandora*'s doleful atmosphere, they began to move into the cold latitudes. Ski clothes and long underwear replaced jeans and tee shirts, and more and more the sky was heavy with icy, cloud-bearing winds that blew whisper breaths down from the sleeping arctic sea.

Nearly two whole weeks went by.

Hawk remained distant and aloof, as if his belief that Dee was "just another user" made him lose any interest he once had in her. Most of his off watches he spent reading or poring over charts in his cabin. And he had little success trying to befriend Marion, who stayed stubbornly loyal to Dee.

On the other hand, Dee was sure she had personally destroyed whatever plans God might have been setting up to win Hawk over and open up connections between them. Connections that might have very well led to the kind of marriage she had always dreamed about. Because, if there was one thing she was certain about after all this, it was that she had fallen hopelessly—and completely—in love with Wayne Hawkins. Whether it was one-sided or not, the slightest touch or glance from him, even now, still sent her emotions careening in every direction.

But Hawk stuck to his decisions. His expressive eyes no longer softened when they met hers. His gaze always turned away too quickly, refusing to rest on her for any length of time. If he spoke to her it was only out of necessity and always with the utmost casualness. Which was more hurtful than if he had stayed angry.

Even the name-calling disappeared. Which, rather than being a relief, made Dee feel even more miserable.

"Take my advice," Starr said to her one night when they were alone on deck together, "and don't let yourself fall for him."

It was one-thirty in the morning and the wind was bitter cold.

Dee was sitting in the lee of the heavy canvas they had laced along the cockpit railing for a windbreak, sipping her hot coffee and brooding. "Is it that obvious?" she asked.

"Obvious—I've got sympathy pains just watching you torture yourself with guilt. It's not your fault. Hawk has a lot of his own problems to deal with. No use getting yourself tangled up in something that started a long time before you ever came along."

"What is he, a monster in disguise?"

He got up to lean over and check something on the side of *Pandora*'s hull for a moment before sitting back down again. "You can hear what people say up here clear as a bell if the side port's open," he explained. "But he's got it closed. Where was I?"

"Monsters."

"He can be one, all right. How's the saying go? When he's good, he's very, very good, but when he's bad..."

"He's horrible," she finished for him. "How come you stick so close to him, then?"

"Because he picked me up out of the gutter, that's why." He got up again, lifted the locker beneath his seat and retrieved a bottle of *Southern Comfort* from its recesses. He poured a liberal portion into his coffee, looked over at Dee to offer, but she put a hand over the top of her cup in reply.

"That doesn't sound like any monster to me," she said.

"I've been married three times," he confided. "First wife died. Second two... ah, they were just passtimes, mostly. Anyway, when Hawk drifted through, the last one had just finished cleaning me out. My fishing business was about to go bust, and I was pretty low. Met him in the bar one night. Next thing you know he had invested in the business. Bailed me out of debt is more like it, and we were partners."

"That doesn't sound like a man with such problems, either."

"He did it in spite of his problems. Like it was second nature to him, like... breathing. That's the thing about Hawk. He always does what's right, even if it's for the wrong reasons. He just crashed and burned ten years of marriage in a messy divorce and what does he do? He helps out a drowning old duffer like me nobody else will give the time of day to."

"Ten years?"

"Ten miserable years to hear him tell it. I guess she really did a number on him. Rich, lawyer-type career lady that walked all over him to get to the top, then dumped him once she got there. No kids. Just money, money, and money."

He tipped a little more whiskey into his cup. "Anyway, that's why Hawk has a vendetta against anything female. At least he did until you came along. Between you and *Pandora*, I thought maybe he found the right road again. Now, I don't know. All the old symptoms are back and he's closer to toppling over the edge than ever."

"What kind of symptoms, Starr?"

"It isn't my place to say. I already said too much. But I'm getting a little attached to you myself these days. You're a nice gal. I wouldn't want to see you get hurt. Truth is, Hawk's not the kind of person someone as nice as you ought to be chasing after. After he gets what he wants, he'll just cut and run."

26
Suspicion

"Don't worry," I said encouragingly, as I was unable to speak that dreadful word..." ~ Nellie Bly

"What's this?" Marion asked when Hawk emerged from the companionway at dawn and handed her a folded wool blanket.

"A peace offering," He sat down in the seat across from her and reached for the coffee thermos. "It's one hundred percent wool. Even if it gets wet it'll stay warm."

She was quiet.

"Come on, Mare. It's been almost three weeks. How many times do you want me to say I'm sorry?"

"I'm not the one who needs to hear it, Hawk. Dee's miserable."

He sighed, took a sip from the steaming cup, then put a hand in the pocket of his jacket to keep warm. "She isn't miserable because I lost my temper, Marion. She's upset because she lost the reins on this whole thing and I'm not playing into her hands anymore."

"That's the farthest thing from the truth there is.

Dee's not that kind of person. It's just a...twist of fate that it even looks that way."

"It's a twist, all right." He looked tired.

She contemplated the handsome, troubled gaze that stared moodily into the dawn and felt sorry for him. Whatever his reasons for withdrawing into himself, he was lonely, spent, and trying to make amends. Who was she to insist that he make them first with Dee? After all, didn't the deepest wounds take longest to heal?

"You don't have to give me the blanket off your bed, Hawk," she finally said. "Apology accepted. I just wish we'd all try thinking the best of each other instead of the worst every time. Including me." She took a tissue out of her pocket and dabbed at her nose that had long since grown irritated in the wind. "Red sky in the morning, sailor take warning," she quoted the famous lines then got to her feet. "I've been feeling rain in the air all night long."

"Barometer dropped into the storm zone. Better sleep while you can. It looks like it might be a rough one."

"Don't you want to have breakfast before I go down?"

"I'm not hungry, I'll get something later."

She handed him the blanket.

"No, you take it," he insisted. "I don't have the wet spot. I just have the ghost."

It was amazing, Marion thought, how much better a person could feel after airing their differences. Keeping things all locked up inside and holding a grudge, that's what wore a person out. She hadn't changed her mind about Hawk's actions or even her opinion of how he was treating Dee. But she felt better about him. At least standing watch with him every day wouldn't feel so much like the judgment seat anymore.

She missed Starr. She missed that big comfortable hulk sitting there in his worn-out jeans and suspenders, with his plaid flannel shirtsleeves rolled up past the elbows of his long underwear. He drank too much but he didn't put on airs. And he made a person feel like they didn't have to waste time putting on airs for him, either. He thought a little too highly of Hawk. But then it was difficult for anyone not to be taken in by the warmth and friendliness Hawk doled out whenever he felt like it. Hadn't she just been taken in by it herself?

No matter. If she had to be Hawk's partner she would rather have him be the smooth-talking charmer who meant only half what he said than the dark brooding stranger he had been lately. Charm she could live with. Dark, brooding secrets gave her chills.

Marion pulled the green, acrylic blanket with the damp center from her bed and shook out the thick, gray wool one to replace it. It wasn't until she was tucking in the corners that she noticed the black lettering at the hem. She bent down for a closer look and then froze.

It had the words Wyngate State Hospital stamped on it.

Dee had only been asleep since Marion took over the watch at two and was harder to wake than usual. "Now what?" she groaned at the intrusion. "It can't be my turn already, and I don't want any coffee!"

"It's me—Marion!" her friend persisted in a hushed but urgent whisper. "Dee, this is important!

You have to come to my cabin for a minute. I have to show you something!"

"Now?"

"You bet your life now. Come on!" She dragged her out of bed. "But be quiet..." She peeked down the companionway to make sure it was empty before darting across to her own door that was still ajar.

"This better be good, Mare," Dee whispered, "because I'm exhausted."

"Look." Marion pointed to the blanket hem that was turned up across the corner.

Dee bent down for a closer look. "I don't believe it! Where in the world did it come from? How did it get here?"

"Hawk gave it to me this morning." Marion's tone had the death-bell ring, again. "And I think it makes perfect sense!" She closed the door behind them, after a quick glance down the empty companionway and whispered. "It explains everything. Where else would he get a signed-off title of the boat if not from Peterson? You said yourself someone was blackmailing him. And the only people who were ever around him besides you were Wyngate staff."

"Marion, that's just too frightening! What would he be doing there? He's not a doctor or anything."

"How do you know? Did you ever ask him what he retired from?"

"He retired from the military, remember? And besides that, he just isn't the type."

"They have medical people in the military, Dee. They don't all just march and carry guns. And he's been out of the military long enough to have befriended Peterson, just like you did."

"But do you realize how cold and devious he

would have to be to pull something like that off? I can't picture it, Mare, he's too... well, he's just too emotional."

She gasped. "Oh, good heavens, that's even worse. But you're right. It does make more sense."

"What sense?"

"How emotional he is." Marion opened one of the drawers beneath her bunk and withdrew a pair of thick flannel pajamas to change into. "Think about it. He's perfectly charming one minute and then brooding and moody the next. He spends hours in his cabin."

"We all do, ever since this blowup about the journal. It's turned the whole trip depressing."

"Not like him. If you ask me, I think he's got all the symptoms of a manic depressant. Bi-polar, I think they call it these days. And maybe he wasn't on the Wyngate staff at all, Dee. Maybe he was a patient."

"Marion! Oh, don't say another word!" Dee pulled the collar of her jogging suit closer against her neck at the chilling thought.

"That's the way they are, you know. They go to extremes. And I'm telling you, Dee, when I saw the way he grabbed you up that day and carried you off like some caveman..."

"He was just upset."

"Upset," she clarified, "is when you say, honey, I wrecked the car, and he maybe puts his fist through a door. But going after a person like that and then sulking about it for three weeks, making the rest of us miserable...that calls for psychiatric help. They get progressively violent, you know."

"He didn't hurt me, Marion."

"He did something. I've never seen you so upset

before."

"I was just emotional, because he got to me somehow." She looked her friend in the eye. "I love him."

"Dee Parker! I can't believe what I'm hearing! There's thousands of wonderful, eligible men in the world without having to consider someone like Wayne Hawkins!"

"He reminds me of my brothers."

"Oh, gads. Someone to fight with and go on adventures. That's fine for kids, Dee, but there's no place in the modern adult world for that kind of life. You wouldn't want it if there was.'"

"I'm not so sure I wouldn't."

"It's like the movies." She hung her damp clothing on a peg behind the door, to dry. "Great fun and excitement to watch from the safety of your seat, but hair-raising horror to live through in real life."

"I don't know what to do." Dee ran a hand through her tangled hair. "I've never felt like this about anybody before. Not like this. It's all so disturbing!"

"I know what to do. We pull this boat over, get off in Tokyo and take the first plane back to the States. That's what we do."

"And leave the boat and diamonds all to them? Marion, you can't be serious! If we stick it out we could be set for life. Just imagine the good we could do."

"I'm deadly serious. And what good is set for life if you're dead?"

"Dead?"

"Yes, dead. This infatuation is clouding your judgment, Dee. I've never known you to be so naive."

"Whatever Wayne Hawkins is," she declared, "he is not a murderer! He's just been in a tailspin because he thinks I betrayed him. That I'm a rotten Christian even though I act like I'm not."

"A rotten Christian? I've never known anyone as dedicated as you, how could he say that?"

"It's just like my father always said, Mare. People judge you more by what you do than what you say. And I've never made such a mess in my whole life."

"You can't save everyone. Don't be so hard on yourself."

"But he's so miserable. Do you think he'll get over it?"

"Oh, he'll get over it. He'll be all charm and sweetness getting over it. Next thing you know, he'll sweep you right off your feet. But it's a mood swing, Dee, and he's only interested in you because you're here and he's...an over-sexed male! I hope you remember that. People with his kind of problem seem to need constant reinforcement from others. Whether it's approval of their behavior or a warm companion to sleep with."

"Marion, for heaven's sake!"

"I'm just being frank. Because even after the despicable way he treated you, you seem to be too starry eyed to see it."

"We can't assume he has mental problems just because he..." Dee looked out the porthole and was startled at how turbulent the slate gray sea was beginning to look. At the same time, she could hear in her mind Starr's hushed voice quoting, *"When he's good, he's very very good, but when he's bad..."*

The thought was so disturbing it made her

shudder.

"I guess we'll just have to wait and see," Marion said. "But he was either on staff at Wyngate or a patient. There's no other way to explain this blanket being here. That he would be so blatant as to come right out and give it to me is downright frightening!"

"Maybe he didn't know it was a Wyngate blanket," Dee suggested. "Maybe Nels brought it aboard. On a visit or something."

"I thought Peterson told you he hadn't been out of that hospital in almost five years."

"He did."

"Then I'd say that pretty much rules out Peterson. So I for one intend to be on my guard at all times. You've given him all the papers, now, and he hasn't said one word about it since. Not one word, Dee. That's because we're not needed anymore. Next thing you know..." She began to smooth cold cream over her face. "There's going to be an accident."

27
The Accident

"I went in very bravely and took my place on the captain's left..." ~ *Nellie Bly*

It was not the same as the rough weather they had encountered off the Oregon coast. This was a surging, full-blown gale. It kicked waves up to thirty feet that sent *Pandora* crashing and pounding over seas that buried her under tons of water half the time and left her groaning and shuddering the rest.

No amount of reefing sails or adjusting the rigging could stabilize her. The self-steering gear could not function in such erratic weather, and watches had to be reduced to two hours on and two off, around the clock. Nobody stayed on deck alone. Each person kept their safety lines on above and below decks to avoid the danger of being swept overboard by some random wave while trying to clip one on in the tossing cockpit.

Any lingering disputes among *Pandora*'s crew, melted before the face of such grueling work and harrowing seas. The storm was unrelenting. For a day and a half they got little sleep, lived off damp sandwiches and coffee, and were hard pressed to stay dry.

Hawk was an unyielding taskmaster whose word went undisputed, even though he sometimes seemed to ask the impossible.

If anyone lay down to rest it was only on one of the settees in the main salon. They wedged themselves, fully clothed, between the table and the bulkhead to keep from being thrown to the floor with the violent motion.

Starr was as steady and comforting as a dependable giant, whose sheer strength pulled them through time and again. He seemed less unnerved than Dee and Marion and had great confidence that Hawk's judgment would see them through.

Marion and Dee did their best at whatever tasks they were given and in spite of their fears, worked tirelessly right along with the men. They learned to make sandwiches and coffee in the pitching roller-coaster galley, and they could handle every chore on deck but steering, which they could only manage for brief intervals. Neither of them had enough strength or endurance, yet, to hold the wheel steady against the pounding seas for any length of time.

So it was that toward the end of the storm's second day, Dee was roused out of a fitful sleep by Starr as he thundered past her through the salon and up the companionway ladder in two bounds. By the time she reached the decks herself, he was already hauling an unconscious Marion aboard by her safety line, hand over hand.

Hawk hadn't moved from the wheel.

"What happened?" she cried against the wind.

"Hawk—she's bleeding!"

"One of the stays broke loose and I had to jibe." he shouted back. "I yelled at her but she didn't move fast enough. The boom knocked her overboard."

"Marion!" Dee helped Starr carry her down below, where they laid her out on the floor. "Marion!"

"Get a flashlight," he said, "and the first aid kit from under the steps there. I think I saw a pretty bad gash in her forehead when I pulled her aboard."

Dee reached for the flashlight that was always at the navigation table and used it to peer into the step-locker for the first aid kit. By the time she brought it back, Starr already had Marion's knit hat off and jacket unbuttoned.

Dee pointed the light beam at her.

"Holy fright!" he stared at the gaping wound that shown back from the middle of Marion's forehead like an extra eye.

"I can't put a bandage on that! That's a hole the size of a blasted —"

"Apply pressure!" Dee rummaged through the box for a gauze pad with her free hand. "Here, hold this on there!"

"You hold it on there." He got to his feet. "I'm gonna go take the wheel so Hawk can come down here. He's the medic."

The words chilled Dee to the bone.

A few minutes later, Hawk grabbed the hatch cover and swung himself down through the companionway, finding it easier to drop the seven feet than try to keep his foothold on the slippery ladder. "Let's see what we've got here." He took the flashlight from Dee and knelt down beside her. He lifted her hand away along with the gauze to look.

"It won't stop bleeding!" The rising dread she could feel in the pit of her stomach nearly made her ill. "And she's out cold!"

"Well...it can't wait." He replaced her hand even though the gauze was already soaked in blood. "It's going to be a bear of a job under these conditions. Think you can help? Or are you going to be like Starr and crap out on me?"

"Of course I'll help. She's my dearest friend! I'll do whatever I can."

"OK. You just hold on there until I get some things."

Hawk closed the main hatch so no light would spill out onto the decks to mar Starr's vision when he turned them on. It was imperative that his capable friend be able to adjust their course to accommodate the dangerous swells, and to do so, he had to be able to see them before they were on top of *Pandora*.

Then, a few moments after he disappeared down the aft companionway, the engine roared to life and the cabin lights came on to their full brightness. For weeks now, they had been letting the charge dwindle in an effort to conserve fuel they would need more along the coast and rarely used anything but the red navigation lights at night anymore.

""Marion..." Dee tried to coax a response from the ashen face, noticed that blood was beginning to trickle through her fingers and felt a sudden dismay. "Marion, please wake up!"

"Don't try to bring her around." Hawk returned with a green metal box with a red cross on it. He had taken off his jacket and pushed back the sleeves of his brown fisherman's sweater. "Better if she isn't awake for a while. She's going to have one huge headache when she comes to."

"Oh, Hawk, she needs a doctor! Can't we radio for help or something?"

"We're in the middle of nowhere in a howling gale, Dee. She'd bleed to death before we could get help out here. Don't worry, I can handle it." He filled a pan half with water at the sink.

Hawk had hardly picked it up when he felt the familiar surge of a giant roller beneath them and lost it as they crashed down. He swore under his breath and started over.

"Get her jacket off," he said when he returned. He wedged the pan with a lid on it into the space between the table leg and the settee.

"But the bleeding! I don't dare—"

"Don't worry about the blood, it's slowing down. Head wounds always look worse than they really are." He opened the metal box, took out several wrapped packages of gauze and two small bottles—one of which he poured into the pan. Next came a thin rubber tube that he draped over his shoulder for a moment while he used both hands to roll up the sleeve of Marion's sweatshirt. Every movement was smooth, practiced, and made with no hesitation. As if he had done it a hundred times.

At that moment, Dee could easily picture him in the gray scrubs of Wyngate, and the thought frightened her. She watched wide-eyed as he deftly tied off the rubber tube above Marion's elbow and tore open a package to reveal the silvery, thread-like flash of a hypodermic needle.

"What are you going to do!" she cried.

He paused and looked up at her, surprised at the traces of sudden panic. "I'm going to make her as comfortable as possible before I start poking holes in her. You think you can relax a little?"

"What is that?"

"Morphine." He turned the bottle upside down and eased the needle through the cap.

"That's illegal!"

"Dee, it's a common ingredient to any cruising medicine chest." He flicked the side of the syringe with his finger and pushed up the stopper until a few drops of liquid appeared on the needle. He swabbed the inside of Marion's arm with an alcohol pad and concentrated for a moment until he was sure he had found the vein. "So...either calm down and be a little more help...or back off."

Dee looked away. There was a shuddering lurch as *Pandora* plowed her way through another wave.

Hawk withdrew the needle and blood spurted. "I didn't even feel that one coming."

Marion whimpered and began to stir.

"One more time, Mare," he soothed. "Hold her head still, sugar. She starts thrashing around before this takes effect and she's going to come right up off the floor."

There was another steep, unannounced roll and this time it was all they could do to keep Marion and themselves from sliding across the floor.

"If I don't do it fast, she's not going to get any at all. This keeps up, she'll hate me for making a mess of her arm."

Marion's eyes fluttered open and she looked with frightened panic into Dee's.

"Everything's fine, Mare," Dee assured, though

her voice was shaking. "It's all right now, everything's..."

"Hawk!" Marion whispered. "I told you...I..." A visible wave of pain swept over her,"Oh, I feel like I..."

"Try not to move," Dee pleaded.

"Dee, I...feel like I'm dying! My kids...my..."

"Just the morphine," Hawk replied to Dee's sudden gasp. "It's hitting her hard and all at once. Trade places with me now, so I can get busy."

He knelt down with Marion's head between his knees and motioned Dee closer. "Come on, get in here." He put one of her hands on Marion's chin and the other on top of her head. She had to rest her forearms against his knee to do it. "Don't let her head move. If you start to feel sick, lay your head down but don't let go of hers. Got it?"

She nodded.

"It'll be a messy enough job as it is." He opened another package. The contents were a curved suturing needle complete with thread. He wrung a washcloth out of the pan of antiseptic water and removed the bloody gauze from Marion's head. "If it bothers you., don't look."

Dee couldn't look. She leaned her head down against his knee and felt cold chills every time Marion's face tried to move in her hands.

Hawk swore at *Pandora*'s every jolt, but he continued the steady tying and snipping, pausing only to wipe away fresh blood when it became too difficult to see what he was doing.

Dee only looked once before turning her head away.

"Still with me, sweets?" he asked.

"Yes."

"Number eight and we're done. She'll have a concussion but I don't think there's any fracture. Starting to bruise, though. Talk to me, Dee."

"I can't."

"Take a few deep breaths."

"Hawk, where did you learn all this?"

"I started out in the Boy Scouts."

"Seriously?"

"Seriously, you wouldn't want to know. But if it makes you feel any better, injuries like this..." He snipped off the last of the thread and set the scissors aside to reach for a bandage. "Are my specialty. All done now, you can relax."

Dee straightened up slowly, her back stiff and tired from leaning over for so long. She looked up at Hawk.

For the first time in weeks he did not glance away, but let his gaze soften and linger, causing a rush of conflicting emotions to course through her.

"What's wrong, baby?" he asked with a gentleness that reached out and enveloped her. "She's going to be all right. I promise."

"Oh, Hawk, why didn't you pull her in?" she suddenly blurted out. "Why did you just stand there and wait until Starr came out? Why?"

"I told you, a stay broke loose. If I let go of the wheel just then we could have rolled. Maybe even lost the foremast. She was on a safety line and Starr came as soon as I called."

"But she could have drowned and you just stood there! You didn't even try to—"

"You're too tired, Dee." The tone sounded as if he could sense every suspicion she had. "Don't say anything you might regret later."

While Hawk cleaned up and put the medical kit away, Dee dressed Marion in a dry flannel gown. Afterward, he carried her back to her cabin and set her down gently. He clipped the mesh hammock up into place so that she would be as stable as possible in *Pandora*'s constant pitch and roll.

Dee tucked the wool blanket close all around her friend and—when the Wyngate lettering shown for a moment, looked up quickly to see if she could read some trace of sinister knowledge or recognition in Hawk.

If there was, she couldn't tell.

"She's going to sleep for at least six hours. Guaranteed." He switched off the light as they left and closed the door behind them. "So should you."

"I have to take my watch."

"Starr and I can handle the deck. I want you to go to bed."

"I can do it," she argued. "I'd rather—"

He reached out and stopped her as she passed her own cabin, opened the door and steered her gently but firmly inside before closing it, again. The effect of him shutting her away in the dark room suddenly felt too overwhelming. The long weeks of inner turmoil, the accident, lack of sleep, and the constant rolling and pounding of *Pandora* all whirled together to magnify the impression.

"Hawkins!" she called out to him in a tone that was edged with despair.

The door swung open again, and he looked in.

"Don't shut me out anymore. Please don't!" He stepped inside and she reached up for him, her words tumbling out in a rush. "I can't stand it! I never said I was perfect, I'm only trying to be. And I can't stand that you would turn away from the things God wants to give you, just because of the way I've acted. I'd die first! Because I love you, Hawk, I—"

His mouth stopped the words with a long answering kiss before he swept her up long enough to set her down on the bed. The response was so reassuring a wave of sheer relief swept through her.

"I love you, too, sugar. And I love whatever makes you so quick to give yourself up for someone like me. I never thought of God thinking about me, much less having anything to give me. That's just—"

Pandora suddenly rolled and he reached for the bulkhead to steady them, making the only effect a slight shifting of her weight against his. "It's just too good to be true."

"It is true!"

"Well, if Starr hadn't been out there by himself, so long, I'd let you prove it." He kissed her again. "Right now, I have to go. But I'll be back when the storm's over."

He left her then, and after he was gone his presence lingered like poignant music, with all the sensations returning again, and again, whenever she thought of him. It wasn't until just before she drifted off to sleep, that she realized she had been— literally— swept off her feet.

Exactly like Marion had predicted.

28
Acceptance

"I had a very strong determination to resist my impulses, but yet, in the bottom of my heart was a little faint feeling that I had found something even stronger than my will power." ~ Nellie Bly

By the time Dee woke the following morning, the storm had blown itself out and *Pandora* was moving at a swift graceful clip, once again. The slanted decks were finally steady and no longer rolling or erratic.

Dee felt wonderful. After peeking in at Marion to find her still asleep, she showered and took her time getting dressed.

She looked into the mirror and was startled by her own reflection. After a month of outdoor living, she had acquired a rich tan of a depth she hadn't achieved since she was sixteen and devoted an entire summer to get. The makeup she had brought along paled in comparison, so she set it aside. Instead, she made do with a little eye-shadow and lipstick of a slightly deeper shade than the pink turtleneck sweater she was wearing. She was ready in a mere ten minutes. One could definitely get ready for the day, faster, when there was less to do.

She twisted her hair up into the clip and pulled a chocolate-colored knit hat with a fur brim over it all. Then as she rummaged in her make-up bag for a small bottle of perfume, she heard a muffled moan from Marion's cabin, and set things aside to look in on her.

Marion was engaged in a slow motion struggle to disentangle herself from the hammock.

"Dear...Lord! I've got the worst...hangover I ever—" Marion's hand went to her bandaged head. "Owww! What happened?"

"Just take it easy and try not to move too fast." Dee helped her sit up and propped pillows behind her back to lean against. "Don't you remember anything?"

"I was adjusting one of the sails and—oh, Dee— Hawk hit me!"

"What?"

"He did! I heard him yell, and then he hit me!"

"The boom hit you, Marion," she insisted, even though the accusation brought that same feeling of dread back into the pit of her stomach. "He tried to warn you, but you didn't hear. It was the boom that knocked you overboard. Put a terrible gash in your head and you had to have eight stitches."

"Stitches!" Her hand moved to her head again and she traced the bandage with her fingers. "Who on earth?"

"Hawk did."

"You let him do something like that to me? What if I get gangrene or something? How could you!"

"I didn't have any choice, Marion. You were bleeding so terribly I... don't worry. It was all very professional. He just..."

Their gazes met and there was a long, uncomfortable silence.

"I told you," Marion breathed finally. "Didn't I tell you?"

Dee sat down on the foot of the bed and ran a hand over her brown ski pants. "It doesn't have to mean he worked at Wyngate, though. It could be a coincidence."

"You should have come right out and asked. Say, did you work at Wyngate? Yes, or no."

"I can't put it that way, Marion. Not when he already said he never heard of Wyngate before I brought it up. To ask if he worked there, now, would be accusing him of a lie. I don't want to upset him again."

"Dee, have you lost your senses? He's as good as proved himself. How many normal, everyday people would have been able to sew up somebody's head? Would you have?"

"Oh, I couldn't!"

"That's my point. You'd have done your best with a butterfly bandage and wrapped it up. I'm surprised he didn't kill me! And if he didn't, then..." She raised a warning finger for emphasis and a pain shot through her arm. "Ouch! My word! What happened to my arm?"

"He had some trouble with the morphine."

"Morphine!"

"The boat was rocking and banging like you wouldn't—"

"Morphine! You let him give me drugs? What if I was allergic?"

"Shhh! Marion, you want them to hear us? I told you everything was perfectly sterile. Never used. I watched him tear open the packages, myself."

"If I get addicted, what am I going to tell my kids? I'd be a disgrace to Bill's memory! I—"

The door clicked open and they both froze.

"Good morning, ladies," Hawk's tone carried the usual pleasantness they had become accustomed to before he lost his temper. "Are we having some trouble in here?"

"She's...upset about the stitches," Dee spoke up first.

"There was no choice, Marion." He put a hand under the older woman's chin and turned her face up to look carefully into her gray eyes. "No uneven dilation. Can you focus on my finger?"

"Dee!" Marion's voice was barely a whisper.

"Bet you've got a bear of a headache, though," he soothed. "Go get her a couple aspirin, sugar, while I check and see if there's any—"

"No, I want Dee to stay!" Marion's voice had the ring of a petulant child and Hawk's eyes softened as he looked down at her.

"That was a terrible experience, Mare. I'm sorry it happened. Think you can forgive me?"

"My mouth tastes like seawater, my head's killing me, and you—you had no right to give me drugs!"

"You'd have thought I was torturing you if I hadn't. It was so rough down here you got about twice too many holes poked in you as it was."

"But a woman my age could be addicted!"

"Well, if the pain gets too bad, let me know, and I'll give you some more."

"Good grief, what do you take me for? I'll die first. I don't care if—"

"Just kidding. I don't think a woman of your

strength and will power needs to worry about addictions."

"Don't try to butter me up. I'm put out with you, Hawk. Extremely put out! If I didn't know better, I'd think—"

He leaned over and kissed her on the cheek.

The gesture startled her. "Oh, I...suppose I'm just irritable."

"Understandable," he assured. "So you're officially relieved of duties until you feel better. Breakfast and a couple aspirin will do wonders."

"I'm not hungry."

"How about some tea and toast?" Dee suggested. "It'll just take a minute."

They left Marion's cabin and as Dee went to the sink to fill the teakettle, Hawk came up behind and put his arms around her. "Are you still the same girl I left last night?" he asked.

"Yes."

He leaned down and whispered against her hair, "The whole gift and not just the package?"

"Yes."

"Then I don't need anything else." He tightened his arms around her until she set the kettle down and gave in to the embrace. "Stay this way, Dee."

"I will. But, Hawk, I have so many questions."

"Come on up on deck and ask away. Are you up to taking the watch?"

"Are you kidding? Eight straight hours of sleep in the middle of the night—where they belong. Of course, I am. You and Starr must be exhausted. Want me to make a hot breakfast?"

"We had something around four after the storm

passed. Now that we've got the self-steering on again and made repairs, I can send Starr down for some sleep." He kissed the back of her neck and it sent a chill through her. "I'm not good for much longer, either, so hurry on up as soon as you're finished here."

By the time Marion was settled and Dee finally went up on deck, Starr's snores were already reverberating through *Pandora*'s passageways. Hawk was stretched out on the low side of the cockpit, propped comfortably against the canvass windbreak. He was methodically peeling an orange and tossing the pieces of rind over the side.

"Did she eat?" he asked.

"She drank some tea." Dee zipped her jacket up snugly against the cold wind, amazed once more at how cozy the cabin stove could keep things down below. "But she only nibbled at the toast. Said it made her sort of sick."

"I was afraid of that. Tossing sailboat's no place to ride out a concussion. But I guess it could be worse. At least there's no fracture. Step into my office, sugar, so we can talk."

Though the storm had died down there was a cold thirty-knot wind blowing over choppy seas, and it was a comfort to sit in the shelter of the canvas rails. It was even more of a comfort to share a place with Wayne Hawkins that he had moved over and made for her and to feel in that casual gesture, a sense of acceptance and belonging.

Dee suddenly dreaded the thought of stirring up disturbing subjects, again. All she wanted to do was nestle into that inviting embrace and stay there.

"So what are all these questions?" He handed her

a section of his orange. "Better hurry, or you'll miss your chance. When I finish this I'm going to take a sleeping bag out of that locker over there and check out for at least two hours."

"You're not going down to your cabin?"

"It's lonely down there. The way yours was last night."

Having looked forward to this moment, Dee was surprised at the flicker of hesitation she felt. But she had always found her judgments to be reliable and in her heart she felt she could trust Wayne Hawkins. Even when her mind flashed memories of the night before, when he had been so unhesitating and smooth, she found herself searching for reasons to believe in him. How could someone so wonderful be anything less than wonderful?

Suddenly, she had to know.

"Are you a doctor or something?" Her mind raced for ways to sound more casual. "I mean, not many people could do what you did last night. And why did you say I wouldn't want to know?"

He finished the last of the orange and wiped his hands on his jeans. "Because it turns most people off, that's all. I got in the habit of avoiding the subject. Especially now that I don't do it anymore."

"What exactly was it?"

"I started off in the Army as a medic." He got up and rummaged through one of the seat lockers for a sleeping bag. "Then went into forensic medicine. Know anything about that?"

"Cause of death investigations," she replied. "Police work, court rooms, and... autopsies."

"Yep. I was the military equivalent of a coroner.

Like I said, it turns a lot of people off."

"I thought you were in computers."

"What gave you that idea?" He unzipped the bag, sat down next to her again and spread it over both of them.

Dee's heart began to pound. "The lady at the port office in Oregon said you were supposed to fix the computer. So I assumed..."

He put his arms around her and leaned back comfortably against the seat. "They just got that set-up put in down at the port and think anyone who can reset when it freezes or recover something they lost is a computer genius. You feel good, Dee."

"Then I suppose you spent a certain amount of time at hospitals."

"Some. But why all the sudden curiosity? Looking for common threads to explain your impulses?"

"Maybe."

"We have a lot in common, Dee. More than you realize. But for the moment, let's just stick with the impulses."

29
Heart to Heart

"Well, by all that is wonderful, where am I?"

~ *Nellie Bly*

Just before Hawk finally settled down to get some sleep, he brushed the curls back from Dee's face and kissed her again. "I'm having a hard time believing you're real. Not going to disappear or anything, are you?"

"I'm not the disappearing type."

"Who are you, Dee?"

"Really?"

"Really."

"Well, I think I better give you the short version." She twisted her hair up into the clip and put her hat on as she talked. "In case you need a little more time to get used to what you've gotten yourself into."

"I don't think I'll ever get used to you. But go ahead."

"I'm Dorothy Jane Parker, youngest of five.—"

"Dorothy Jane Hawkins."

"Hawkins." Dee conceded with a smile. "Youngest of five children born to a fire-breathing

242

preacher and a saint straight from heaven. Dad's words, not mine. Because he says only a bona fide saint could ever live with a preacher. Anyway, they run a conference center up on the Wenachee Pass, in Oregon. Along with my two older brothers and their families."

"That explains the religion. Now what about the—"

"It isn't a religion, it's a relationship." She looked straight into his eyes for emphasis. "Like yours and mine, only without all the misunderstandings."

His eyes twinkled with amusement. "You sure can put a twist on things, sugar. Where's the adventure fit in?"

"That part's just a matter of preference I'd have to blame mostly on the way I was raised. My front yard was a lake. My backyard was a state park that still holds some of the densest mountain wilderness in the country. My brothers and I had free reign of it."

"So why aren't you tramping around in some jungle trying to save the world? How did you end up with a journalism career?"

"Let's just say I read a biography of Nellie Bly at a very impressionable age. She didn't just speak up about things that were wrong, she actually did something to change them. In some very adventuresome ways, I might add. I wanted to be like her."

"That's all it took?" He laughed, and the sparkle in his smile caused a warmth to spread through her. "So you are trying to save the world. That's an impossible job, sweets."

"Not the whole world. Only whatever I encounter along my own road. But it's a lot harder than I thought. So far, I haven't been able to come close to the kind of results her reporting produced. I guess I'm just not brave enough."

"I don't know many people brave enough to take off on a fifty-six foot ketch with a couple of strangers. Even for the money. Especially these days."

"Thanks, but unless I can do something worthwhile with the money, what good is it? My biggest fear is that, deep down, I might turn out just as ordinary as most people and not be able to handle it."

"You're more than most people can handle already. But how come, with that pretty smile and those long eyelashes, you made it all the way to thirty-one without getting caught by some guy who had his hopes up for you?"

"I had four brothers who chased away every boy who was ever interested in me. After that it was a habit. And after that, there seemed to be a terrible shortage of appealing men. I was wrapped up in my work…and the years went by."

"How did I get so lucky?"

"It wasn't luck, it was God's timing."

"Now, there's something I'd like to believe. It wasn't my charm, I know that much."

"That's not exactly true, either. You swept me off my feet, Hawkins." She sighed and snuggled close to him. "Starting with that first kiss."

"I meant that kiss."

"I know."

"You had me the day you dropped in without knocking, though," he admitted. "The first time I laid eyes on you. Only I didn't want to go through another attachment. Truth is, I just spent ten years married to the most beautiful witch in the world who did nothing but try to destroy me."

"Starr told me." A gust of cold wind rippled through his hair and she ran a hand through it. "And he told me not to fall for you because after you got what you wanted, you'd probably cut and run. Are you going to cut and run, Wayne Hawkins? Now that you got what you wanted from me?"

"I haven't got enough of it, that's for sure. It works both ways you know. If you turn out to be another witch, I'm done for. I don't have it in me to go through that twice."

"I'm not the wicked witch, I'm Dorothy." She moved away from him long enough to pull the fur-lined hood of her jacket up over her hat and tie it snuggly beneath her chin. "The follow-you-all-the-way-to-the-Emerald-City- type Dorothy. Be careful what road you lead me down, Hawkins."

"I will."

He slept for three hours.

Still unwilling to be far from her, he stayed on deck and finally drifted off to sleep after she promised to wake him if there was any break in the clouds.

Three days of being tossed by the storm had driven them too far off course to simply resume their original heading. Since the loran signals used by aircraft did not come in as clear this far out on the water, the only way to determine exactly where they were was to take an old fashioned reading with a sextant.

When Starr finally stumbled up on deck with a cup of warmed over coffee, he found Dee nestled against one of the canvass rails on the boat's lower side, bundled into a down, rose-colored ski-jacket she had put on over the top of her sailing jacket and lifeline. She had gloves on and was reading a Louis L'Amour book.

Hawk was asleep somewhere under the sleeping bag on the seat cushion below her, without even his head sticking out.

"About time he gave in and got some sleep. But man, it's freezing up here." He set his cup down for a moment, to bring his own hood up over his dark head and tie the strings. Then he picked up the cup, again, took a long swallow, and spat his first mouthful over the lee rail. He set it aside a second time and began to rummage through the seat locker across from them. "This needs something."

"The storm might be over," Dee said. But I haven't seen the sun all morning and it's after noon, already. I hope this isn't going to be the way it is from now on. Too cold!"

"Well..." He poured half his coffee over the side and added something from a flask to the brim. "The barometer's either broke or we're in for trouble. It's still stuck hard in the storm zone."

"What does that mean?"

"It means we're just getting some kind of lull, here, and the front's still bearing down on us."

"Oh, no!" Dee looked up at the dark clouds that pressed close against the slow, rolling, molten sea. "Can we take it, Starr? What if it's worse than last time?"

"Long as we do our jobs, she can take it." He glanced up at the foremast. "We're the ones with the error factor. She's made for this kind of stuff. They don't make 'em like this anymore. Over seventy years old and she's still as sound and pretty as the day they first rolled her off the blocks."

"Hard to believe."

"These days it is. Nice to know a few things are still around that last. You tired?"

"Not yet. After a full night's sleep, I feel like a real person.'

"I think I'll make something hot, then. If the weather kicks up too soon we might not get another chance. Personally, I'm sick of sandwiches."

"Look in on Marion when you're down there, will you?"

"I tried, but she threw something at me. I guess she got a look at herself in the mirror, and thought she'd been dead for two days." He finished the last of his coffee. "I never saw a woman so mad at the world for helping her."

"Maybe it's time for more aspirin."

"I'm not going in there. She's a dead shot. Hit me right on the head with one of her books." He pulled a rumpled paperback romance novel out of his back pocket and flipped through the pages.

"You stay up here for a few minutes then, and I'll go. I'm a little worried about her."

She put a foot down on the seat and stepped over Hawk. "Starr?" She glanced back at the sleeping bag to make sure he hadn't wakened. "Have you ever heard of Wyngate State Hospital?"

"Wyngate? Sure. Everybody's heard of Wyngate."

"Hawk hasn't."

"He sticks around Oregon long enough he will. Couple years back there was a rumor they were doing some kind of experiments over there. Just like in those Nazi prison camps. It was only a rumor, though. You can't get away with that kind of stuff nowadays. Media would eat you alive."

"That's funny you would compare them to the Nazis."

"Maybe I've got Nazis on the brain with all this talk of Keller and everything. Just popped into my head."

"I spent two months investigating Wyngate."

"That's right, you are the media. So what did you find out? Nothing, I bet. There's always spooky stories floating around about state hospitals. They're scary places."

"I found out they're doing illegal medical experiments over there. And selling human organs for transplants on the black market." She glanced at Hawk again. "That's what I found out."

"Can you believe that?" He sank down onto the seat opposite Hawk and shook his head. "What are they going to do now? Shut it down?"

"I don't know. The police were still looking into things when I left. But I have a feeling some of the Wyngate staff are going to start scattering in all directions. Especially since the whole story is out, by now."

"Dangerous job you got, Dee." He handed her Marion's book to take back down. "Certain people could get upset at the person who let that kind of cat out of the bag."

"That's why I'm on vacation."

"You call this a vacation? I never worked so hard and with such lousy hours, in my life!"

"Yes, but if you stick it out..." She scanned the horizon out of habit. "The pay could be awfully good."

"That's a fact." He laughed. "If the weather doesn't get us, or the other guys don't beat us to it, or the Ruskies don't get ticked. Sometimes I think the older I get, the worse kinda fool I turn into! But, here I am. Just like the—"

"Starr, there's something out there! A flash of light or something. There it is again, see?"

He followed her gaze.

A speck of brightness blinked twice and disappeared.

"Uh-oh." Then he yelled, "Hey, Hawk!" with such urgency that Hawk rose up from under the sleeping bag like a whale breaking free of the sea.

"What's wrong?" He crossed the cockpit in one smooth motion.

"Take a look at this, boy," Starr reached for a pair of binoculars and peered through them. "We got another boat coming up on our tail."

30
Distress Signals

"Someone suggested that a revolver would be a good companion piece...but I had such a strong belief in the world's greeting me as I greeted it, that I refused to arm myself." ~ Nellie Bly

Hawk peered through the binoculars and then lowered them. "I didn't expect to run into anybody this far out."

"Maybe they're just cruising," Dee offered. "Most boaters are, you know. There aren't many out diamond-hunting around here."

"There aren't many taking any delightful little cruises to Siberia, either," he answered dryly. "It's not exactly inviting, even at this time of year."

"But isn't this the way to Tokyo?" she asked.

"If we haven't been blown too far south in that storm." He handed the glasses back to Starr and reached for his jacket. "We should have passed by the Tokyo heading a couple days ago."

"The way they're moving out there," Starr informed them, "looks like they're under power. If

250

that's the case…" He lowered the binoculars. "They could catch up to us a little after dark."

Hawk stepped up to sit on the top of the cabin house where he could see over the canvas rails. "Well," he finally replied, "we can't take any chances. Let's get the guns out and make sure they're good and visible when they pull up alongside."

"Guns!" Dee looked at him with a shocked expression. "We can't get involved with guns!"

"There's no law out here, sugar, you have to have guns. People get their boats hijacked out from under them all the time. Less apt to happen if your guns are showing. Hand me the glasses again, Starr."

"Anybody who has guns," she declared, "will sooner or later come up with a reason to use them. I'm a very firm believer in that."

Starr took a rifle case out of one of the seat lockers. "I'm a firm believer in covering my own butt."

"Hawk," Dee put a hand on his knee. "If we get involved with guns we're not just innocent travelers anymore. It puts us into the big leagues."

"We never were innocent travelers, baby." He lowered the glasses and looked down at her. "You stepped into the big leagues when you felt the urge to leave town in a hurry and gave in to it."

"You want me to clean the grease out of this thing?" Starr removed the rifle from a large plastic bag inside the case. "Or just wipe off the outside and make it look operational?"

"We're not playing games, here," Hawk replied. "So lock and load."

Dee felt a chill go through her that rivaled any the wind had brought on. She stood still for a moment, looking from one to the other, and realized they were both deadly serious. "I'll... I'll fix something hot for us." She started slowly down the ladder. "Spaghetti or...stew or something."

Normally, there would have been an enthusiastic vote of choice from both men but neither of them said anything. Hawk was looking through the binoculars, again, and Starr was already busy wiping the gun barrel off with a flannel rag.

Dee left them to their schemes and headed straight for Marion's cabin.

"Marion?" she knocked tentatively before going in. "Are you awake?"

"Gads, yes...come on in," came the reply. "Maybe you can help me." Marion was seated in the center of her bed dressed in a bright multicolored caftan, trying unsuccessfully to tie a matching scarf over the top of her head. "My arm is so darn sore, I can't hold it up long enough to tie the knot."

"Here, let me do it." Dee sat down beside her and took over.

"I was trying to wash some of that dried blood out of my hair in the shower. But after about two seconds in the bathroom I got so nauseated, I had to give up. Thought I'd try this instead. I sure can't go around looking like I just stuck my finger in a light socket."

"You shouldn't have tried to get up by yourself, Mare. You have a concussion."

"Nobody told me that! How come nobody told me that?"

"You haven't exactly given anyone a chance. Starr said you threw a book at him."

"He walked in right when I was changing. I tried

to scream, but it sent a pain through my skull like the next world war. So I threw the book, instead."

"There. How's that feel?"

"How's it look, that's the important thing. It feels like a cracked watermelon."

"Better take some more aspirin." Dee reached for the bottle and shook two out. "I'm sorry I got you into all this, Mare."

"Well, it wasn't like you twisted my arm."

"I'm afraid we're in way over our heads."

"What happened?" she asked after she washed down the pills with cold tea. "Did you find out Hawk worked for Wyngate?"

"No, but I don't care anymore. Oh, Marion, you were right! What good is fifty million dollars if we're dead? I can just see the headline now: **Pandora Expedition Disappears at Sea, Entire Crew Presumed Dead.**"

"Tell them we want off in Tokyo, Dee. It's the only logical thing to do."

"They're beyond logic and we're way past Tokyo."

"They won't be beyond taking our share of the money. Tell them to drop us off somewhere else, then. Isn't that what they wanted all along?"

"Yesterday, they might have agreed. Today, there's another boat out there trying to catch up with us."

"What?"

"Our partners are setting up a regular arsenal on deck, getting ready for a...a shootout."

Marion gasped. "Good grief! What are we going to do? We'll all be killed! Oh, I'll never see my kids again!"

"Don't panic yet." Dee's voice conveyed more reassurance than she felt. "I've got an idea. I just haven't worked up quite enough nerve to do it."

"Dee, it scares me when you use that tone. That's the same way you talked the night you came up with the idea of sneaking Peterson out of Wyngate. Now look where it's got us!"

"Well, I can't just stand by and let them shoot somebody can I? Things have gotten way too out of hand."

"Isn't there a lifeboat around here? Maybe we could slip away before the shooting starts and wait for a rescue."

"Are you kidding? We're hundreds of miles from nowhere and it's freezing cold out there! You can't tell down here with the stove going, but it is. Besides that, who would rescue us?"

"Can't we call the Coast Guard?"

"There is no Coast Guard this far out. Not ours anyway. But..." She took a deep breath. "I think I can call someone else."

"Who?"

"Eddington gave me a contact for one of our ships out here, in case we got in trouble. He said we could get help in twenty-four hours."

"Do it, Dee!" Marion gave her a nudge and then winced. "It's only sensible."

"The trouble is, this other boat is going to catch up with us before that. By dark, Starr said." Dee looked out at the surge of gray sea rushing past the porthole. "If things start going crazy, we could be in more trouble because we called. Hawk would be irate."

"He's going to be irate no matter what. At least we could get off the boat. And I'm ready to get off, Dee.

This situation has gotten too wild for a woman my age. Look at me! I'm going to have a scar that looks like an ax murderer tried to kill me, right across my forehead! I'll have to live with it the rest of my life."

"Maybe if I could do it without Hawk knowing." She thought about the possibilities. "It might look like a coincidence by the time they get here. Then I wouldn't have to admit I was the one who called."

"Who cares what he thinks? If he's going to start acting crazy and shooting at other boats we don't have any choice. And Dee..." She lowered her voice to a whisper. "We've already seen what happens when he loses control of himself. Would you like to see him in that state with a gun?"

"No, of course not. And that's the only reason I'm even considering this. Bringing in the guns changes everything. I couldn't stand it if something happened to him."

"To him? What about us? Dee, you're talking crazy! You're talking like you wouldn't be relieved to get away and never see him, again. This whole thing is turning into one big ghastly nightmare!"

"I can't help it, Marion. I told you I'm head over heels in love with him. He could be crazy as a loon and I don't think it would make any difference. Besides that, I..." She looked hesitantly at Marion's horrified expression and finished, "I married him in San Francisco."

"You what?"

"I said I married him. In San Francisco."

Marion blinked twice, as if it took those two seconds for the thought to completely register. "I can't believe it! I'm shocked. Why...nice, normal men with good futures ask you out and you put them off for weeks until they lose interest. Then some over-sexed, manic depressive asks you to marry him on the spur of the moment, and you do?"

"I don't regret it."

"Well, I'm absolutely floored! No wonder you can't think straight. But I'm telling you, Dee, you certainly have a knack for complicating an already complicated situation."

"You still think I should call?"

"Absolutely, I think you should call. Of course, you should. And under the circumstances, I don't see how it could make things any worse than they already are."

"All right." She sighed. "I'll do it right now. They're so busy talking guns and watching that boat up there, they'll never know."

Dee went into her cabin, fished the number Eddington had given her out of her canvas bag and headed for the radio.

Marion shuffled behind in spite of Dee's warnings and had to sit down before she got halfway to the navigation desk.

"Keep an eye out," Dee said. The navigation desk, or nav station, was where the charts and sextant were kept, along with all the electronic equipment that aided navigation. A VHF radio and a GPS, a depth sounder and even a computer that did most of the calculations for them. The HAM radio was on a shelf in the left corner.

Dee got butterflies in her stomach just turning it on. She set the channel to the number her notes indicated, pressed the red button on the mike, and read out the call numbers. Her voice was quavery. Nothing happened, so she tried again.

When a man's voice finally snapped back, loud and clear, she jumped.

"Turn it down!" whispered Marion. "Or they'll hear it up there!"

Dee found a knob marked volume and turned it down.

"Acknowledge, sailing vessel *Pandora*." The voice came softer this time. "What is your position? Over."

"My position..." Dee faltered. "Marion!" She whispered. "I don't know our position! What am I..."

"This is *White Fox* to *Pandora*. Do you acknowledge? Over."

"Yes." Dee pushed the button again and replied. "We acknowledge, *White Fox*. Uh... over."

"White Fox to *Pandora*, can you put the skipper on, ma'am? Over."

"Oh, no," Dee whispered. "I better just..."

"Hang up on them!" Marion urged as if their lives depended on it.

"*White Fox* to *Pandora*, acknowledge please. We have a transmission for Major Wayne Hawkins. Contents classified. Request you put him on. We will stand by. Over."

"Hang up and say you were disconnected!" Marion pleaded. "Hawk's liable to kill us both if he finds out!"

"I can't, Marion, did you hear that? Classified, he said. Oh, no, now I have to put him on! If we don't we could get in trouble for...treason or something!"

31
The Gathering Storm

"Notwithstanding all annoying trifles it was a very happy life we spent in those waters." ~ Nellie Bly

Dee climbed halfway up the ladder so that just her head was above deck.

Hawk and Starr were at the starboard rail, intently engaged in a discussion about firearms as they were cleaning the rifle and another handgun.

"Hawk." Her butterflies turned to trembles that threatened to betray her. "Somebody wants to talk to you."

"What?" His look was skeptical.

"On the radio," she explained. "Somebody wants to talk to you."

"I don't have the radio on." He set the hand gun aside and got to his feet. "The last thing I want is a radio audience when we're on a deal like this. Are you fooling with the radio, sugar?"

"Just come on, they're waiting."

"As long as we don't acknowledge, they won't

know we heard." He followed her down the ladder. "So, just turn it off, and..."

"I already acknowledged."

He threw her a frustrated glance and picked up the mike. "This is *Pandora* skipper. Go ahead."

"Major Wayne Hawkins?"

"Who is this?"

"This is *USS White Fox*, Major. You are hereby reinstated for special duty."

"What the—"

"Orders are to change your course heading to zero, three, niner, and wait for intercept. Over."

He stood in a stunned silence for one long, disbelieving moment before the voice came over the speaker again.

"Standing by *Pandora*. Please acknowledge. Over."

He brought the mike up slowly, as if in a trance. "Acknowledge *White Fox*. Changing course heading to...zero, three, niner...*Pandora* out."

He replaced the mike and turned off the radio. "How did that happen?" His voice still carried traces of unbelief. "They just pulled me back in! Did you hear that?" A barrage of frustrated profanity followed.

Dee interrupted just to put an end to it.

"Can they do that?" she asked. "Legally, I mean."

"They can do anything they want." He swore, again, then walked back to his cabin slamming the door.

"Oh, Marion!" Dee felt her emotions churn. "How could I do that to him?"

"You didn't do it," she replied. "The government did."

"This whole thing is my fault and it just keeps

getting worse and worse!' Dee hurried through the passageway and opened his door.

He was standing by the stern windows, looking out, with one hand braced on the bulkhead above him.

"Hawk, I'm so sorry." She put her arms around him from behind and leaned her head against his back.

"I had no idea. I..."

He put a hand over hers but didn't turn around.

"Why did you have to fool with that thing?" "Eddington told me they could send help in twenty-four hours if we ran into trouble. With that other boat out there...the guns and everything...I thought we might be needing some help."

"You should have asked me first."

"I guess I was afraid to."

"Afraid of what? Me?" He turned around and looked down at her, as if trying to figure her out, then gave up and sat down on the window seat. Resting a forearm across one drawn up knee, he returned his gaze to the cold following sea beyond the stern windows, again.

Dee sat down next to him and was quiet.

"I'm the one who ought to be worried. I can't figure out what kind of a mess we got ourselves into, here. It isn't just lost diamonds. Not with all this heavyweight stuff around. And I don't have the kind of job they would call me back in for. Even if I had to testify on some past case, they wouldn't reinstate me." He shot her a penetrating glance, as if the realization just came to him. "OK, it's because of you."

"Hawk, I said I was sorry. I don't know what else I could possibly..." Sensing tears coming on, she fumbled in her pocket for a tissue.

"Come here." He reached out to draw her gently against him. "Lawful, wedded husband, remember? Whatever happens to one happens to both of us. I might be easygoing but I'm no quitter. We stick together, no matter how this thing works out."

A sense of relief flooded over her, and she leaned her head against his chest, letting the peaceful feeling of those words invade her. "I'd do anything to take back what I did."

"In the long run, it's probably best. It was just a shock, that's all. Special duty...man, I'm not up to it."

"What do you think it means?"

"It could mean anything from turning all our information over to them to getting hauled off this boat and sent to who knows where. Whatever it is, it's a lot bigger than us. Your friend Eddington's little plan for using us as bait must have backfired."

"I'd hardly call him a friend. And he's had plenty enough time to check into Wyngate. By now, he should know our only connection to all this was Peterson and his diamonds. He was convinced before we left San Francisco, or he never would have let us go."

"He let us go because you hit some sort of pay dirt for him, that's why he let us go. I think the diamonds must be a piece of a bigger puzzle. One that he didn't exactly feel like telling us about. And I think maybe while you were busy uncovering society's latest corruption out there at that hospital, you accidentally uncovered some kind of espionage ring."

"Espionage!"

"Those were the charges they had on you. Espionage. That's why the big guys are so worked up.

But there's still something not quite right about all this. It bothers me Eddington didn't confiscate that ring. It makes me think he's got more at stake here than just a big case."

"I told you, Marion had my purse and the ring was in it."

He shuddered at some inner thought. "I hope we're not being set up to take the fall for this guy while he ends up walking away with the goods."

"Hawk, that's an awful thought!" Dee looked up at him with a startled expression. "He's a law officer, for heaven's sake."

"That doesn't mean a whole lot anymore. You can find corruption as easily in the big places as the small ones. Those guys are like spiders. They're in the lowest hovels and the richest mansions. All they need is a dark place."

"I don't think he's that type."

"How do you know?"

"I just know. I get a feeling about things like that. Especially people. And the—" She was about to say the Lord told her but she didn't want to bring up another volatile subject. "I just know."

"Well, those guys can be pretty smooth. And he did too much research on all of us just to brush us off in Frisco and let us go our own way."

"Maybe he realized he made a mistake," she suggested.

"If it was a mistake, sugar, he wouldn't have given you the contact information or put a tracking device in your camera. Not to mention the kind of pull it takes to get somebody reinstated." He shook his head at the unbelievable thought. "That was a slick move. It's the only thing that could have stopped me. Instantly. Not just stopped but turned into one of their pawns."

"It could be for our safety. We haven't thought of that."

"Safety? I've been playing the cruising bum for two years and no one so much as cared. Now, all of a sudden there's a United States ship out there asking for me by name? Like I said, it isn't me they want, it's you. You stumbled right into the big time, honey. Just before I went and stumbled into you."

"Do you think Eddington's really looking for Keller?"

"He's looking for Keller, that's his cover-up. But maybe Keller is just some kind of code name. Or more than one person. Whatever it is, there's a lot more to it than just an old man and some diamonds. What exactly did you come up with at that hospital?"

"Medical fraud. Some illegal experiments by one of the surgeons. Selling healthy organs on the international black market. With everything together, they've probably made a fortune by now."

"That's bad but it's not the kind of stuff the military gets involved in. Something tells me Eddington isn't exactly FBI, either. More like CIA." He ran a hand through his hair again. "If your investigation of the hospital toppled some sort of undercover ring that was embedded, then that boat on our tail could have some dangerous characters on it. In that case, we would be in for something worse than any pirates we might run into."

"What do we do? Can't we turn on the motor and try to run the other way?"

"The engine wouldn't push us along any faster than the sails and maybe even a lot slower if the weather kicks up, again. I might have gone for some evasive action a half hour ago, but I don't have that choice anymore. Now I've got to change course and do what I'm told. Should add a little time to our safety factor, though. Other than that, our best bet is to try and stall until *White Fox* gets here. We're just going to have to ride things out."

They sat quietly for a few moments, each unwilling to let go of the other.

Finally, Hawk brushed the side of her face with a kiss, squeezed her tight and got to his feet again. "I better go change our heading. Then we should have that hot meal you were talking about because on top of everything else, the barometer's still dropping."

"I'll make spaghetti," Dee replied.

He walked out the door but after a few seconds, returned long enough to stick his head back in again. "And after that, you can move the rest of your things into here, Mrs. Hawkins. *Pandora*'s doing a pretty good clip, so I think we can count on at least eight hours before they catch up with us. Even if they are under power. We ought to be able to snatch a couple of those hours to ourselves." He winked, flashed her that winning smile and left.

Because of the change in course, it was well after ten by the time a sleek-looking forty-eight foot sloop with a broken mast finally limped up alongside *Pandora*. Since they were so far north, it was barely after sundown. The name *Seascape* painted in dark lettering along the hull could still be made out in the gathering dusk.

"Ahoy the boat!" a shadowy form with a man's voice shouted to them as the three stood watching warily from the cockpit. "I say, could you give us a hand? We'll toss a line over."

"Not so fast," Hawk held the rifle in the crook of his arm. "We're not taking on boarders."

"Oh, come on, man. Can't you see we've had a rough time of it? Lost our mast in the storm. We've had a terrible accident, and one of our crew was injured!"

"Oh, no," Dee whispered. "we've got to help!"

"Lay off about fifty yards," Hawk said firmly. "We can talk in the morning."

"But we're taking on water! Knee deep in it over here and I've only got two women aboard."

"Hawk, please."

"Shhh." Then loudly, "You're not sinking and we don't have anything in our medicine box you wouldn't have over there. So lay off and we'll talk in the morning."

"How about just taking the injured girl aboard?"

"Not a chance."

There was an uncomfortable silence broken only by the sound of Starr spitting over the lee rail.

"Not very decent of you, captain," the stranger spoke again. "Seeing we used most of our fuel to get over to you."

"You should have called first."

"We tried VHF but you didn't seem to be monitoring. Can't you see we're desperate over here? You've at least got to let us raft alongside. I'm throwing you a line."

"You throw anything over here..." Hawk raised the rifle to his shoulder. "And I'll shoot you right off that deck, mister."

32
Gunfire

"It was too dark to see each other, but I know our faces were the picture of dismay." ~ Nellie Bly

After a long and uncomfortable silence, the sloop backed off. The three of them stood there, watching the distance between the two boats widen, as if by some magic the intruder might change into a thrashing sea monster should they take their eyes off it.

"All right," Hawk said when they were a safe distance away. "I'll take the first watch. I want a gun on deck all night long."

"I feel just awful turning them away," Dee pulled the hood of her jacket up to keep off the cold wind.

"It's too shady, Dee," he replied. "Any self-respecting yachtsman would have limped his way into the nearest port, not waste time chasing another boat around. They weren't sinking and they never called in a mayday. It's our fellow treasure hunters trying to move in because they can't keep up with that kind of damage. And if they tried motoring all the way, they'd run out of fuel."

"How do you know they didn't call in a mayday?

We didn't have our radio on."

"It's common practice for anyone in the area to aid another boat in distress. Since we were closest, *White Fox* would have informed us if they knew about it. They didn't."

"I'm with Hawk." Starr turned toward the companionway. "That's the oldest trick in the book, pretending you're in trouble. They're either pirates or crazies. You wouldn't want either kind coming aboard. I'm going to make a pot of chili and put it in thermoses. It looks like we're going to be back on cold sandwiches again before long, and I need something to do."

"See if you can get Marion to eat something," Dee suggested. "She hardly ate a bite all day."

Hawk went to sit on the top of the cabin house where he could see the sloop as it lumbered along behind them under reduced power. He rested the rifle across his knees while he put up his hood against the wind. "Marion's not coming around as fast as she should be. What's she so upset about? It can't still be the way I treated you that day."

Dee was startled that the dreaded subject had come up so casually. Especially since she had subconsciously pushed even the desire to know those answers to the back of her mind. Her complete acceptance of Hawk during the last twenty-four hours had given her an alliance with him that she dared not undermine. She had been given a second chance and she was determined not to fail, this time. No matter what things looked like she would believe nothing other than the fact that God was in control. Working things out for them, in spite of all her mistakes.

Whether she saw any evidence of it or not.

Yet, she knew that honesty, no matter how difficult it might seem at the moment, was always best in the long run. She settled herself into the corner seat below her husband, where she could be close enough to talk but still out of the wind and decided to come right to the point.

"That blanket you gave her came from Wyngate," she finally replied. "It has the name stamped on the hem. She thinks you must have worked there or something. That you've been using us all along." She sighed and turned to glance at the other boat but couldn't see over the canvas windbreaks from where she was sitting. "That you may even have been the person who was blackmailing Peterson, right from the beginning. That's how she thinks you got the yacht's papers."

He was so quiet Dee looked up at him. But the dark and the hood of his jacket hid his face from her.

"What do you think?" he finally asked.

"I can't think anymore, Hawk." She leaned her forehead against his knee with a sigh. "I just know I love you and you wouldn't hurt any of us. No matter how much money is involved."

She could sense his relief in the reassuring way he put his hand on her head. "I don't know how that blanket got here," he said. "Peterson must have brought it aboard himself, somehow. On a pass maybe, I don't know. I never noticed it before. As for the papers, I found them with the logbook and I just wrote my name in. What does she think I am, some new version of Dr. Frankenstein?"

"Something like that." She replied with his own

familiar phrase.

"No wonder she turns white every time I go in there."

"Oh, Hawk, this whole thing has brought the absolute worst out of all of us. Suspecting each other like this. I don't know if it's even worth it anymore. What good is all the money in the world if something happens to any one of us?"

"We're not exactly in a position we can turn back from, sugar. We're locked into this thing now. Especially with *White Fox* telling us what to do. Did that guy who asked for help look familiar to you?"

"I don't know. It was too dark to tell. But don't you think he acted more scared than dangerous?"

"He was too pushy to be that scared. Something odd about him. And they didn't have any lights on down below when they pulled up alongside."

"Neither did we," she reminded him.

"We have our nav lights on. You can always see a red glow from the ports if they're on. They don't have any."

"Maybe they lost electrical power. They definitely lost their mast."

"I think the storm caught them by surprise. Otherwise, they'd have waited until we got the diamonds to make their move. This way..." He set the rifle aside and slipped down onto the seat beside her. "Dee, listen to me. If anything happens and things get out of hand..."

"Oh, Hawk!" She shook her head at the thought. "I'm not even going to think like that!"

"Listen now. I want you to stay with *Pandora*. *White Fox* will find the boat. But it's almost impossible to find someone in the water. You understand me, sweets? You've got to promise me."

"What makes you think I have any more chance than the rest of you? I wouldn't take it even if I had it. I wouldn't! This whole situation is my fault, and I'd rather—"

"You're the one with the information they want. Hear me? And you may be able to buy yourself some time with it."

"Well, I wouldn't. And I refuse to talk like this, Hawkins. We're all in this together, you said so yourself."

"We have to talk like this, sugar. There has to be a plan B."

"Radio for more help, then. Tell *White Fox* what's going on."

"They're on their way. Making radio contact now would only spook our visitors into doing something hasty. I don't, for a minute, believe he's only got two women with him over there. And I don't want to get anyone killed. They've got to be monitoring. Which means they probably even heard our conversation with *White Fox*, this morning."

"Oh, I'd never forgive myself if something happened to any of you. And when we get out of this mess, I promise—"

"Shhh." He pulled her close. "We're all consenting adults here, Dee. Responsible for our own decisions. You just made things a little more hair-raising, that's all." The spicy aroma of Starr's chili began to waft up from the companionway. "Cheer up, sugar. At least we bought ourselves a little more time for *White Fox* to get here."

"Till morning anyway"

****

At dawn, Dee went below, with orders to stand by the radio to call in a mayday in case anything went wrong, as Hawk and Starr began to catch lines thrown over from the other boat in order to pull the sloop up alongside. *Seascape* had taken on so much water during the night that *Pandora* could no longer refuse assistance. But Hawk was still cautious. He insisted the sloop's skipper come aboard first, so that Starr could hold him at gunpoint while he made an inspection of the other craft. If the situation turned out to be irreparable, he would let the remaining crew aboard *Pandora*. The man readily agreed.

As the two boats drew together, Hawk could see he was in his late fifties. Though wearing a hooded jacket, the trim gray mustache indicated someone of meticulousness and distinction. Hardly the pirate or thief variety.

"I'm Robert Stevens," he said formally as they helped him aboard. "My wife, Ellen, is below with the injured girl. I gave her morphine for the pain but she's been delirious ever since the accident."

"I'll be back in a minute." Hawk motioned Stevens to sit down. Then he looked over at Starr. "If he moves, shoot him."

"This is really most distressing!" Stevens complained. "To be treated in such a manner after what we've been through. We've had a miserable night, as you can see, and I assure you, we only—"

"Save it." Starr spat nervously over the rail and

watched Hawk disappear down the sloop's companionway. "The less I know about people I might have to plug, the better."

"We're sailors, the same as you!" Stevens breathed the words out in a frightened whisper and then was quiet.

****

Aboard *Seascape*, Hawk eased himself down into a foot of water and floating debris.

The salon and galley were dark and cold, with no effort having been made to clean up or restore the comforts of light and heat. He turned one of the stove burners on until he heard the hiss of escaping fuel, then turned it off again. It wasn't empty.

There was a heavy odor of cigarette smoke, and as he moved through the dark corridor, he began to feel the overpowering urge to leave. "Mrs. Stevens?" he spoke the name before he opened the first cabin door.

It was empty, with only a black duffel bag swinging slowly back and forth on a nearby hook to signify that it had been occupied.

"In here!" A woman's voice called from the forward cabin.

The door opened before he had time to turn the handle.

An older blonde-haired woman stood there, dressed in blue foul-weather gear and black gloves. Her hair, pulled back into a once fashionable knot at the back of her neck, was now damp and coming undone. Her face showed the strains of cold and stress.

"Jenny's in the forward berth." She motioned him inside. "Maybe you can help?"

Hawk bent down to draw back the blankets. It was difficult to see well in the meager light that filtered in through the porthole, but he could tell the young woman was unconscious. He brushed back a tangled mass of dark hair to lay a hand on her forehead.

It was cold.

"All right, what the devil's going on here?" His hand moved instinctively to feel for a pulse at her throat. "This girl's dead."

He heard the cabin door snap shut behind him and then the click of a lock. He reached to open the porthole and shout a warning but it had been tightened down with a tool and would take a tool to loosen it. It faced the open sea and not *Pandora*, so he quickly looked for something to break it out with, yelling, "Shoot him, Starr—shoot!"

****

Dee couldn't see the woman from her place at the radio down below but knew she had come up on deck when she heard her voice drift over to them from the other boat.

"He's asking for the medicine box," she said. "Could somebody please get it for him?"

With a sigh of relief, Dee headed for the locker under the companionway stairs to get it. Just then, she heard scuffling on the decks above and–seconds later—she heard the unbelievable sound of a splash as someone tumbled into the water.

She froze. One, two, three seconds... before she

could overcome the shock enough to turn and race back to the radio, grab the mike and press down. "Mayday—mayday—mayday! *White Fox*, this is *Pandora*. *White Fox*, this is *Pandora*, do you—"

"Put it down, Miss Parker," said a chilling voice behind her. "Move away from the radio and sit down."

Dee turned and found herself face-to-face with the woman from the other boat, whom she now recognized as the head nurse from the sixth floor at Wyngate.

The woman was holding a gun and motioned with it toward the settee. "Where is the journal?"

"What have you done?" Dee's voice shook with emotion.

"Leveled the playing field, obviously. Your friends are…" She withdrew a cigarette and lighter from her pocket with her free hand and paused long enough to light it with a practiced ease. "Lost at sea, I'm afraid. So I suggest you be sensible and cooperate."

33

Intercept

*"The doctor looked clever and I had not one
hope of deceiving him.' ~ Nellie Bly*

The words fell on Dee like a crushing weight and she suddenly felt like she couldn't breathe. Then the hatchway darkened for a moment as Stevens came down.

"We're all set." He unbuttoned his jacket and threw back the hood to reveal close trimmed gray hair. "Our things are aboard and we've cast off the other boat."

Dee recognized him immediately as the older gentleman she had seen several times in San Francisco. But the woman he was always with had been gray-haired, not this nurse she would have recognized immediately.

"Bring the medical case down," the woman replied, "we haven't much time."

"So. This is the notorious D.J. Parker." He looked Dee over with a cold calculated scrutiny. "I am Dr. Eric Von Hayden, young lady. The latest victim of your poison pen."

Dee couldn't help the sudden gasp as she recognized the name of the head surgeon at Wyngate, who had received the full brunt of her accusations in the final installment of her series. She had never actually seen him.

"She doesn't look anything like Jennifer." He studied her as if she were an object instead of a person. "But with a head injury we might be able to get by."

The name triggered the memory of the young aide in the elevator, and the smell of night-blooming jasmine. Dee realized her intuition had been right. The girl must have been working with them all along. From the very beginning. Then a thought flashed through her mind that Peterson could have been collaborating with them, too, for all she knew. And now she had dragged her friends (and her husband) into it all—to be killed and tossed into that deep, cold sea.

"We've got to do more than get by, Eric!" the woman snapped, revealing the tell-tale signs that her nerves were not as cool and controlled as they had first seemed. "Nothing must seem out of place when we're boarded!"

"Calm down, Anna," he replied. "We've faced worse. You're just tired."

"It's that horrid storm!" She blew smoke out as she sighed. "This whole set back. As soon as we get underway, I'll—"

"Turn this boat around!" Dee cried out against the casual, mind-numbing chatter. "Go back and get them."

"Take off your jacket, Miss Parker," The nurse

ground her cigarette out in the galley sink. "And roll up your—"

"If you want the journal..." Dee glanced after the retreating back of Dr. Von Hayden as he climbed out of the companionway and up on deck again. "Then you turn this boat around. Otherwise, you'll never lay your eyes on it."

"We'll see. We have a little something that will make sure you cooperate with us. And we will have that journal, Miss Parker. Probably in less than ten—"

Dee darted toward the aft cabin, and the gun went off. It sounded like a cheap firecracker. But the telling thud of the bullet into the bulkhead just as she slipped into the passageway was real enough. She raced into Hawk's cabin and slammed the door, only to realize there was no lock on it, so she ran for the adjoining bathroom.

Only a half-louvered door separated the small room from the main cabin, and Dee was horrified to find there was no lock on that one, either. The best she could do was wedge herself between the solid half of the door and the commode, stay low to the floor, and pray she could avoid any flying bullets that came shattering through the louvers.

But no bullets came.

She heard footsteps and then the chink of something being set down outside the door. There was a quiet hiss of...water heating...or air escaping through an open valve. Then a sickly smell and a horrible heaviness pressed down. The last thing she remembered was hearing the outer door snap closed.

When she opened her eyes, she sensed Hawk close by. But her happiness melted into a horrifying despair when she reached out to him. She could not move. She had a splitting headache and her ears were ringing. Reality fell like a crushing weight. The reason she felt Hawk's presence was because her head was on his pillow and it still carried the distinct scent of his aftershave.

She had no idea how much time had passed but she could see a bit of gray daylight through the open porthole. There was no way of knowing if it was dawn or dusk or somewhere in between. Something felt different about the boat, though. They were rocking, dead in the water, on a considerably choppy sea.

She could hear muffled voices outside the door.

Someone squeezed her hand. "It's all right, Dee, I'll get you out of this, I swear. Just hold my hand. Can you hold my hand a little? Can you say something?" he whispered.

It was Scott Evans.

Dee couldn't speak because her entire head was wrapped with gauze. The small slits for her eyes and nose were suffocating and she felt a rising sense of panic. She did manage an ever-so-slight movement of her hand in his to indicate that she had heard him... but how had he gotten here?

"They'll kill you if I don't go along with them." He continued to whisper close to her ear but she couldn't see him. "They killed my girlfriend, Dee. Because she wouldn't cooperate. But you and I have one last chance to get out of here. It's our only hope. You've got to trust me. Dee, do you hear?"

"She's in here." It was the nurse's voice.

Heavy footsteps followed.

"We've made her as comfortable as we could. This bed has the least motion of all the others, so we moved her in here. There was too much swelling to stitch the wound but we gave her morphine. As you can see, we had to wrap everything and make her as immobile as possible. This is her fiancée, Evan Myers. I've already shown them your passports, Evan, they just need to check everything over."

"This delay could cost her life." Scott's voice was distraught. "There's a surgeon waiting in Tokyo but we've got to beat the weather!"

"Her father had one flown out from the states when we first called in the accident." The nurse's voice was soothing.

"Sorry, Mr. Myers, but our orders are to board every vessel in the area. If all your papers check out and we get full cooperation, you can be on your way in about fifteen minutes."

"Everything is just like they said up forward, sir," another man's voice drifted in from the companionway. "All the papers check out and they've got a picture of them on this boat that goes back a good twenty years."

"Kind of you to say so," said the nurse. "That picture was actually taken in the sixties, when we were on our world cruise. But there's no mistaking it was *Andor*."

"Let's just get on with it!" Scott implored.

They all shuffled out and then Dee could hear the unmistakable sound of an idling engine a short distance away.

White Fox had arrived but they were getting ready to leave! Were they all blind? What was this charade Scott was putting on? The only plan he needed was to open his mouth and call them back.

And where was Marion?

The thought of Marion being dumped into the

water the same way as Starr sent a shudder through her. All of them were dead and that caused a blind despair to swirl into an unbearable sense of loss. Where was God? Where were the angels?

All of a sudden, terrible sobs that should have wracked her entire body with their release, welled up inside her until her heart and throat felt as if they might burst. Yet, the great and heavy stupor of whatever monster drug they had used, allowed only a whimper to escape her. She moved frantic eyes but could still not see anything other than the ceiling and a sliver of the open porthole beneath it. The only things in her direct line of vision.

All was quiet until she heard the nurse's voice through the porthole as everyone moved up on deck.

"This was supposed to have been the vacation of a lifetime. But I don't think we'll go beyond Tokyo, now. It's all been so upsetting!"

It was very convincing. Whatever her real name was, Dee knew it was not Ellen Stevens, even as Dr. Von Hayden was no yachtsman named Robert Stevens, either.

"You can get underway," the voice of the man in charge replied. "Everything checks out. We still have another vessel in the area to board before the weather gets prohibitive. Appreciate if you'd stay in radio contact until further notice, though, Skipper."

"I'm not the skipper, I'm just the deckhand." It was Scott's voice this time. "Mr. Stevens up there, he's supposed to be the guy who knows everything about sailing. Nearly got us all killed in that storm!"

"Let's not trouble anyone with our personal differences, shall we?" Von Hayden spoke. "What we've been through the last few days was close to a hurricane, as I'm sure these men will attest to. What happened to us could have happened to anybody. Ready to fend off, gentlemen?"

"Yes, sir, we are. Let's get a move on, Henry. Thompson, let go those lines so we can shove off. Good luck, Skipper. Sorry for the inconvenience."

"Inconvenience." Scott sounded as if he were close to a breaking point. "My fiancée could die over your inconvenience."

"We have a doctor aboard *White Fox*, Mr. Myers, if you want us to transfer her to sick bay."

"I've got a doctor right here but he isn't a brain surgeon! Just leave so we can—"

"It doesn't help to shout, Evan," the nurse interrupted. "They're only following orders."

"Haul up the foresail, Ev," said Von Hayden. "That's about all we're going to need in this wind to get underway, again."

After that, Dee heard only the sound of boots along the deck and then the idling engine of a launch shifting into gear before it pulled away. She tried her best to scream, or cry out, but succeeded in nothing more than a muffled moan. They were leaving. Eddington's plan was not working.

Next came the familiar sound of lines running through winches, and Pandora leaned into the wind and picked up speed… sailing through the choppy seas as beautifully as she had for Hawkins.

34
White Fox

"I am positive she is somebody's darling." ~ Nellie Bly

At 7:20, Eddington and his partner came aboard the *USS White Fox*. Their small float plane had landed in choppy seas a short distance from the ship, the last leg of their journey having brought them from a United States aircraft carrier cruising some hundred and fifty miles off the coast of Japan. Because of the weather the plane did little more than tumble its passengers onto the waiting launch before taking off, again, into the darkening sky.

"You head for communications and set up the equipment," he said to Reynolds as he took the last ladder up to the main deck two steps at a time. "I'm going to the bridge and find out what's going on. We should have had an intercept by now."

As he ducked through the door, the captain looked over at him.

"You Eddington? Looks like you had a rough trip."

"What's the last radio contact you had with the

Pandora?"

"Sometime around dawn this morning we picked up a partial mayday."

Eddington breathed out a sigh of frustration.

"Let's head on down to communications and we can talk to search and rescue." The captain picked up his hat. "Mr. Ramsey, have some coffee sent down, will you? This guy looks like he's spent the last two hours in a deep freeze," he called to a lieutenant on watch.

By the time they arrived in the communication center his partner had already set up their equipment. "Got 'em, Ren?" Eddington peered at the small scope over his shoulder.

"Yeah, barely," his partner replied. "They changed course, Ed."

"What?"

"Looks like they're heading south. Right for the Tsugaru Straits. The most direct route to Vladivostok."

"Well, what happened? He was on zero, three, niner before we left the carrier. I thought sure he'd stick with it. I would have bet money!"

"That's nowhere near the search area." The captain took his hat off and scratched the close shaved gray hairs with the same hand before setting it back on again. "I better call my helicopter back."

"Search and rescue, sir," a young man on the ship's radio announced. "They just spotted a demasted sloop. Heading zero, three, niner... radios are down, but they're going to lower someone in to assess the situation. Standing by."

"That doesn't make sense," Eddington moved

over to stand behind the man as if he could watch the radio like a TV. "*Pandora*'s a ketch. Did Hawkins report any storm damage when you talked with him yesterday?"

"No, sir, he didn't," the young man replied. "It's possible it could have happened before we got here, though. The vessel we boarded this afternoon had a crew member seriously injured by the rough weather, last night."

"You boarded somebody?"

"We boarded a vessel earlier this afternoon." The captain took a fresh mug of coffee brought in by a steward as he talked. "But they were just cruisers blown off course on their way to Japan. No reason to detain—"

Eddington stopped the captain. "They made the switch already! Get me a—"

The man at the radio perked up and listened to his headset.

"Unplug that thing so we can all hear, son." The captain came to stand next to Eddington.

"Just a routine weather transmission, sir." The man flicked a switch so that the tail end of the message rang out over the room.

"*... along the east coast and the island of Honshu. Typhoon Hikari is expected to reach the southern tip of Hokkaido before midnight.*"

"Right through the Tsugaru Straits," Eddington moaned. "What else can go wrong?"

"Don't worry about us," the captain assured. "We might get a little backlash from the tail but this far out there's no need to worry too much about it."

"Not us—*Pandora*!" Feeling suddenly stifled by the warmth, Eddington unzipped his thick leather jacket and moved back to the scope to look over Reynolds shoulder, again. "At her present heading, she's going to run right up over the back of that thing. We've got to change course and try for another intercept."

"I can't change course." The captain looked over at him as if he had lost his mind. "I'm in the middle of a"rescue. Even if I could, I wouldn't run my ship up the back end of a typhoon, I'd get court marshaled."

"Captain, I—"

"*Fox Wing* to *White Fox*," the radio sparked to life over the room again. "Confirm sailing vessel *Seascape* located with three crew members aboard, one dead. Skipper is Major Wayne Hawkins. Standing by for damage report."

"Let me talk to Hawkins," Eddington headed back for the radio.

"The radios are down, sir," the young man reminded him. "Any messages will have to be relayed through the pilot."

"Tell him this is Eddington, here, and I need to know who's aboard *Pandora*."

The radio operator repeated the message into the mike and then there was a long, agonizing silence while it was relayed to the man on deck. A minute and a half later, the pilot's voice broke into the heavy silence of the communications room where all eyes were now turned toward the operator.

"This is *Fox Wing* to *White Fox*. Skipper confirms D.J. Parker, Marion Bates, Scott Evans, Anna Keller, and Doctor Eric Von Hayden..."

"Bingo..." Eddington breathed as he listened to the rest.

"...says to tell Eddington they took the bait. The

rest is disrespectful, sir, over."

"Let's have it, let's have it!" Eddington nudged the young man impatiently.

"Request full message, *Fox Wing*. Over."

"He says, for Eddington to stop messing around. Get off his butt and go after *Pandora*. He wants his wife back. That was a paraphrase, sir. Over."

"Dang..." Eddington straightened up slowly as the full realization dawned on him. Those ladies are in some big trouble."

"Get me that damage report," the captain snapped. "And an exact location so we can change our course accordingly. We should be able to pick them up in..." He glanced at his watch.

"Captain Fergusen," Eddington said, "if we take time to rescue the sloop, *Pandora* could reach the protective waters of the Russian coast. That's if they manage to beat that typhoon through the straits. Either way, we've lost them unless we change course, right now, and concentrate all our efforts in that direction."

"I already told you we can't do that, Eddington," the captain said firmly. "That sloop might not make it to port in this weather and there's a death under questionable circumstances involved. If they get the slightest backlash from that typhoon, they're as good as finished."

"But, sir—"

"We're going for the rescue."

"*Fox Wing* to *White Fox*. Hawkins requests permission to take sailing vessel *Seascape* to nearest Japanese port. Says he can make it. I can't get them all off in one trip and the way it's kicking up out here, I won't even be able to get my man back aboard if we don't hurry. Over."

Eddington sensed he was losing control of the situation and tossed a pencil he held back onto the desk, again. "Captain," he spoke quietly to the ranking officer, "Can we talk privately? What I have to tell you, is classified."

35
The Pandora Effect

"Some strange magic seems to rob one of all care."
~ *Nellie Bly*

The captain cast him a knowing glance and then motioned him to follow with a resigned sigh. "Let me know as soon as that damage report comes in," he said, as they left the communications room.

Eddington followed silently along the long gray corridors until they entered what was obviously a private cabin. After they were inside he handed over his identification and sank into a chair across from the desk where the captain had already seated himself.

"Just what I figured." Captain Fergusen tossed the wallet back to Eddington. "Another one of you guys who aren't really here."

"What we have, Captain, is..."

"I'm well aware that national security takes precedence over everything else, Agent Eddington. Just give me what I have to know."

"Our objective is the arrest of a Soviet agent."

"The chaos that country's in these days, you'd think they'd be busy with other things."

"They're busy, all right. Besides being a channel for U.S. military information for over twenty years, this one heads up one of the world's most lucrative black market rings ever dreamed of. Enough to finance half a world take-over, if that's what they were up to."

He paused "Well, what is it? Drugs? Selling arms to crazy Arabs? What?" the captain prompted.

"To be exact, the sale of healthy human organs, sir. For transplant and experimentation."

Captain Ferguson was quiet for a moment. "One up on the drug trade, that's for sure," he finally admitted.

Eddington leaned forward and rested his forearms across his knees. "Captain, we've spent years trying to track this guy down, only to finally find out that he was just a clever decoy for something much bigger than selling two bit military secrets to the Soviets."

"Was he selling military secrets?"

"Yes, sir. And that's what threw us off. That and the fact that the real culprit in this thing wasn't him at all. It was his daughter. Anna Keller. She used her father as a front for years. When he finally found out and balked, she killed him. Just like that," he snapped his fingers. "Her own father."

"And that's her on the boat out there, is it?"

"Her and a Dr. Von Hayden. He's the master-mind behind the black market ring. With the high cost and low availability of healthy organs, I guess the hospital set-up turned out to be more lucrative all the way around." He felt the unnerving agitation of wasting valuable time but he pressed on. "They've got an elaborate organization set up, with years of experience behind them."

Eddington sat up straight again, drummed impatient fingers on the arm of his chair, then caught himself, and quit. "They've already covered their tracks at the asylum, leaving absolutely no trace of evidence behind. They've even managed to point some pretty incriminating evidence at Parker—that's Hawkins's wife. She's an investigative reporter out of Portland, Oregon, who first blew the lid off this thing."

"So the boat we boarded this morning was the *Pandora*? I find it hard to believe my officers were that easily misled."

"They had probably switched it back to the Dutch name by then. *Andor*. These people are masters at the art of deception. I'm telling you, sir, if we don't catch them red-handed now, our chances of ever catching up with them would be next to nothing. Especially out of the country and with the kind of connections they have, now."

Eddington sighed and shifted uncomfortably in his chair. "I'm not trying to be dramatic when I say they could actually spearhead the biggest wave of widespread euthanasia the world has ever seen. Something that would make the Holocaust look like child's play."

"Now, that's a scary thought."

"I'm not kidding."

"I know you're not, son. You've just thrown me quite a curve, here." The captain was quiet for a moment, thinking. "If these people are what you say, what makes you think they still might have Parker alive?"

"I'm hoping they still think she has information they need. But I'd feel responsible if something happened to her, because...well, like he said over the radio...I used her as bait."

"You mean she didn't volunteer for this duty? Don't tell me she's a civilian."

"It's a special case."

"No case is special enough to use unsuspecting civilians as bait, Eddington. That would make us no better than the terrorists, wouldn't it. I hope you're going to tell me she at least knew what she was risking."

"I haven't been so unethical. No, sir. That's the thing about this case, it... well, it brings the absolute worst out of people. If you know what I mean."

"No, I don't think I do." He reached for a silver bowled pipe that was resting in an ashtray on the desk and a blue foil pouch of tobacco to fill it with.

"This ring has been active for over fifty years. Fifty years! Can you believe that?"

Fergusen looked up from his small task and noted the unusual light in Eddington's eyes. "I think I'm beginning to."

"And you know how many agents have worked on this case during that time? Three hundred and twenty-two. All victims..." He leaned forward in his chair a little. "Of something I call the Pandora Effect."

"The Pandora Effect?"

"Sort of a legendary curse. But what it really is, Captain, is greed. It's got an ungodly, powerful pull attached to it but it's greed all right. Pure, unadulterated, basic greed. Does terrible things to people. No, I haven't been unethical, sir. But I'll admit I sort of dangled that greed out there like a carrot and used it to crack this case." He sat back in the chair, as if he could hardly believe it himself.

The smell of the captain's pipe smoke wafted toward him with a tantalizing aroma, and having only recently quit smoking, the temptation was almost overpowering. He reached into his pocket for a stick of gum.

"So what are we talking about here, Ed?" The captain steered him back to the facts at hand. "That gets people so worked up and...beside themselves."

"Fifty million dollars in diamonds, that's what we're talking about." He tore off the wrapper, popped the gum into his mouth, and continued to talk around it. "That's what they're all headed for. That little crack shot reporter stirred up the old legend, again, managed to topple the hospital ring practically by accident, and has Anna Keller and Von Hayden running right along after her. The old man kept it to himself for years, until she came along. They gotta have it, now. Those diamonds are the big money they're going to need to set up somewhere else.'

"Just how did she manage to do all that? Single handed, that is."

"By befriending the real Heinrich Keller, at just the right time. After he found out his daughter was blackmailing him. I think he convinced Parker to go after the diamonds for him. She didn't know he'd get killed for it. And she didn't know all these others would come after her if she tried."

"Seems at that point, somebody..." The captain

paused long enough to give him a penetrating stare. "Should have felt responsible enough to tell her what she was up against."

"Oh, I did. But at that point, she was as hooked as everybody else that ever bumped into this legend. You might say she was already a victim of the Pandora Effect."

"Which is what you were counting on."

"Yes, but I never expected her to actually get tangled up with those two," he admitted uncomfortably. "Just flush them out is all. That was a slip up, all right. Now, I've got to do whatever it takes to help her, because..."

"Because you want those arrests, no doubt," the captain finished for him. "Seems this Pandora Effect is working you up pretty good, too, Ed."

"I won't deny it. I'm as human as the next guy. But it happens to be my job, sir. And it just happens that I've finally cracked this thing after working on it, on and off, for the last ten years. I don't mind saying I'm more than a little excited about it. A fifty year old case! But at the same time I'd feel terrible if I lost Parker to do it. You see, I..."

He cast a calculating glance at the captain and realized he was going to have to tell the whole, naked truth. "I left out a vital piece of information that might have greatly influenced her decision to cooperate with us." The former zeal drained out of his expression like a receding tide and he looked away from the older man as if it took all the pleasure of winning away.

"What information?"

"There are no diamonds anymore," Eddington finally confessed. "The famous Pandora box that contained the Strassgaard collection was recovered by native seal hunters and sold to a private collector. Back in 1973."

36
Descension

*"I felt lost. My head felt dizzy and my heart felt
as if it would burst." ~ Nellie Bly*

Dee began to feel sensation coming back into her arms and fingers and started pulling at the gauze wrapped around her face. But there was such a lot of it! The launch was gone, along with any hope of catching anyone's attention through a porthole. She had thought of many ways she could have done that while lying there. A flashing mirror had been her best bet. But it was too late for that, now.

Scott had not come back in. The seas were steadily rising with the gathering storm and he was being kept busy on deck. Meanwhile, the temperature was dropping uncomfortably in the cabin but she kept the porthole open, so she could hear what was going on up there. But where was the nurse? She hadn't heard her voice for a long time. Ellen was not her real name. Von Hayden had called her Anna.

Whatever kind of truth serum (was there really such a thing?) they had planned for her had obviously been postponed, due to Dee having barricaded herself in the bathroom. Forcing them to drug instead of kill her before *White Fox* caught up with them. She had no doubts these people wouldn't hesitate to kill her as quickly as the others.

The others!

Oh, Lord, what had she done? God, forgive me, she thought over and over to herself as the phrase played in her mind like a disk stuck on repeat. How many more people would have to pay the price for her mistakes? She should have let go of this thing in San Francisco. The minute she discovered what was really going on. Now look what such foolishness had cost! And what on earth had made her think treasure hunting for stolen goods—that had a curse on them— could lead to anything but trouble?

"The wealth of the wicked is laid up for the just..." is what had captured her. Oh, what a perversion of scripture she had committed! Not to mention, *"Greater love hath no man, than he lay down his life for his friends."*

She knew now the only reason Peterson had "laid down his life" was because he would have ended up on trial as a war criminal, no matter how old he was. No wonder he had opted for the same way out as his famous commanding officer.

"God, forgive me!" It was the first thing out of her mouth when she finally pulled the last of the gauze away. More of a slur than a sentence but at least she was getting some mobility back. It would be a hard thing to die without being able to pray. Oh, but the others had no time to pray. "Lord, how could something like this happen when I was trying to do something good for somebody? Lord, where are you!"

Suddenly, the most awesome feeling came over

her. The most incredible sensation of God's presence she had ever felt in her life. Well, this was it, then. She must be closer to death than she realized. Everything was over for her. Any minute, they would come in and force her to give over the journal. And considering her threshold for pain was not something she was proud of, she knew she did not have the makings of a heroine. So if she was going to die anyway, she would rather be shot than tortured. And the only way to do that...

Was to get rid of the journal.

That way, if there was such a thing as truth serum, she could only tell the truth. Suddenly, an incredible idea came to her. If she was going to die, she should at least leave something behind. Something that would "stay with the boat," as Hawk had suggested, even if she couldn't. She would leave an account of everything that had happened. The same way the real Peterson had done. Only she wouldn't write anything down or hide it. Instead, she would send an email to Devlin, back at the newspaper.

Not that they were anywhere near a connection way out here. But that wouldn't matter. Her mail program was set to send as soon as her computer turned on, and it would go through no matter who pushed the button, once it was within range. That way, whether friend or enemy found her laptop, the confession would get into the right hands. And that's what it would be. A confession. Because there was no one more than herself to blame for what had happened here. She only hoped she could do it before anyone came in.

Especially Scott Evans, who had obviously been

manipulating her for months. Taking advantage of her respect for a senior reporter. Someone who was too much a part of this intricate deception to be anything less than a major player in it. Whatever his role, it didn't matter, anymore. He had passed up the one chance to save them both when they were boarded. Whether for money or anything else, it was the wrong choice for the wrong reasons. Innocent people had died. And if she even had half enough time left to explain all this, she could...

It occurred to her, then, how she could barricade the door with something (anything) and it would at least buy her the time she needed. The wooden closet rod. It lifted up easily because it was set in like a shower rod, in case there was a need to get through to the crawlspace where one could check the aft bilges. She even piled her suitcase and the two duffels that were in there against the door. Her own things that she had brought in only this morning. Along with a heavy mesh bag that held Hawk's diving equipment. But the very thought of him made her suddenly feel ill and she had to head for the bathroom.

She needed a drink of water, only she didn't dare turn on the faucet because it would engage the pump. Then they would know she was awake. So she swished mouthwash around in her mouth, instead, and spit into the sink. The drug must have made her thirsty. After that, she quietly got her laptop and opened it, thankful that the sound was turned down. She couldn't think about Marion, Hawk, or Starr. She didn't dare, or she would never have the strength to do this one last thing.

She kept to the basic facts in case she should get

interrupted, working under the blanket so that she could shove the laptop quickly down to the foot of the bed if she had to. Yet, by the time she had the file in the outbox for sending, it was still eerily silent on the other side of the door. Maybe she better send a goodbye to her parents.

Halfway through that she was entirely overcome with sobs and had to bury her face in the pillow to keep quiet. A pillow that still smelled faintly of Hawk's aftershave.

"It won't work, you know. No one ever gets out." Von Hayden's voice drifted through the porthole.

"So who asked you?" Scott was at the helm, almost directly above her.

"They...they have backup plans!" Von Hayden sounded like he was struggling with something heavy. "For deserters. No one...ever gets out."

"Yeah, and if I wanted to desert all I had to do was speak up when the Navy was here. Did I do it? Not when you still have something of mine, I didn't."

Dee pulled the blanket back from her laptop, clicked on the podcast program, and turned it to face the porthole. Not that the web cam would catch anything but the rich hues of the smooth wooden bulkhead. But the voices would still come in clear.

"I'm not interested in anything of yours. I'm not even interested in you. My own business is more lucrative than... Oh, this wretched thing doesn't seem to be doing what it's supposed to! There's something stuck in it."

"Your business isn't operational, though. So, right now, you need me as much as I need you." He laughed, as if the thought was a sudden pleasure.

"Tables have turned, haven't they, Doc."

"Shut up and fix this thing!"

"There's nothing wrong with it. Just getting too rough out here. Won't be long and it's going to take all of us to keep a handle on things."

"Then you better be as good as Anna says you are. This boat is bigger than the other one. Are you sure you can handle it?"

"Whatever Anna says." Scott said the name in a tone that was almost mocking.

Dee had never heard him talk that way. In fact, if she hadn't listened to that same voice for all of her five years at the *Columbia Herald*, simply because his desk was across the room from hers, she wouldn't have believed it was the same man. The Scott she knew would have been complaining of the cold by now or at least, throwing up over the rail. In fact, she distinctly remembered him saying that he didn't like boats and never set foot on them. He had even traded his cruise for a plane ticket the one time he won Devlin's feature award.

He did have a bottomless need for money, though. And a fortune in diamonds might have been more temptation than he would ever admit. It occurred to her that there was every possibility he had given her the Wyngate lead for no other reason than to extract the necessary information from Nels that he had been unable to get from the old man, himself. But whatever his reasons, it was obvious these other two depended on him. She couldn't imagine how he had managed that kind of confidence. Scott Evans was more crafty and deceitful than she ever could have imagined.

"Get some sleep, Eric. You're no good to me half-dead. You have about an hour before it gets really wild out here."

"I'll stay on deck. I noticed a sleeping bag in one of these seat lockers, I'll get under that."

Dee dived for the pillow and tried to stifle another sob. What kind of people could so easily use the things they had stolen from others without so much as a second thought? Suddenly, there was a startled cry from Marion's cabin and a near hysteric barrage of German before the nurse began to call out for Heinrich.

But just as the chilling thought occurred to Dee that Von Hayden might actually be the notorious Heinrich Keller Eddington was looking for, it was an answering stream of German—from Scott—that echoed back down through the companionway. She only understood one word. *Mútti*.

It was the German equivalent of mama.

"Get up and take the wheel, so I can see what she wants," he said. Not the slightest trace of an accent. Nothing, in all the years Dee had known him had ever led her to believe he was anything less than a patriotic American. Why he had overseen that charity event for wounded veterans, last Fourth of July.

"No need," Von Hayden's voice was muffled, as if he had covered most of his head with the sleeping bag, already. "She's just dreaming. I gave her a sedative."

"You what?"

"She was close to hysterics. If she doesn't get some sleep, she'll have a breakdown."

"You give anybody anything, I want to know about it. Hear me? We need help up here when things get bad, or we'll be worse off than last time."

"Anna said you could handle this boat singlehanded."

"Not in some freak typhoon, I can't."

"Practically grown up on it, she said. All those years the three of you were making your endless circles around the world for people who would just as soon cut your throats as use you. Some grandfather you had. Man was strong as iron right up till he died. You aren't half the man he was at your age!"

"You think so? My grandfather had nothing to do with the operation at the asylum. I'm in charge. Only no one knows that because I've been using his name for a long time now. So what do you think about that? It was me from the very beginning. Meantime, you better hope I can remember enough about sailing to get us out of this, because we're headed for a typhoon."

"Then change course and run from it. What are you thinking?"

"I need distance between us and the Navy. We have to get through the Tsugaro Straits. Someone's waiting for me, there."

"And risk getting us all killed? For a few lousy diamonds? I've had enough of it! That journal might not even exist!!"

"It exists, I've seen it before. Dee has it."

"You and your mother are so insane over it, you can't see anything else. This is worse than when she brought the old man here, on a pass, thinking he might tell her where they were if she helped him. But he had her number. Took off the first chance he got. I had to call in the police to get him back, almost blew the whole operation. For a few lousy diamonds! I'm not going through that again. I want no part of it."

"I said I'd get that journal and I will. I'll make Dee

tell me where it is. She's too smart when it comes to hiding things. I never found anything but the map before we left and I turned her whole place inside out. If she's transposed it onto some file on her computer, it could take weeks to find. Weeks we don't have."

"Weeks you don't have, maybe. Me, I have no intention of making myself a sitting duck, chasing after some famous hoard of jewels every treasure hunter and their brother knows about."

"They're mine, and I'm going to get them, Eric.'

"That crafty old codger knew all along this is how things would play out. Even dead, he's smarter than you!"

"Get up and take this wheel, so, I can go down there."

37
Those Who Are About to Die

"I thought it very possible that I had spoken my last word to any mortal, that the ship would doubtless sink..."
~ *Nellie Bly*

Something came over Dee when she heard those words. The thought that Scott Evans had actually planned on her ability to befriend Peterson, gave her a worse sense of invasion than when she discovered he had broken into her house. It proved he was not acting out of any wild desperation for money but from some twisted perspective that had gone deviant a long time ago. He might even be insane.

And he was going to kill her.

"Lord, forgive me. I've never wished anyone dead in my life," she spoke out loud as she closed the laptop, shoved it down beneath the covers, and headed for the closet. "And I never tried to hurt anyone, either." She reached for her canvas bag. Was she seeing things, or had the hatch cover always been slightly ajar?

If Scott was Peterson's grandson, he would know

every inch of this boat. She had forgotten about that pass through the bilges. If you didn't mind crawling on your stomach along the inside ledge, the way Starr had done just last week, when he thought there was diesel fuel leaking into there. But what did she have left that was heavy enough to weigh down the hatch cover? Nothing. At least nothing she was willing to remove from her barricade at the door. Oh, what did it matter? There was always some way to get in, and she was wasting time. It wasn't until she fished around for a few moments that she remembered the journal wasn't in her bag anymore. Hawk had it last.

Probably still in his desk drawer. Sometimes the most obvious places were the last ones anyone would look. It was finally getting dark now, so she switched on the light. Which threw an immediate shaft through the porthole and onto the churning, rising sea. But she didn't care. Enough was enough.

She pulled open the drawer and started rummaging. Not there. The small frustration almost crumpled her again. "Lord, where is it? Where could it possibly—"

"Dee." Scott's voice...still up on deck...and still at the wheel. "What are you doing down there?"

"Oh, wouldn't you like to know, Heinrich!" she muttered. "Wouldn't you just like to..."

Maybe there was a safe behind Peterson's picture. Like there was in back of the painting in the main salon. She reached for it but it didn't swing open like the other and she saw that it was actually screwed to the wall. There was a screwdriver in the drawer, somewhere, she had just seen it.

"Come up here—can you hear me, Dee?"

"I've heard enough from you, all right." She spoke to herself as she worked at loosening the screw. Couldn't budge the one side (too tight), so she tried the other. It started turning almost immediately. In a few moments, she had it out and was able to pivot the picture up to reveal the space behind. The two journals were inside.

Dee snatched up the one she had taken from the safety deposit box, turned around, and was promptly tossed onto the floor by the sudden jolt of a wave. The boat dipped crazily toward the churning sea, just as the screwdriver rolled off the desk. The long screw followed after and clattered across the floor. "Too much sail up, gentlemen." She reached for the edge of the desk to pull herself to her feet.

Pandora steadied and leveled a little, obviously being steered by a practiced hand. All right, so he knew what he was doing up there. He could sail. She ran back to the bed, not so much on purpose as the force of another rising swell sent her plummeting toward the low end of the cabin until she had to either leap or crash into it. She leapt. Just as a splash of cold sea spilled in from the open port.

"Dee, come help reef the main before it gets too—"

"Help yourself, Heinrich Keller, Junior." She called out loud enough for him to hear this time and thrust her hand through the porthole to hold the journal directly in the beam of light. So, he could see exactly what she was going to do.

"Wait. Don't!" He let go of the wheel and leapt for it so fast, she was caught off-guard when he actually grabbed hold.

Her grasp held only for a few seconds before he

wrenched it out of her hand. In the same moment, *Pandora* swerved into the wind. Von Hayden yelled and jumped for the abandoned wheel as the vessel began to roll onto its beam ends. His sudden yank caused the boat to jibe with a loud crash of rigging, before the backwind jerked it over onto its other side. Scott was flung into the churning water as if he had been shot out of some giant sling.

Dee heard a gasp for air, caught a fleeting glimpse of gray sweater going under, and then frantic clawing against the side of the boat in an effort to catch something to hold onto. A split second later, she heard him call out.

The panic in his voice, along with the desperation of those words, echoed through her as if she had been struck by something physical. Words that faded into the dark churning sea within a mere few seconds but seared themselves into the depths of her very soul. An agonizing string of German words, of which she only understood, one...

"*Mútti!*"

She slammed the porthole closed to stop another torrent of water rushing in and stumbled her way toward the stern windows. But by that time, she could see nothing but an angry following sea. When the decks began to tilt at a steep, dangerous angle and Von Hayden didn't correct it, the thought occurred to her he might not know what to do. Was he busy helping Scott back onboard? Another wave crashed into them, sending Dee to the floor again.

Was this how it was going to end, then? Were they all going to drown at sea?

Why hadn't the Lord protected them? Had she

strayed so far from her roots that she was no longer traveling (as her father always put it) on Divine assignment? Was there no way back from here?

Call upon Me in the day of trouble and I will save thee.

The scripture flashed through her mind, and she took hold of it, just like the lifeline that was trailing out behind them. "Lord, if there's a way out of this—if you show me the way out of this—I promise, I—"

There was a familiar surge, and the yacht rose up and up, until the boat leveled out on the crest, paused and shuddered, and then went racing down the back of another giant swell like a toboggan in winter. Proof that the storm was coming up behind them like some growling hungry monster. She heard a splash off the stern and realized Von Hayden must have thrown out a sea anchor, in preparation for reducing sail.

"Anna!" he called out. "Anna!" But there was no answer from the forward cabin.

All at once, Dee heard a heavy grating sound behind her, and as she turned, the wooden hatch cover in the closet rose up slowly, as if of its own accord. She gasped at the sudden horror that Scott had found the lifeline, climbed back onto the boat and crawled through the bilges to get in here. But just as she leapt to fling herself against it, she caught sight of a familiar swath of multicolored scarf instead.

"Marion!" She pushed the heavy cover aside and dragged her friend out of the hole. "Oh, Marion! I thought you were dead!"

"So did I!" she replied in a hoarse whisper. "I fell into a dead faint the minute I lifted this bilge hatch, and—I've been passed out in that hole for—I don't know how long!"

"You've been in the bilges all this time? Oh, Mare that was genius!"

"Starr told me to get in there. That little passageway that runs along the starboard side of the engine room. I was hiding in it." She pulled the trailing end of her caftan up behind her and wrung bilge-water out of it before getting unsteadily to her feet. "He said he had a bad feeling about everything, and—and oh, Dee! I thought they shot you!"

"They missed." Dee helped her over to the window seat but was reluctant to let go of her for fear she was just a vision that might disappear.

"Where are the guys? Are they..."

Dee couldn't answer, except to cover her mouth with her hand as if she could stifle the sobs that were rising up in her.

"I thought so!" Marion put an involuntary hand to her chest as if it were difficult to breathe. "But—I just can't believe it!"

"They got dumped off," Dee practically choked on the words. "Left on that sinking boat. It all happened so fast, I'm not sure."

"What about *White Fox*?"

"They came and they went."

Marion gasped. "They couldn't have! I would have screamed my lungs out no matter how much it hurt—I can't believe it!"

"They released some toxic kind of nerve gas in here. I was just coming out of it when we were boarded but I couldn't move, holler or anything."

"You'd think somebody would have recognized you!"

"They had my face covered with bandages. Said I

was someone else and had a brain injury. That my parents and a surgeon were waiting to meet us in Japan. Anyway, they convinced *White Fox* we were the wrong boat and they let us go. Just like that! So we're on our own, Mare."

"What are we going to do?"

There was a surge and a roll, and they both reached for the wall to hang on. "We could try the radio," Dee replied. "But I can't even relay our position. What good would that be?"

"How many of them are there?"

"Just Dr. Von Hayden and the nurse. Scott fell overboard—oh, Mare, it was awful!"

"Scott Evans? Our own Scott Evans?"

"Marion, he's Heinrich Keller! And for all I know, he could have climbed back aboard on the end of that lifeline, already! I thought it was him coming out of that hole, just now."

"I thought Peterson was Heinrich Keller."

"I just heard him confess to using Peterson's real name—he's been doing it for years. Probably ever since they locked Peterson up in Wyngate. He's worse than the original, too. Anyway, he's Peterson's grandson and I'm convinced now that Peterson was the real Heinrich Keller. Who knows? Maybe they were in cahoots when they first started out. That old man had an amazing knack for getting people to do things."

"What are we going to do, now?"

"We're going to go down with this boat if we don't help them, but...they'll kill us when we're done. Oh, it...it just doesn't look good for us, Marion!"

There were a few moments of silence as the full

impact of that thought set in.

"We've got to do something! We can't just sit here."

"The only choice I can see is if we want to drown or be shot," Dee replied miserably. "I'm so sorry, Mare!"

Pandora plummeted down the backside of another wave and Marion reached for the wall and held on. "Gads, It feels like we've got way too much sail up."

"We do. But I don't care. It's keeping Von Hayden busy."

"Well, they'll get it taken care of sooner or later. We've got to think of something."

"It's just Von Hayden up there right now. The nurse is sleeping off some kind of sedative in your cabin. Hey...hey..."

"Do you have an idea? I knew you'd come up with one!"

"While he's busy, we could get a rope and tie her into your cabin." There was another long pause as they both thought about it. "No...no, that wouldn't work. She'd just climb out the hatchway."

"What hatchway?" Now Marion began to get excited. "There's no hatchway in my cabin, only portholes! That's why there's that little crawlspace alongside the bilge. In case of fire or something."

"Yes, but what's to stop her from getting out the same way you did? She knows this boat better than we do."

"Dee, I was scared stiff. How could I tell who might come after me? I wedged it shut with a crowbar from the engine room."

"You're kidding!" she whispered. "Marion, that was brilliant! Let's go for it, then, that's our only hope. We better hurry, though. She can't stay out much longer, especially with Von Hayden calling her every few minutes."

"What if he comes down here while we're doing it?"

"He'd have to tie off the wheel first, wouldn't he? I mean, he can't just let go of it. Maybe if you sit on the galley sink and peek at him through the porthole, we'd have plenty of warning before he actually came down."

"What if she comes out first?"

"Well, I'll... I'll...take that little can of pepper spray I have on my key chain and squirt her with it!" Dee hurried to the closet to search through her canvas bag. "I don't know if it will work. I've carried it around for three years and never even tried it."

"I wouldn't count on it, then. I better back you up with a frying pan. Whoever comes first, you squirt them and I'll smack them!"

"Gosh, that sounds awful. But it's the only thing we can do. Here it is, but I wonder..."

"Just come on."

They quietly removed the barricade to the door and crept stealthily through the companionway. The galley was tilted at such an angle that Marion hardly had to step up to sit on the counter. She peeked out the porthole. Von Hayden was still hanging onto the wheel.

Dee slipped into the engine room to get some rope and went to work quickly on Marion's door. It was eerily quiet inside as she tied the handle securely to the handle of the bathroom across the companionway. She had barely finished and was still on her knees when Von Hayden's voice bellowed from the cockpit, again.

"Anna! Anna, come up! Can you hear? I need your help! Anna!"

There a momentary thumping and stumbling, then a startled scream from the woman when she realized she was locked in. After that there was such a loud riotous pounding against the door, Dee could actually see it flexing against the hinges. Followed by an angry barrage of hysterical German. Dee only understood one word, repeated over and over.. Heinrich!

"He's tying it off!" Marion's voice sounded as if she were about to go rushing down the highest loop of a roller coaster. "Hurry up—here he comes!"

38
The Last Stand

"No one but a man can do this?" ~ Nellie Bly

Dee hurried over to take her position opposite Marion on the other side of the companionway ladder.

"No, wait..." Marion peered out the porthole over the sink. "Wait...he's heading for the upper deck, instead."

A tremendous thundering sound of flapping canvas filled the air as a sail was let loose, and the boat eased back into a normal thirty-degree angle. Marion rose up with the counter top, increasing her position to an almost deadly advantage with the frying pan.

"It sounds like he released the jib sheets," Dee whispered. "I think he's going to try it alone."

"No—here he comes!" Marion barely had time to whisper before Von Hayden took hold of the hatch cover and eased himself wearily down through the opening.

"Anna! What the devil are you hollering about! I— what's this? What—" He took in the length of knotted rope trailing along the floor, then met Dee's gaze for one split second before the sudden thunk of the frying pan. "Ouch!" He grasped his hooded head in his hands. He tottered.

Dee pressed down the tiny cap of the pepper spray container, and to her surprise, a fine stream hit Von Hayden square in the face as he was still reeling from the shock of having been struck with the pan. The result was immediate. He coughed, gasped, and dropped to his knees, trying to wipe the burning liquid from his face as he fought for air. In the next second, Marion brought the pan down once more, with a little more force this time, and dropped him flat. But instead of being knocked out, he simply lay on the floor, writhing and moaning.

"We better just tie him up. He's too hard to knock out!" Dee reached for the other end of the fifty-foot rope she had tied the cabin doors closed with.

"It sure isn't like the movies." Marion lay the pan aside, rubbed a hand over her injured arm, and then climbed down to help. "Let's tie him to the table so he can't move around."

They secured his hands to one end and his feet to the other, pulling him tight until he looked trussed up and hanging from a spit. Then, just as Dee was wondering why it had suddenly gotten so quiet up forward, a gunshot rang out.

"Oh, Lord help us!" Marion's face turned pale as another shot thudded into the teak door and then another. "She's going to shoot her way out!"

"I don't think she can." Dee rose cautiously to her feet, making sure to keep behind the bulkhead and out of line with the companionway. "If it was any other kind of wood but teak, she probably could, but—"

The next shot was an unmistakable zinging of brass as the bullet crashed into a hinge. Then the creak and strain of wood, before the obvious sound of the door giving way. "Heinrich!" Anna screamed through the partial opening before lapsing into another barrage of German.

"The radio, Marion—hurry! She only has one more bullet left, and then I'm going to run up to that crack and squirt her with the pepper spray!"

"But what if it's an eight gun? What if—"

"Hurry!" She had to raise her voice to be heard over Anna's. "They'll at least pick up our mayday, and—"

The gun went off again, zinging off the second hinge, but instead of breaking apart like the first one had, it held. One click of an empty chamber, then another and the clatter of the gun thrown against the door. In the same moment that Anna began to rattle the last loose hinge with both hands, Dee bent low and darted down the companionway. She positioned herself just beneath the opening Vee at the top where the door was hanging askew, aimed her little can, and waited for the woman's face to appear.

"Miss Parker." No trace of an accent. "You haven't got a chance. In less than an hour, this boat is going to rendezvous with our—"

As soon as the disheveled blonde head leaned out, Dee pressed down on the cap and released a two second stream of liquid fire before the aerosol sputtered out and dribbled a puff of it down her own arm, enough to make Anna fall backward and gasping onto the floor of the cabin. It was also enough to make Dee's own eyes smart and water from the vapors rising off her clothes.

She stumbled her way to the galley sink, turned on the pump, and stuck her sleeve under the faucet to dilute the potent chemicals. At the same time, Marion's voice quavered into the microphone. "Hello, out there, *White Fox*? This is Marion Marie Bates from Portland, Or—"

An earsplitting scream rang out over Von Hayden's low moans and Anna's muffled sobs. The first thought Dee had was that the radio had been broken and there was water rushing in. She blinked back a blur of still-stinging tears, staggered over to Marion, and picked up the mike swinging back and forth on its cord, to see for herself. By that time her friend was standing, frozen, like Lot's wife who had turned to salt when she looked back at a disaster.

"What—is it broken? What's—"

"Look at that!" Marion's voice was little more than a raspy whisper as she pointed to the barometer hanging on the wall. "It's stuck over as far as it can go on that little peg, and it says hurricane! Oh, what else—what else! Even if they hear us, we could—"

Dee felt a chilling fear wash over her, but still couldn't see clear enough to focus on it. "Anything short of a hurricane..." she murmured the words out loud, remembering. "She can take anything short of a—"

"Acknowledge *Pandora*, this is *White Fox*," the radio suddenly crackled loud and clear into their chaos. "Reverse your heading. Repeat. Reverse your heading. You are running up on the tail of Typhoon *Hikari*. Stand by for—" The message was cut off by a familiar voice. "Dee, is that you? This is Eddington—

what's your situation there? Over."

"We have Dr. Von Hayden and the head nurse from Wyngate in custody!" she shouted back into the receiver. "But Marion and I are alone. Hawkins and Starr were—" She let go of the button because she couldn't bring herself to say it.

"Hold on, Dee," Eddington's voice was reassuring. "Major Hawkins and Henry Starr are alive and en route for the Japanese coast in a disabled vessel. Now, if you girls can reverse your heading and hold on, *White Fox* can intercept at... oh, one hundred. Over."

A relief close to delirium swept over Dee and she slumped down onto the floor.

"They're alive!" Marion cried. "Did you hear that, Dee? They're—" She grabbed the mike, herself, pressed down the button and hollered, "What time exactly is that, Mr. Eddington! So we know how long we have to hold out! Over!"

"One o'clock in the morning, Ms. Bates, and it sure is good to hear from you, ma'am. I don't know how you two managed but we can talk when you get here. And keep the radio on this time, girls. One more loss of contact could cause a nervous breakdown around here. *White Fox* out."

Buoyed by each other and the news that Hawk and Starr were alive, Dee quickly dressed in warm clothes and foul weather gear. Since Marion couldn't get hers out of the forward cabin, she borrowed from Dee and they climbed onto Pandora's wet, windblown decks. After weeks at sea, they knew what had to be done and how to do it.

There was no room for mistakes. Not if they were going to get the boat turned around fast enough to outrun a typhoon. Which would be a tricky undertaking in such heavy weather, all by itself. Their prospects looked more than daunting, and without a shadow of doubt, there was only one possible way they could succeed...There would have to be angels helping.

39
Inheritance

"We were afraid that you were dead..." ~ Nellie Bly

It was pitch dark, in considerably calmer waters when *Pandora* was finally boarded by duty officers. This time Eddington and Reynolds were among them to arrest the notorious suspects, who looked anything but dangerous after their unusual confinements. Their eyes were swollen shut, and Anna Keller—with hair tumbled down and clothes askew—looked all of her sixty-two years.

Dee and Marion were so exhausted they gathered a few of their things and gladly exchanged places with four able-bodied seamen who would finish taking the yacht to the nearest Japanese harbor. It was nearly two in the morning by the time the women finally traded the cold rolling decks of *Pandora* for the longer, slower, more gradual roll of the *USS White Fox*.

While Reynolds settled the prisoners in the ship's brig, Eddington led Marion and Dee to the officers' dining room, where sandwiches and hot coffee were waiting. Since neither of them had eaten for twenty-four hours, they were starved. With faces flushed and eyes bright from coming into the warm room after so many hours in the cold, they piled their few bags in a corner and removed heavy jackets before sitting.

"That was a fine piece of work, ladies," Eddington said with a genuine show of relief at having finally recovered his entire flock of decoys without casualty. "Shoot, with a little push and some training, I could probably get you gals jobs at the agency."

"No thanks," Marion demurred. "I'm relegating myself back to the rank of grandmother."

"Have you heard from Hawk?" Dee asked him. "And how did Starr manage—"

"I don't know any details. We're not in radio contact." Eddington took half a ham sandwich from a plate that was piled high. "But we'll hear from them as soon as they reach the coast. About two or three days."

"Two or three days on that broken boat? In all this bad weather?"

"Can't they be rescued?" Dee pressed.

"They refused assistance so we could come after you," Eddington replied. "But if anyone can make it, they can. That Hawkins is a world class sailor. Pretty resourceful," he added on a more positive note.

"He told us he was just a cruising bum, Mr. Eddington," Marion clarified. "They're going to need help."

"Excuse me, ma'am, but anyone who can sail a forty-foot yacht singlehanded around the world is no bum. Especially a retired medical examiner. They don't just give those kinds of credentials away. What sort of a story was he feeding you girls?"

"Nothing compared to the one all this seems to have brought on," Dee accused. "Were you responsible for having him reinstated, Mr. Eddington?"

"I did that because I knew it was the only way he'd cooperate. When I realized what you all were headed into, I had to do something fast. Shoot, I'd end up with my head on a block if I lost four civilians. I knew I could count on him, though."

"How did you know?" Dee asked.

"Because of his past record. He's one of those beyond-the-call-of-duty types. If they can't carry out orders the way they're told, they'll find some other way to get it done. Earned himself a medal about eleven years ago."

"Doing what?"

"Details are classified." Then seeing the look of disappointment on Dee's face, he added, "But since you're his wife, I guess it wouldn't hurt to give you a general idea. He participated in a rescue of a downed American aircraft in a...questionable area. Commanding officer was wounded and he performed emergency surgery in the field. Saved his life. Then got everybody out, alive." He smiled at the look of admiration in her eyes. "You got yourself a hero, Miss Dee."

"Well I'm just flabbergasted!" Marion marveled.

"How long will he have to stay reinstated?" Dee asked. "Will it delay our search for the diamonds?"

Eddington set his half-eaten sandwich aside with an uncomfortable sigh. "I have a lot of explaining to do, here. Might take a little time. Are you sure you wouldn't rather get some rest and talk in the morning?"

"I'd rather talk now." Dee felt a slow apprehension at the thought that he had painted a glowing picture of Hawk as a prelude to announcing he had been lost at sea.

"You ever been turkey hunting, Dee?"

"Turkey hunting?"

"First, you walk out in the woods where you think the turkeys are, and—"

"Mr. Eddington, I fail to see what this has to do with—"

"Give me a minute now, I'm getting to it." He was wearing a dark Navy issue sweater and he pushed up the sleeves before leaning his forearms on the table. "You go out where the turkeys are, hide behind a log, and make a sound like another turkey. Pretty soon, a real one comes by to check things out, and..."

He made a gesture like he was sighting down the barrel of a rifle. "Bam! You got yourself a turkey. Now there's no easy way to say this, so, I'm gonna come right out and admit I used you to get the turkeys. But no one was as surprised as me when I looked down my sights and saw a couple of vultures sitting there, instead."

"But I thought you were after Keller all along," Dee said.

"Keller. But Keller turned out to be a sophisticated network of extortionists that were two steps ahead of me and right on your tail. You were playing into their hands, and I had no way to call you back in—or even warn you—because Hawkins didn't have his radio on! My backup plan didn't work out."

"You mean reinstating him?"

"That reinstatement isn't official. I just haven't had a chance to tell him, yet."

"But he was reinstated before we even connected with that other boat!"

"Shoot, that was just a message I had relayed a couple days before. Ren and I were stuck out on an aircraft carrier because of the weather, when everything started coming down." He picked up his sandwich again. "You wouldn't believe the strings I had to pull even to get out here. By the time I did, *White Fox* had already let *Pandora* slip through their hands."

"Well, it wasn't as if you didn't try to talk us out of it in San Francisco." Dee took a contemplative sip of the strong black coffee she was holding onto just to take the chill off her nearly frozen hands. "I don't think you could have said anything to change our minds about it anyway. We were sort of... spellbound."

"There is one thing I could have said." Eddington took a deep breath and looked her right in the eye. "There are no diamonds out there, Dee. Not in Siberia anyway."

"What?"

Marion's mouth dropped open. "You mean you let us walk right into that trap for—for nothing?"

"I did try to talk you out of it."

"No diamonds!" Dee was shocked. "If you'd have told us there were no diamonds, we'd have been talked out of it! How could you do something like that? Especially if you already knew Heinrich Keller was dead."

"I didn't know he was dead until after San

Francisco. I just knew you were the vital link. And if he still thought the diamonds were there, I figured he'd stay in touch with you. It wasn't until we looked into Wyngate that we realized they were so far ahead of us. Been following right behind you the whole time."

"We were nearly killed!" Marion pushed her colorful drooping scarf out of her eye and gave him a piercing glance.

"I'm sorry about that, ladies, I really am. If I'd have known what you were really up against out here, I'd never done it. That's a fact. I still don't know how you two managed to overpower them before they got rid of you. They didn't leave any witnesses, anywhere else, not even Keller's own son."

"We have the help of angels, Mr. Eddington," Marion informed him. "On account of Dee's father is a pastor."

"Marion, that isn't why we have angels," Dee objected, "everybody has at least—"

"Angels or no angels." He grinned. "The thing is, it looks like Keller even did away with Anna's son, at some point, because he hasn't been on the radar for years."

"You mean Peterson's grandson?" Dee took a deep breath before she could steady herself enough to explain. "I know where he is, and Peterson didn't kill him, Mr. Eddington. He fell overboard because I was trying to throw the journal in the water."

"Dee!" Marion gasped at the thought.

"Well, I knew I couldn't stand up under any kind of torture, and—"

"Dee Parker!"

"Marion, you know what a baby I am when it

comes to pain. That awful thing had a curse on it! I thought sure he would climb back up on the lifeline but when we got out on deck, I found half of the line in the cockpit. Von Hayden must have cut it off before he even—"

"Hold it!" Eddington dropped the drooping sandwich he was still hanging onto back on the plate, got to his feet, and started pacing back and forth, as if he was about to come undone. "Are you telling me they were both using that name? Like some code word to communicate with?"

"For the last five years, it was only Scott"

"He was on that boat with you, too."

"He's been working at the desk across from mine for the last five years," Dee went on. "Under the name of Scott Evans. Anna was his mother, and Peterson—my Peterson—was his grandfather."

"That whole family was rotten!" Marion declared.

Eddington stopped in his tracks. "There's the last piece of the puzzle, right there. Anna Keller was married to some Dutch fisherman after the war. She was only fifteen. Public records say his name was Nelson Peterson. Heinrich Keller killed him and assumed his identity. This is the first I heard about Anna's son working with them but it makes all kinds of sense. He was just the type they needed to make international connections for the organ donor ring. Spoke several languages, too."

"I don't think he was doing it willingly, though," Dee reasoned. "He and Von Hayden were too much at odds with each other. It was the diamonds that had the hold on him. He could never get the location out of his grandfather. But that does explain why Anna hated her father so much."

"That's no excuse to go around killing and stealing other people's body parts!" Marion huffed.

"Of course not, but it makes sense." Dee pulled her black knit cap off, realized her clip was missing, and began shoving the damp, unruly curls back up into it again.

"I'm just surprised she let Ms. Bates go. That isn't her style."

"They didn't know I was there. I was hiding out in the bilge."

He looked from one to the other, as if he hadn't heard right. "Between you hiding out in bilges and Dee tossing over the only thing that could buy her more time, I know I could get you both on at the agency. Well...you've got a friend anyway, ladies, I'll say that much. And if there's ever anything I can do for either one of you—anything—you just let me know."

"Hopefully, we won't ever get into a fix like this again," Dee replied.

"Probably not, but..." Eddington sank back into his seat, picked up his drooping sandwich, and then tossed it aside. "There is one last thing I have to discuss with you."

"For heaven's sakes, now what?" Marion took another half sandwich, opened it long enough to remove a wilted piece of lettuce and then closed it up again before taking a bite.

"What else could there possibly be? As it is, I'll never forgive myself for everything that's happened." Dee lamented.

"Well, don't take it too hard," Eddington replied. "You were up against professional criminals. They were plotting against you for over a year before they even made their move. And, as often happens with these types, they were at odds with each other. Seems that colleague of yours really was trying to make a change. He was going to pull out after he got hold of the diamonds. Left an account of the whole story in his personal effects on the other boat. Hawk sent it in with the helicopter, thinking it might help locate you if we couldn't catch up."

"But I thought you said you didn't know Scott was with them," Dee reminded him.

"I didn't. He signed his name as Scott Evans, so I didn't know the connection. Said he and his fiancée, Jennifer Young, had just signed on as crew. But when Jennifer started complaining about some of the activities they were involved in...like following you around back in San Francisco, dressed as a couple of old people..."

"Oh, gosh—that was her I saw in the restaurant."

"What restaurant?" Marion asked. "The only person you pointed out to me, that day, was Mr. Eddington, here."

"The day after that, when I was in the *Fish Grotto* with Hawk."

"She caused more trouble than they wanted to deal with, so they poisoned her. I figured they did the same to Scott, until Hawk said he was aboard *Pandora* with all of you. Jennifer was a decoy, dead or alive, for slipping out from under *White Fox.*"

"Which they used me for instead. Oh, it's all so awful." Dee put her head in her hands and suddenly felt exhausted. "I'm ashamed we ever got caught up in something so—so sordid! I really don't know what came over us. It's like we were all..."

"Possessed," Marion finished for her.

"Maybe it's a good thing the diamonds are gone," Dee reasoned. "Who knows what depths we would have sunk to if we still thought they were out there."

"All this for something I'll never see," Marion sighed.

"Actually," Eddington said in a lighter tone, "I think that could be arranged. Now that we've got the bad news over with, let's get to the good part. The wealthy Japanese collector who bought the Strassgaard Jewels when they were recovered back in seventy-three, is interested in finishing out the collection. In case you'd like to sell that ring."

"You mean I get to keep it?" Dee raised her head to look over at him. "I don't have to turn it over for evidence or anything?"

"I could confiscate it for evidence," he admitted. "But it isn't an integral part of the case. You came by it honestly, and there's no one else left to claim it. So after months or even years in litigation, it would probably come back to you, anyway. And since you've both been so instrumental in all this, and..."

"Saved your hide," Marion finished for him.

He laughed. "You've done that, all right. I think it's only fair you hang onto it. Unless you're ready to sell, that is."

"Oh, I am ready to sell," Dee insisted. "I can't wait to sell it. That ring has brought us nothing but bad luck from the moment I first took it out of the box!"

"All right, then. The man's name is Kim Yakawa. He's a businessman in Tokyo. Made his money in high tech electronics, and he's willing to pay a million point five for it."

"A million point five." Dee whispered.

"It's worth more because it once belonged to a cousin of the Russian royal family. Historical value and all that. Not such a bad profit for your efforts. Right? He owns the *Blue Moon*. A fancy, upper class resort over on the coast there. I talked to him last week and he said if I could get my hands on it, he'd be willing to talk.'

"I'm so happy we're all alive, I'd split five ways if you wanted to."

"Dee Parker." Marion objected. "We have to have a round table with the other partners before you go agreeing to anything like that."

"I couldn't take the money, Miss Dee," Eddington smiled warmly. "It's illegal for me to accept any monetary reward in connection with a case. But I do appreciate the vote of confidence."

"What did you have in mind, then?" she asked.

"Just a little favor. That's how we do things like this. But I do feel responsible to let you know…" he warned with a teasing twinkle coming into his eyes, "that it could be a little dangerous."

40
Assignment to Danger

*"I answered the summons with pleasure because I longed
to help those of God's most unfortunate children whom I
had left prisoners behind me." ~ Nellie Bly*

Dee put on a mint green kimono, took the towel from her head and shook down her hair. The last of her rose water bath was trickling through the drain of the oval-shaped, jade green tub, in the luxurious bathroom of an executive suite at the *Blue Moon* resort.

"I'm back," Marion called cheerily from outside the door.

"Let me see," Dee replied.

The door opened and Marion stuck her newly permed head in, with its stylish wave. "It isn't quite me but it covers the crack."

"It isn't always going to be a crack. Before you know it, you'll have a barely detectable scar there. Anyway, you look ten years younger, Mare. I think it's wonderful."

"Thanks. That's what the lady at the shop said, but

I figured she said that to everybody. Any calls?"

"Only from me to Eddington."

"Dee, you've got to quit bothering the poor man. He said he'd let us know the minute he heard anything. Let's think of something to do. Go shopping. Or out to eat or something."

"That's all we've been doing for four days. I can't make myself get interested anymore. Especially when they could call any time, now. Two or three days, Eddington said. It's been four, Marion. Four and a half to be exact. I'm starting to worry."

"Well, it doesn't help to—"

The phone rang and Dee ran past Marion to snatch up the pearl-white receiver on one of the nightstands. "Hello?" And then less enthusiastically, "Yes...yes, thank you," before hanging up.

"Not them, I take it." Marion guessed.

"Not them. The boat's ready, though, and we can move back aboard anytime. You know, as much as I've enjoyed all this pampering, I really can't wait to get back to it."

"You're bitten, Dee Parker." She picked up a magazine from her own bedside table that was open at a half-finished crossword puzzle. "Bitten with the treasure hunting bug. You've got all the signs."

"Hawkins, now. Remember?"

"It'll take a while, I still can't believe it. And I still think he's bipolar, even if he did do all those glowing things Eddington said. He's going to hit the roof you know, when he sees what you've done to his boat."

"It's my boat, too, and I've improved it. He can hardly be mad about that." She took a few tissues from a decorative box and sat at a small table to remove her nail polish and then paint more on.

"What's a five letter word that means to acquire knowledge?"

"Learn." Dee rummaged through her make-up bag for the polish.

"Nope, it has a "u" in it. I think we should move back to *Pandora* today, or we're going to have to take out a loan to pay the bill on this place. Especially with all the room service we've ordered. We're rich, but we're not fifteen hundred dollars a day rich. It's a once in a lifetime fling."

"At fifteen hundred dollars a day, Marion, we don't pay for room service. We don't pay for the sushi or the fruit or anything else we ordered. It's included in the bill. We even get to keep these kimonos."

"That's a relief. At a hundred and twenty dollars a day for snacks, I was starting to worry. How about the word, study...that fits."

"All compliments of Mr. Yakawa." She dipped the small brush into the opaque liquid and began to paint. "Including the hotel bill."

Marion's mouth dropped open. "You took his offer! I wondered what you two were whispering about when I was looking at the Strassgaard jewels— oh, those jewels!"

"We weren't whispering. And from now on, I'm steering clear of anything that even comes close to having a curse on it. Believe me. One pass was plenty good enough for me."

"Well, you really missed something because they were so breathtaking I could swear they were breathing all by themselves, right there on that pillow."

"Double shudders. Did you pick them up?"

"Good grief, no. I didn't want to be some electrical socket for evil." She plucked a perfectly ripe, red grape from a nearby fruit basket and popped it into her mouth. "I can see right now, though, I should have been listening closer to you two, so, I could have jabbed you in the ribs when you agreed to do something like this again."

"It isn't just the necklace. Mr. Yakawa is a very persuasive man."

"Sure he is. Him and Eddington together. But it's like a vampire curse, all this mystery stuff. Keeps popping up, after you think it's dead. Look at yourself! Two months ago, you would have been head over heels about a million point five. Not given the time of day to any hoo-doo story of some Ming Dynasty necklace, lost during—"

The phone rang, and Dee leapt for it.

Seascape had finally docked in the seaport town of Akkeshi, on Alsukeshi Bay, at the eastern tip of Japan's Hokkaido Island. Because of damages, they had been unable to hold their course through the recent storm and had not returned to it until the weather died down.

The two men were exhausted but well. And so relieved over the news that Dee and Marion were safe that they accepted their quarantine from customs with relatively good humor. Since they had arrived without papers, and *Seascape*—chartered out of San Francisco for a week—was now listed as stolen, they had to remain aboard the yacht until Eddington could fly in and straighten things out. At the same time, the agent was convinced Hawk was going to greet him with a well-deserved punch in the nose, so, wisely asked that Dee and Marion go first.

Three hours and twenty minutes after the phone call, Eddington made his appearance at the customs office, while Marion and Dee were shuttled by Harbor Patrol out over a choppy bay to where *Seascape* was moored.

Other than the jury-rigged, makeshift mast, it seemed none the worse for wear after its hazardous voyage. It looked deserted when the patrol launch pulled up alongside, and Dee, unable to contain herself any longer, was the first to board and head down the companionway.

Her foot hit something on the way down the ladder, and a coffee pot went clamoring to the floor.

"Sugar? I can't believe it!"

"Hawk!"

"Come here, baby, come here!" He swept her up and held her tight, as if he might never let go, again. Dee half-laughed and half-cried, ran her hands lovingly over the loose, blonde curls while she kissed and was kissed, letting herself revel in the joy that he was alive and really there. Only Starr's booming voice as he stumbled in from the forward cabin separated them long enough to exchange hugs all around, before Marion came down, and it started all over, again.

"Dee said you fell off the boat into the freezing water, Starr!" Marion looked him over as if he had been raised from the dead. "How ever did you—"

"Down jacket and a hard head, I guess," he replied. "And it's a good thing. By the time I got myself aboard the boat, here, she was nearly sunk already. Hawk was locked in the forward cabin. He never would've got out in time."

"You kept the boat from sinking?" this spoken as

if he had fought a war single-handed.

"That wasn't anything." Starr avoided the admiring gaze with a self-conscious shrug. "Just went around and closed all the sea cocks, is all. There weren't any damages below the water line. They meant to sink her, the evidence, and Hawk right along with her."

"I was fit to be tied when I saw *Pandora* slip over the horizon and nothing I could do about it. I actually prayed one of Dee's prayers." Hawk tightened his arms around her waist as he talked.

"Which one?" she asked.

"God help us! Figured I needed the big guns. And He did."

"It worked, too!" Starr laughed. "I put an amen on the end of it and even swore to stop drinking!"

"Starr!" Marion's voice rang with amazement. "Maybe Dee was right about—"

"Only in the morning," he added quickly. "Nothing to get all worked up about. Some things a man has to take on at his own pace, even if he is headed in the right direction. Anyhow, they destroyed all the radio equipment, so we couldn't put in a mayday. But I sure thought you two were goners! Once they found the journal and once Marion cut loose with one of her screams."

"I'll have you know I didn't scream one time. Not until they were tied up." Marion bent down for the coffee pot that was still on the floor. "Did I, Dee?"

"Not until she realized what it meant for the barometer to be pegged," Dee replied. "We were so cool and calculating, Eddington said he could probably get us both jobs at the agency."

"Where is that bum anyway?" Hawk growled.

"I'm going to punch him right in the—"

"Hawk, don't you dare," she warned. "He saved our lives, for goodness sake. And if it hadn't been for him, we never would have met Mr. Yakawa."

"Who's Mr. Yakawa?" Starr asked.

"The man who has the diamonds," Marion blurted out. "Brace yourselves, boys...we have all made fools out of ourselves for nothing. The Strassgaard Jewels were recovered in nineteen seventy-three by a pack of seal hunters."

"What?" Both men spoke the unbelieving word in unison.

"The rest I'll let Dee explain."

"Marion..." Dee glanced uncomfortably over at her friend. "I was hoping to put off business details until tomorrow. Or at least until they've rested and had a decent meal."

"Business details..." Hawk looked down at her with a familiar suspicion. "You can't just drop a bomb like that and not explain things. Let's have it, sugar."

"Well, I was...a little disappointed about the diamonds."

"A little," Starr complained, "I'm downright disgusted. It's embarrassing! If I'm going to make a fool out of myself, I'd at least like to have something to show for it. What have we got to show for all this?"

"We've got each other," Dee reminded him. "And I've never been so happy for anything in my life! We still have *Pandora*, too. And we have a million dollars."

"A million dollars!" Starr breathed the words out in near ecstasy.

"A million, point five," Marion corrected. "Less

whatever it cost to have all that high tech equipment installed. And you can bet it cost plenty, too."

"Marion!" Dee objected again. "You've got to quit springing things like—"

"What high tech equipment? On *Pandora*? Hang it all, Dee, you should have asked me!"

"You weren't there and I had to make a snap decision."

"Holy fright, here we go again," Starr muttered.

"Listen," Dee tried to explain. "Do you honestly think we could go back to the hum-drum of everyday life, after this kind of experience? We're not the same people we were when we first started. None of us are."

"I've got to admit," said Marion, "after I called my kids to make sure everything was OK, the thought of going back to Portland was a bit depressing. What do I have to go back to? I mean, an exciting speaker at writer's club just isn't going to do it for me anymore."

"Try baiting hooks for land duffers," Starr challenged, "see what that does for you. Especially when most of them have the pukes. Dee's right. We can't go back to what we had before. But the diamonds! We're never gonna get a deal as sweet as that again."

"Tell them, Dee," Marion said.

"We have been offered an incredible opportunity," she began carefully. "To actually be financed for something we probably would have jumped at the chance to do all by ourselves. Mr. Yakawa, has agreed to back us—as a team—to recover a practically priceless necklace, called the Blue Moon."

"The Blue Moon." Starr murmured.

"It's a necklace that was worn by the Empress of China back in...oh...say, fourteen eighty-five," she went on quickly. "Legend says, a barge that was carrying the famous jewels went down in the Yangtze River in the year—"

"Dee..." Hawk 's voice carried a tone of warning.

"It's worth a fortune!" she insisted. "And Yakawa is willing to spend one for us, just to find it for him. He's got this private museum—you should have seen it—and he's—"

"I've heard of Yakawa, sweets. He's known for backing high risk recovery operations. He's got a dig going on right now in West Africa that two men died on last year."

"How do you know all that?" she asked.

"I read an interview of him in a treasure hunting magazine a while back. We're not the only ones interested in treasure hunting, sugar, it's big business. Guys like him get their kicks out of financing life-threatening expeditions."

"But with a boat like *Pandora*," she insisted, and the right equipment..."

"It's in China, sweetheart, let's get serious here. If you think Russia is dangerous, I'll tell you right now, China is out of the question."

"But we wouldn't have to land there, actually. Just go up the river a little ways, and—"

"Out of the question, baby. Did you hear me?"

"If we didn't actually have to touch down," Starr reasoned, "*Pandora* is the sort of boat I'd put my trust in any day. After what we've been through in this one, I'm even more convinced."

"I'm convinced *Pandora* is a boat with a

destiny," Marion said dreamily. "Guided by the angels to do good things in the world."

"You know, Marion," Starr turned to her. "I thought that stuff was a bunch of junk when we first started out. But for you two to be alive...well, there's no way to deny something bigger than all of us took a hand."

"Yes, and it was angels. Wasn't it, Dee? She ought to know, her father is a pastor."

"I agree but not for that reason. But the boat with a destiny part is the most lovely idea." she agreed.

"But even with angels, sneaking into communist China is not a lovely idea," Hawk argued. "Like I said before, there are hundreds of other treasures to go after, if you want to keep doing it. Sunken ships and all that. And as long as you didn't put anything in writing for this Yakawa character, then we're not legally—"

He stopped mid-sentence when he caught the look on Dee's face. "You didn't."

"I did it mostly for you, Hawk. I thought you'd jump at an opportunity like this. And to get the kind of glimpse into China no one has seen for generations. It's the assignment of a lifetime! Gosh—I can see the headline now: **Treasure Hunters Topple Kidnapping Ring While Recovering Ming Dynasty Necklace**. I could maybe win the Pulitzer!"

"Kidnapping ring!" Hawk ran a hand through his hair and then smoothed down his mustache in a gesture Dee had come to realize was an expression of total frustration. "Don't even tell me whose idea that was."

"But with what Yakawa is going to pay us for it, I could add two more buildings and a hundred more kids to Dan's orphanage! And as far as the danger, Hawk, Eddington assured me that as long as we were determined to go anyway, he could back us up with—"

"If Eddington thinks we're going to run point for him on another one of his cases again, I'm going to punch that—"

"Hawk..."

She looked up at him in a way that was so appealing it sent a wave of emotion all through him.

"You wouldn't believe who those criminals took hostage." Dee said.

He knew right then he would give in to her.

But he took her by the arm anyway and ushered her toward the aft cabin. "Step into my office a minute, sugar." But it was only a half-hearted pretense at standing firm. He already knew he would give her whatever she wanted. He'd give her the moon if she asked for it like that.

Even if it was blue.

The End

*"Therefore, since we are surrounded by such a huge
crowd of witnesses to the life of faith, let us strip off
every weight that slows us down, especially the sin that
so easily trips us up. And let us run with endurance
the race God has set before us."*

Hebrews 12:1

(New Living Translation)

Invincible Nellie Bly
(1864-1922)

Nellie Bly is America's pioneer female journalist, best remembered for two extraordinary things. Being incarcerated into Blackwell's Island notorious institution for the insane (or, ‚the madhouse' as it was called back then), in order to get the true story of how patients were treated there; and a race around the world to beat Jules Verne's fictional character, Phineas Fogg's record of eighty days. Both of these fantastic feats of "stunt journalism" (a phrase coined by the many strange methods she used to get her stories) not only brought her fame in her own day, but a lasting name in history, as well. What was different about her?

Nellie Bly lived during an era when many amazing things were being tried and accomplished, by heroic, exceptional people. A time when there seems to have been more discoveries, more inventions, and more events that would ultimately shape our lives today. She was not born wealthy or famous to begin with. Her father died when she was six, leaving the large family destitute. She began her unusual journalistic career at the age of seventeen and when she died forty years later, her name was not only known around the world, she had been influential in social changes, business practices, and charity projects with arms that reached worldwide. Yet, the words most commonly referred to her, today, are "daredevil" and "feminist."

In my own acquaintance (research derived strictly from

what has been written or documented by the subject, themselves) I found Nellie Bly to be another wonderful combination of adventure and Christian character that had (like all good things) such far- reaching effects on society, we can still hear their echoes. One of those special few whose compassion for others drives them to literally move things rather than just being moved by those things themselves. Her responses to human suffering, such as, "I longed to help those of God's most unfortunate children," or, "My heart ached to see the sick grow sicker," are the true reasons Nellie Bly did those brave things she later became famous for.

When she found herself, in later life, reporting as a correspondent for the *New York Evening Journal,* from the trenches during WWI, her response to seeing a soldier die in front of her own eyes, while asking for his children, was, "I cried, unable to stand it...I had no answer to give...I could not endure...and asked the doctor, "Could Emperors and Czars and Kings look on this torturing slaughter and ever sleep again?"..."They do not look," he said gently..."

May there be more people like Nellie Bly in this world who are brave enough to look. I feel richer having met her.

You can meet Nellie Bly, yourself, and tag along on some of her true-life adventures, by reading her own books that are available, free, online. *Ten Days in a Madhouse,* *Around the World in 72 Days*, and *Six Months in Mexico,* as well as numerous articles can be found at:

NellieBlyOnline.com

Other books by
Lilly Maytree

Novels:
Gold Trap
The Pandora Box
Neptune's Lady
The Rising
An American story

The Stella Madison Capers:
Home Before Dark
A Thief In The House
Sea Trials
The Pushover Plot
Lost In The Wilderness
The Last Resort
Voyage of the Dreadnaught
The Complete Stella Madison Capers

For Writers:
Unspoken Rules
Writing Rules!

For Parents:
The Nature Of Children
(And how to deal with it)

Behave Yourself!
Teaching children to discipline themselves.

About the Author

Lilly Maytree is an inspirational adventure novelist who decided to prove to herself that some of the things her characters did could be done in real life. A decision that sent her careening along on a very long voyage through the Inside Passage to Alaska with her captain husband aboard a sailboat called the *Glory B*.

She eventually ended up on a faraway island that was so beautiful she never went home. She lives there on a float house, tucked into a little cove in the wilderness, with the *Glory B* tied up alongside, ready for more adventures. Which she loves sharing with readers. It has even been said that she time-travels (but that's probably just a rumor). To find out what she's doing right now, simply visit:

LillyMaytree.com

You can also get in touch with her by sending an email to: lilly@LillyMaytree.com. It might take a few days if she is adventuring far away... but she always comes back sooner or later.

This Book was published by:

If you enjoyed it, please consider leaving a review in any of the places you like to buy books. To browse other books like this—both fiction and nonfiction—visit:

LightsmithPublishers.com

We appreciate you taking the time to read. We hope you will also take a look at the FREE EBOOKS we offer each month.

Thank you for reading this book!

You might also like Lilly's novella *Home Before Dark.* You can download it for FREE over at:

LillyMaytree.com.

Home Before Dark an excerpt...

Home Before Dark Here is the first of the Stella Madison Capers, the story of how everything started, and how she escaped from a catastrophe that seemed to come out of nowhere. Which is the nature of catastrophes but it's so hard to be logical when you're in the middle of one. It's also the story of how she met the colonel (if you're interested in that sort of thing).

Something happened in Stella Madison's life that she never dreamed could come close to someone as careful as she was. But it did. In fact, if it hadn't been for sheer Providence and the kindness of strangers (who quickly became friends), she wouldn't be here to this day.

Lesson learned: trouble comes to everybody and usually in bunches...

"Many have puzzled themselves about the origin of evil. I am content to observe that there is evil, and that there is a way to escape from it..."

~John Newton.

Home Before Dark
A Stella Madison Caper
Book 1 (an excerpt)...

1

When opportunity first knocked on Stella Madison's door, she thought it was the devil. Had to be. That's because an unexpected change in circumstances was the last thing a person in her situation would look for. But there it was. Glaring up at her from the letter she had just opened to read with her second cup of morning coffee. "Dear Ms. Madison, we regret to inform you that the building in which you are living..."

But why go into all that. It wasn't the real problem, anyway. The real problem— not counting the emotional stress and strain of moving at her age (a women in her sixties!)—was the fact that she hadn't a penny beyond her monthly expenses to do it with. She lived on a fixed income. And even though she had always kept current with her driver's license, she didn't own a vehicle. Hadn't driven herself anywhere in years. It made her wonder how she would go about even looking for a new place, much less move all of her things into one.

Stella had a lot of things.

To be perfectly honest, she had accumulated about twice as many things as she originally came with, ten years ago. Any way you looked at it, she was in a pickle, and with only thirty days to get out of it. Thirty days! Could big companies really do that to people? Well, they could. So, obviously, she needed a plan.

After having lived in her own familiar world of comfort and safety for so long, the thought of taking a job was appalling. But desperate times called for desperate measures. She could endure anything for a short time, and this situation was only temporary. All right, so she had vowed never to set foot in that crazy rat-race of a working world, again. Things were upside down out there! Not to mention the natural disasters, where people like her were not only overlooked, but got trampled.

Which is why Stella had made it her priority not to depend on anyone but herself.

And, the thought of having to answer to somebody (probably half her age) after having grown so independent, was about the most distasteful thing she could think of. But she would just have to get a grip on herself and buck up. The trouble was, it had been over ten years since Stella had "worked" at anything.

What on earth could she do?

She had always been good with children...only she didn't have the strength and energy to meet the demands of kids these days. Not to mention it was now illegal to discipline any of them. Working at the local coffee shop was out, too, as she had never been fast enough with numbers and cash machines to keep people happy. Selling something was not an option. The only things she had that would be of the slightest value to anyone else were books. Stella loved books and had spent the greater portion of her life collecting for a personal library that now numbered in the thousands.

There were not only bookcases in every room of her small, one bedroom apartment that overlooked the sea (well, it was only tiny sliver of sea, actually, that disappeared entirely when the fog was in), but also shelves that ran throughout the apartment, about a foot below the ceiling. All categorized by the Dewy Decimal System.

Which suddenly gave her an idea.

She could work at the county library. It was within walking distance, and she was as familiar with it as her own kitchen. What's more, it was quiet... which meant a lot to her. She even knew some of the staff.

Which— as it turned out—was the only reason she was able to land any kind of a job there at all. Never mind that she had once been a schoolteacher, or that she loved to read. According to Ester Fergeson, who spoke up for her, the Clerk I positions were the only ones that ever came open anymore. Unless someone above that either died or retired. A Clerk I position was a person who restocked shelves. For an extremely minimum wage.

So it was that Stella Madison, with her lively blue eyes and striking white hair that tucked neatly under, began working five and a half hours a day at the Whitcomb Ritter Library. Four days a week, three days before the end of the next pay period. It wasn't until after she had been formally hired that she found out Clerk I people were only allowed part-time. Something about benefits. To be honest, Stella would have been hard-pressed to put in a full day at any job. Considering her situation. And the fact that it was imperative that she be home before dark. (Her number one rule for staying safe was that she always got home before dark. Safety was something a woman alone had to be constantly aware of. There were desperate people who prowled around in the city after dark.)

Her love of books carried her through. Which was a good thing, because according to her calculations, it seemed hardly possible to pay off the cost of this moving thing before her hundredth birthday. A thought that made her wonder if the entire experience wasn't making her rather cynical...an attitude that eventually led to trouble.

The truth is, Stella had problems from the very first day.

Not with any of the procedures. She knew that Dewey Decimal System like the back of her hand. Not with the computers, either: she had been using one of her own for years, now. It made her feel like something of a world traveler to exchange emails with friends on other continents.

She was even rather proud of her social abilities. Which is why it came as something of a shock to discover she couldn't "get along" very well with the rest of the staff. By the end of the first week, she was sure they were all morons. Including her friend, Ester.

Stella's first confrontation with a staff member happened on her very first day, in what later came to be known as "the egg incident."

"Is there a problem?" The senior librarian and supervisor of the shift looked away from her computer screen and peered over the rims of her reading glasses. She was a tall imposing woman, well dressed in a forest-colored business suit and black turtle-neck sweater. Her dark hair was twisted up neatly in one of those fashionable clips Stella admired but had never been able to get the hang of.

"Well, yes, Ms. Thatcher, there is." Stella stepped

into the office and placed a book with a green, nondescript cover on the desk. "While I was re-shelving the six hundreds—the cooking section, that is—I found this copy of The Egg And I by Betty MacDonald."

"And where else should a book about eggs be, if not in the cooking section?"

For a split second Stella's blue eyes widened with surprise before she assumed the woman had simply been too caught up in what she was doing to hear her right. "You see that's the point. I happen to own a copy of this book, myself, and it has nothing to do with cooking. It's about a woman who married a chicken rancher and the miserable years they went through before their divorce. There isn't a recipe in the whole thing."

There were a few moments of awkward silence between them before Ms. Thatcher broke off eye-contact and busied herself thumbing through the pages a few moments. "Obviously a computer glitch," she finally pronounced. "The computers do all the cataloguing these days, and it's strictly by word association. But I see this was published way back in the forties... hasn't been checked out since 1989. Still has the signature slip we used before we automated." She closed the cover with a decisive thump, "Should have been turned over to FL years ago. Thank you, Stella. I'll take care of it."

"What is FL?"

"Friends of the Library. A nationwide organization that handles the sale of all our discards."

"Discards!" Stella gasped (she couldn't help it).

"But this was a beautifully written book —a bestseller. They even made a movie out of it starring

Fred MacMurry and Claudette Colbert!"

"That may be. But it's a new age, isn't it, and this is hopelessly out-dated. I assure you our shelves are loaded down with a more than adequate supply of information on divorce. Or even chicken ranches for that matter. With all the latest and up-to-Around the world."

Stella felt something like a balloon that was slowly losing its air, and stared for a few moments at the tips of her sensible leather slip-ons that were peeking out from under her gray wool slacks. What about all the worlds that no longer existed anymore? How did one go about traveling to them? Suppose a person wanted to "time travel" to experience a different age altogether? See what it was like back then. Maybe even pick up some useful bit of information that is no longer common knowledge these days. And how else was one supposed to become intimately acquainted with great minds if librarians could lop off the connection to the very works where they lived? Why that —Stella shuddered—was practically murder!

No wonder the young minds of today weren't interested in such things anymore. These lovely things were no longer a part of their life experience. Not by their own. choice, as some would have us believe, but by the choice of some (some senior librarian!) who had made the choice for them. Now the children of the future must evolve out of the narrow-minded channels of a single generation instead of having the freedom to tap into the wisdom of the ages, right from their own neighborhoods.

"Outrageous!" Stella's indignation at the very thought of children being denied this ecstasy boiled over while she backed out of the office. As if Ms. Thatcher had suddenly revealed herself as a snake. "I'm going to—to formally complain to the authorities!"

Slamming the door on the way out was an accident.

The next confrontation occurred three days after that and was referred to (in the subsequent deposition) as "the coffee altercation." If it could be said that an incident was something one did, while an altercation was something one did to someone else, Stella should have realized by the very nature of these events that things were escalating.

Only she didn't.

–End of Excerpt–

To get your free download of
Home Before Dark, go to:
LillyMaytree.com,

click the Books By Lilly Maytree tab, scroll down
until you see the *Home Before Dark* cover, then click
on the "A Free Gift For You" button.

Happy Reading!